A FATAL FALL

An absolutely gripping classic British whodunnit

JANET NEEL

A Wilson and McLeish Mystery Book 2

Originally published as *Death on Site*

JOFFE
Ostara
CLASSICS

Revised edition 2024
Joffe Books, London
www.joffebooks.com

First published in Great Britain in 1989 as *Death on Site*

This paperback edition was first published
in Great Britain in 2024

This book is a work of fiction. Names, characters, businesses, organizations, places and events are either the product of the author's imagination or are used fictitiously. Any resemblance to actual persons, living or dead, events or locales is entirely coincidental.
The spelling used is British English except where fidelity to the author's rendering of accent or dialect supersedes this.

Cover art by Dee Dee Book Covers

ISBN: 978-1-83526-011-1

For my brothers
Giles and Alexander Neel

CHAPTER 1

It had been one of those days so characteristic of the Highlands in early August, wet and still, with mist covering the tops of the hills; and the couple in heavy boots and hooded anoraks and soaked jeans, trudging down the long path along the floor of the valley, stopped in a patch of sun to rest and to take off the heaviest of their clothes. As they did so, the fleeting sun lit up brilliantly a tiny scarlet-jacketed figure high on a stretch of rock in a gully several hundred feet above them. Detective Chief Inspector John McLeish, on leave from his desk in C Division at New Scotland Yard, stared transfixed at the climber, forgetting about his own aching legs and soaked clothes. The faraway figure worked its way up the sheer cliff, moving with a dancer's grace, and John McLeish strained his eyes to see.

'That bit is called something impossible in Gaelic, but the lads here mostly call it the Wall.' The tall, slim girl who had been trailing just behind him all down the hill leant heavily against him. 'I may not survive the rest of this,' she said warningly, and he smiled down into her wet, mud-spattered face. Short dark hair was plastered to her forehead above wide dark-blue eyes and a long straight nose.

'They'd not know you at the Department of Trade and Industry,' he said, with love. 'How do you know what that bit is called anyway? I thought you never went out on the hills at all when you were here with the boys all those years ago? I thought you spent the two weeks in the bar?'

'Unfair to go on about it,' she said with dignity, sitting down on a soaking rock and taking off her right boot. 'I've done very well today; we must have done ten miles in awful pouring rain, and I've hardly whinged at all. My feet hurt now. Both of them.' She took her left boot off, and started methodically on her socks. 'Don't stand there looking like a tree, darling John — help me, or find a Mars Bar or something.'

John McLeish, six foot four in his socks and built like the rugby player he had once been, sat down obediently and rummaged in his rucksack, producing a squashed Mars Bar which he divided between them by the simple dint of biting off half of it and handing over the rest.

'You're a good girl,' he told her, watching her with the pleasure of a missionary with a promising convert. 'Not the same girl I took up a hill a week ago.'

She looked at him reproachfully, but he had turned to watch the distant climber, grinning to himself as he remembered the débâcle of the first walk of their holiday. She had insisted on walking in old gym shoes and a tracksuit inherited from one or other of her four younger brothers. Within two miles of starting, she had been reduced to misery by the typical Highland downpour, finding that neither the gym shoes nor the tracksuit were any protection at all against the wind and the rain, and that her ankles turned on the slippery rocks. A most unlikely performance for the competent Francesca Wilson, at twenty-nine one of the Department of Trade and Industry's rising stars, and undisputed leader of her brothers. He had forced her to keep going, there being no other alternatives on that route, somewhere between amused and appalled by her descent into childish rage as she got wetter and more miserable. They had arrived back, furious with each other, at the cottage lent to them by one of the endless Wilson cousins.

They had made it up later, in bed, but McLeish, brooking no argument, had driven her forty miles round the coast to the nearest climbing shop the very next day and had stood over her while she bought proper boots and a weatherproof jacket, commenting the while on the dangerous idiocy of those who walked in these fierce hills without proper clothes.

He turned his head now to watch her stoically wringing out her socks and batting hopelessly at the midges that gathered in clouds round them both. She was never going to be fast on a hill, he had caught her too late, but she would be able to keep up with him if he waited about a bit. She replaced her socks and boots, stood up, and leant against him while they both watched the distant climber hang near the cliff top.

'Nothing to stop him falling at all,' Francesca said, with wonder.

'Yes, there is. He'll be using a sling — just to tie himself on while he does a difficult bit, not to help him climb.' As McLeish spoke, cloud rolled down again on the ridge, hiding the climber.

'John. Darling, do you tell me now that you are really a rock climber? I'm absolutely not going to start doing that.'

'I did a lot years ago, but I'm a bit old now to take it up again seriously, and I was always a bit heavy.'

'I suppose you were.' She considered him, noticing again how a week of hard walking had put on muscle, so that he looked even bigger than he did in everyday life and office clothes. She sighed, squatted down to tighten a bootlace, and stood up, wobbling slightly. Ten miles over hard ground had left her legs feeling like cottonwool; she would have welcomed a proper rest but, with the midges out, it was impossible to stay where they were. She looked across the small stream, a minor river today, full to bursting, and scanned up the cliff to the top of the ridge where she could now just glimpse the red-anoraked figure. Disheartened by being unable to envisage any scenario in which she might have enough strength to climb a rock face following a long walk, she started down the hill, still watching the distant climber. For a second she could not understand what her eyes were telling her, then she stopped in her tracks, shouting for McLeish who was already well ahead.

'John! He's gone.'

McLeish stopped and peered up to where she was pointing, but the mist rolled down again.

'He sort of somersaulted,' Francesca said, incredulously. 'Look, there he is — he's fallen right down the cliff — there!'

McLeish, scanning the cliff, could see absolutely nothing and said so, but handed her the binoculars, standing behind her as she lined them on the spot. He took them from her, carefully. 'Just on the left of that long piece of rock above the corrie. He's almost hidden but you can see a patch of red. What do we do, John?'

'I'll go to him,' he said, handing her back the binoculars. 'You hurry down as fast as you can and get help. Give me the map so I can mark where we are, and turn everything out of your rucksack that might be useful to a casualty — warm clothes, space blanket, food.'

Francesca, who had become accustomed to being treated as a not very experienced member of the Uniformed Branch when her lover decided to get something done, handed over two chocolate bars which she had been hoarding for the last stretch, a crêpe bandage, the map, and a spare sweater. 'There's someone on the ridge — up there — I saw them just as the chap fell. Wearing a yellow anorak. I'd better wave or something to indicate you are on your way, in case he tries to climb down and help. Oh, damn and blast, the mist's down again.'

McLeish strained to see where she was pointing, but the mist was covering the top of the ridge. 'I'll get going. You go down as fast as you can on the path, but be careful. You're tired and your legs are gone, and you are the only one who can tell them below that there has been an accident, and where it is. Hang on, Francesca — show me yourself where we are on the map.' She produced it meekly, noticing that in this real emergency he was unconsciously speaking more slowly. In dealing with mixed groups of policemen, evidently you made quite certain that even the stupid ones at the back knew exactly what they were supposed to be doing.

McLeish kissed her briskly and turned and plunged off, going as fast as he dared across the flooding stream, picking his way over the rocks, and clearing the last stretch with a jump that landed him in a bog. Francesca started walking stiffly down the path as he ran up the first slope, which was thickly covered with an uncompromising mixture of three-foot-deep heather and scattered boulders. She watched him with anxious affection, as he ran across the hill with the easy spring of someone who had done this from childhood, noticing that instead of looking bulky and clumsy, as he often could in a city, he was absolutely the right scale for this desolate, rock-strewn country where you could walk all day without seeing another human being and where the elements were an enemy to be considered seriously. She stubbed her toe on a rock and stumbled, then steadied herself and concentrated on the path ahead, remembering, as McLeish had meant her to, that she was the fallen climber's lifeline.

John McLeish, going as fast as he knew how, was grimly calculating the chances of dealing effectively with what he was about to meet. The climber must, he reckoned, have fallen at least 200 feet. He was most likely dead, but possibly dying or just barely salvageable with a broken back or skull fractures. Not a lot to be done except keep him company, alive or dead, and wait while Francesca alerted the mountain rescue team and they gathered themselves together and got up the hill. Allow her an hour to get down and find them, unfit as she was; allow another hour for the team to be gathered by telephone; and an hour and a half for them to get there — whichever way you looked at it, he was in for a three-and-a-half-hour vigil. So was the casualty.

McLeish cleared the lower slope at a run but had to slow as the hill steepened. The climber was probably still 500 feet above him, he decided, breathing deeply as he pulled up into a small corrie cradling a lochan, and glanced up at the steep, stone-covered slope above it. He forced himself up as fast as he could, boots slipping on the wet scree, feeling the ten hard miles he had already done pulling at his calf muscles. He pressed on, counting his steps to keep himself going fast, and lifted his head only when a few minutes later he found himself at the top of a minor ridge. He stopped, fleetingly, to catch his breath and to glance at his watch — only fifteen minutes from when Francesca had shouted to him.

He looked up and saw a great scar of earth and broken heather just below the rocks at the top of the main ridge. His eye followed the scar down to where a man lay, only about fifty feet away, face down, stretched out, scarlet anorak rucked up to his armpits exposing a naked back, arms stretched out in front of him, a handful of uprooted heather still clutched in his right hand. McLeish, galvanized, ran and knelt beside him, tearing off his own rucksack. The fallen man was still wearing a climbing helmet, and his rucksack was still on his back, or rather on the back of his neck, pushed up with the anorak, shirt and string vest. The face was covered with blood, as were his hands and arms, and he was very cold. But he was alive. As McLeish took his fingers away from the pulse in the neck, the eyelids flickered and the man groaned.

'Don't try to move,' McLeish said, gently.

One eye opened, painfully, and a singularly bleak gaze fixed itself on him. 'I can move my hands.' The voice was a croak, and McLeish watched with respect while the man carefully moved his right hand and arm, wincing, then his left.

'Pins and needles.' The words were barely audible, and McLeish nodded. No paralysis high up, then.

'What about the legs? No, don't try too hard.'

'I can feel them.' The climber drew up his right knee gingerly, then his left, and cried aloud with pain. 'No, it's not broken, it's just cramp.'

McLeish had his hands over the calf muscle, feeling for the lump made by the cramp, but there was a further two minutes of agony for the casualty while he got the spasm out. Incredibly, the man's back seemed to be all right.

'Jesus, I'm cold.'

'Can you sit up if I help?' McLeish supported him as he struggled painfully to push himself into a sitting position, and felt the strength of the muscles in the back and arms as he helped. As he sat him up, he gently tugged down the rucked-up clothes to keep the biting little wind that had sprung up from chilling him further.

'Christ, my head.' The casualty reached blood-stained, torn hands to his climbing helmet but McLeish told him sharply to keep still and undid the buckles which had dug into the man's neck, leaving huge weals and providing an instant explanation for why he was having difficulty speaking. He lifted the helmet off carefully, revealing bright red-blond hair above a battered, swollen, blood-stained face which, even in that state, suggested youth and good looks. He fished out the emergency kit he had made Francesca buy a week earlier, and unfolded the casualty blanket, which looked like a giant sheet of aluminium foil and performed much the same function in insulating an injured climber. He wrapped it hastily round the man, and observed with satisfaction that it rendered him glitteringly visible against the grey-green heather and dark grey rocks. The climber, hunched over, winced under his ministrations and McLeish apologized.

'I think I've a broken rib or two — I've had that before, and that's what it feels like. Thank you for coming.' He swallowed painfully, and McLeish hastily poured some tea from the thermos that he had been carrying to keep Francesca going. Even in that thread of a voice, McLeish thought, watching him gulp it painfully, you could hear that he was a local lad. He dug in his rucksack for some chocolate, and when he turned back to offer it found he was being watched.

'I'm John McLeish,' he said, speaking slowly. 'I'm on holiday here, and I was walking with my girlfriend. She saw you fall, and she's gone down the hill for help. We've likely several hours to wait, so I want to get you as warm as possible.'

'I owe you both, then. I was by myself, and no one would have known where to look. My name's Fraser, Alan Fraser.' He was shivering uncontrollably and McLeish gently wrapped a spare sweater round his shoulders and unwrapped the second emergency blanket to go on top of the sweater. 'I'm not going to be let forget this. Tourists fall off that climb, whiles, but I've been here or hereabouts all my life.'

'You live locally, then?'

Alan Fraser gave him a sideways glance. 'Yes. I'm a professional climber.' It was said with just a faint air of surprise that it should have been necessary to explain, and it reminded McLeish sharply of someone he could not immediately place. With Fraser silenced by another cup of tea, McLeish realized that it was Francesca's brother Peregrine, a glitteringly successful singer, whom this man resembled. Not conceited, exactly — just used to being recognized instantly and not at all accustomed to having to explain who he was. He remembered suddenly a large display of books in one of the Inverness bookshops, with a colour photograph of the author surmounting the stand, the red-gold hair very bright even in the shop. The battered and swollen face in front of him was recognizable even in that state — this Alan Fraser was one of the successful pair who had got to the top of K2 by the North Face on an expedition which had killed three members of the large team and had defeated all but the lead pair. He was a television personality as well, McLeish recalled, specializing in spectacular stunt-climbing on the sea rocks off the islands on the west coast.

'Were you alone? The girl I was with saw someone up there above you, wearing a yellow anorak.'

'Wasn't with me, whoever it was.' Fraser was chalk white and shivering but his mind was working. 'Something fell on me, I think — loose rock somewhere.'

'Were you tied on?' McLeish tried not to sound censorious, but Fraser looked at him sideways.

'No, but I know that climb like my granny's front garden. No, something hit me on the head.'

He started to shiver more violently and McLeish rummaged in his rucksack to see what else he could pile on to keep him warm. They agreed that gloves would be too painful on the lacerated hands, but McLeish set to work on them with bandages. 'Try and eat something else,' he suggested. 'I've got a sandwich left, and we won't get help for hours yet. You're lucky to be here at all, and I don't want to lose you from shock.'

Fraser's smile was like a bright flash in the battered face. 'I must have come down over 200 feet, dragging at the rocks all the way.'

'Francesca — the girl I was with — said you somersaulted?' McLeish decided he had done all he could with Fraser's right hand and reached over for his left, and another roll of bandage.

'That's right. I felt myself go and I knew I'd to get facing the hill, and get my feet under me. I was lucky, too.'

Not that lucky, McLeish thought respectfully; having committed the initial idiocy of not tying himself on, he'd kept his head, he'd checked his fall by every way he knew, and here he was, alive and with luck barely injured, where most men would have been dead or paralysed. He made him as comfortable as he could and settled himself as close as possible, prepared stoically for a long wait. They both dozed and woke, McLeish continually checking that Fraser was warm enough, for about an hour. McLeish had just shared out the last of the chocolate when a disconcerting noise, barely distinguishable from the incessant wind caught his ear and he looked enquiringly at Fraser who was registering incredulity.

'It's the helicopter! I suppose Duncan must have realized it was me.'

McLeish, as incredulous as he, peered into the mist as the noise got louder, and suddenly a helicopter appeared, whole and entire out of the drifting mist, hanging about 300 feet away. It swung ponderously towards them.

'Saw the space blanket,' Fraser shouted, as both men put their hands over their ears and huddled into the hill.

The helicopter put down, as neatly as if it were landing on a large lawn, on a tiny flat patch at the edge of the corrie about a hundred feet away. Two men dropped out, carrying a stretcher, and ran over to them, bent double. McLeish rose to his feet, bracing himself against the noise and the wind.

'His name is Alan Fraser, he's shocked and badly bruised, and there's maybe a rib or so broken, and that seems to be all,' he reported succinctly.

'Alan!' Both men pushed past him. 'We'd not expected *you*. What happened?' They both glanced up the hill, and saw the long dragged slide below the rocks down which Fraser had come. 'What did you have on, lad, full armour? Let's get you away.' The bigger man knelt by Fraser, gently unwrapping the layers of covering. 'The young lady insisted on the helicopter, so you'll have an easy ride.'

'I thought you'd realized it was me, Duncan?'

'No, no.' The big man nodded to McLeish, and punctiliously introduced himself as Duncan Mackintosh, and the other man as his brother Roddy. He looked at McLeish with sly interest as the three of them supported a wincing Fraser to the helicopter, and McLeish wondered if Francesca had found it necessary to pull his rank to get the helicopter out. He looked back at Duncan, and decided that his expression was simply curiosity not unmixed with pity. Francesca must have been at her forceful best.

'She's good at insisting,' he shouted disloyally over the noise of the helicopter.

'Ah, but we knew she was a sensible lass,' Mackintosh shouted back reprovingly. 'It was Francesca Wilson — ye'll remember her, Alan, her and the boys, and the wee boat? She got us out of the bar.'

This was not received wholly kindly, McLeish thought with interest; even allowing for the bruising, Fraser's expression was, at best, ambivalent.

'She's back, is she? With a boat?'

Both Mackintoshes roared with laughter as the young RAF pilot picked the helicopter up as neatly as he had set it down, and headed off through the mist, dropping swiftly towards the valley floor to get below the worst. McLeish wondered detachedly whether Fraser had been an old flame of Francesca's, and what this was about a boat, and decided he would wait until someone told him.

'Dr Mike or Oban?' the pilot shouted.

'Land it at Dr Mike, and we'll see if we've to go on.'

The doctor came out to meet the helicopter, looked deep into Fraser's eyes, prodded his chest, and dispatched him to Oban. 'They'll clean him up there more quickly than I can, and I'm thinking he's maybe a bit concussed. Better safe than sorry, and there's only his mother at home to see after him.' The helicopter soared away.

McLeish, who had watched this inspired piece of laziness with appreciation, found himself in the doctor's surgery with an enormous glass of whisky in his hand. The speed with which the doctor downed an equally large one offered some explanation of why, at this time in the afternoon, Dr Mike felt it more prudent to dispatch a potentially difficult case to Oban. On the heels of this reflection he found that Duncan Mackintosh had downed an equally large one and was waiting for him to drink up so he could be given a lift back in a police Land Rover. With a faint ringing noise in his ears from the drink, he joined Mackintosh.

'We've not seen you in the bar?' Duncan observed, throwing the big vehicle round a difficult corner.

'No, we've been too tired.' McLeish saw his mistake as he spoke but decided to ride over it. 'Francesca is not used to hill-walking, and I was very tired when I came up.'

'She didn't do much walking when she was last here.' Duncan was grinning broadly. He suddenly hurled the Land Rover into a passing-place, and waited motionless for five seconds until a large dark-blue Range Rover crawled cautiously past them, the driver lifting a hand from the wheel in acknowledgement. 'Saw him from the corner. It's Mr Vernon's car. You know him? No? He stays at the hotel here, every year with his family — oh, for the last five years it must be. They're all walkers but they fish as well. Wonder where he's been the day? There's Francesca now.'

Duncan jerked his head to where a small figure above them on the hill was waving. 'I'll say good-day to you, and thank you. Alan was maybe in no state to return thanks for himself, but he could have been there the night but for you two. We'll be seeing you some evening, then?'

McLeish, disentangling his rucksack from the car, realized that this was both an invitation and a reminder of his social duties, and said heartily that he and Francesca would certainly be down, perhaps not tonight but on the day after. He turned to greet Francesca, who was dancing on the hill above him, very pleased with herself.

CHAPTER 2

Forty-eight hours later, bathed and changed after another long walk, McLeish and Francesca locked the cottage behind them and headed for the hotel bar. Around them a clear bright Highland evening shone, the sky darkening into a deeper blue, with the sun still bright out to sea and every inch of the distant hills glittering in its setting light. McLeish breathed deeply of the scented air and thought that if he never went back to his crowded office that would suit him splendidly. Perhaps he could find a job up in Scotland, since he was a full Scot, and come to this place every weekend? He looked down at Francesca, tidy in clean jeans and a white shirt, with a scarlet sweater knotted round her shoulders, and thought that she too looked part of the scenery. Indeed as she had pointed out on their way through the city, every second woman in Inverness looked like her, tall, dark-haired, with long straight noses and blue eyes. He put an arm round her. 'Are you going to know everyone here?'

'It is ten years since we were last here. On the other hand, people don't move much, and we were all here, and we had the boat.'

McLeish decided detachedly that Francesca, her four brothers, her mother and a boat might well have been conspicuous in a small Highland village, even one as used to tourists as this. So it proved. They walked into the hotel bar — a large room amply provided with small rickety tables, faded heavy armchairs of uncertain date and provenance, and even more faded group photographs featuring gentlemen in massive whiskers smirking modestly at deceased stags. Duncan Mackintosh hailed both of them, bought drinks all round and started to enquire about the welfare of the rest of the Wilson family. Francesca being removed to talk to the daughter of the house, McLeish decided the moment had come to find out about the boat that had accompanied the Wilson family, and prompted Duncan Mackintosh with a gentle enquiry. He could not, he realized, have given greater pleasure had he set out with that object; the group vied with each other to tell him about it. It had been, it transpired, a wee *sailing* boat, built from a kit by Francesca's brothers. McLeish, who knew the Wilson boys to be as cack-handed a group as you could find anywhere, blinked at this revelation, and Duncan Mackintosh confirmed, happily, that indeed with every passing day a further bit of the boat had fallen off, or come apart. But the real fun had been when the Wilsons, severally or in pairs, had sought to sail the craft.

'We'd no need of the television the while they were here,' the square, fifty-year-old postman observed, smiling reminiscently into his drink.

'It's not a place for a sailing boat, mind,' Duncan Mackintosh objected, with a sidelong glance at McLeish to see that he was not offended on behalf of Francesca. 'The wind is difficult, one minute there's not a breath, the next minute it gets up and comes from all around, particularly at this end of the loch.'

'You couldna take your eyes off them for a minute. They must have been in the water a dozen times a day.' The postman, Derrick Grant, ruthlessly destroyed this tactful approach.

'We'd only to go and fetch them the once, though.' Duncan Mackintosh clearly felt the tenor of the conversation might be causing offence to McLeish. His audience, reminded of their social obligations, agreed, happily, that despite the continual stream of spectacular capsizes that had so greatly contributed to the entertainment locally available, no harm had come to the Wilson children until Charlie the eldest boy, two years junior to Francesca, had tipped the boat over more awkwardly than usual and cracked his head on the mast. Peregrine, sailing with him, had found himself being pulled on to the rocks by the ebb tide as he tried to keep his dazed brother from sinking. Duncan had been at their side in a commandeered motorboat in minutes. McLeish nodded, liking the feel of a community which would automatically keep an eye out for a gaggle of visiting teenagers, no matter how much nuisance they were.

'Then they made friends with another family with a big boat, is that not right, Derrick?'

'Aye. With a lad a bit older than Francesca,' Derrick agreed, and perceptibly flinched as Duncan Mackintosh indicated that this might be less than tactful given the presence of Francesca's current man.

'I expect it meant the boys were a bit safer,' McLeish observed, disentangling without effort his love's probable motivation, and got a sharp appreciative look from Duncan Mackintosh.

'That would be right,' he agreed. 'Are the wee boys still singing?'

McLeish realized he must mean the youngest boys, the twins Jeremy and Tristram, now twenty-three, and said that Jeremy was in a merchant bank but still sang in a good choir, while Tristram was trying to follow in the footsteps of the twenty-five-year-old Peregrine and become a professional singer.

'He sings as Perry Wilson, doesn't he? He'll have made a bit of money,' Derrick Grant observed with interest, and McLeish agreed that the proceeds of two records which had both remained at the top of the charts for weeks would have been substantial.

'We never heard Perry sing here, you know. He was fifteen then and his voice had broken the year before and he was not allowed to use it.' McLeish blinked at him, momentarily disoriented by the thought of that golden talent muted. 'It was Tristram that was the star. He had made a record of hymns and the like, and was well known. He came to the kirk with the family — we've no instruments there, so the precentor gives the tune and leads the singing. It was like the angels come to earth to hear him and Jeremy.'

They would have been thirteen and at the full power of their treble voices. 'Of course Francesca and her mother and Charles have fine voices too,' Derrick Grant added courteously. 'So the missionary we had then asked them to sing for a concert he was getting up, and people came from everywhere, and we'd a lot of visitors, too. I can see Francesca now, playing for the boys on the old piano where half the notes stuck. We got the new one from that concert.'

A missionary? McLeish wondered wildly, then remembered that the Church of Scotland would use lay preachers in areas which they could not provide with a full-time clergyman. The Wilsons had paid their debts, then, though that talented bunch of extroverts would doubtless have appeared anywhere they were asked, for any cause. He realized that the group was watching him, and just managing not to speculate aloud about how he coped with this lot.

'You're a Londoner too, I understand?' Duncan Mackintosh enquired, reposing a comfortable beer tummy against the bar.

'Yes. I work for the Home Office,' McLeish said firmly.

When asked about his job casually he usually replied that he was a civil servant, but Francesca had pointed out he would have to do a little better than that in this community. 'They'll think you're a tax man or the Customs and Excise, either of which would be death to any social life,' she had stated with her customary authority. 'You'd better work for the Home Office. There are lots of jobs there of such unutterable dullness that no one would have the heart to enquire in any detail. Couldn't you be responsible for liaison with Treasury on pay and conditions for firemen, and invent any detail you needed? No one would be any the wiser, including Home Office ministers if present.'

McLeish, continually amused by the contempt with which the Department of Trade and Industry spoke of all other Departments of State, had agreed that the Home Office was the right place for him to be attributed to. More cautious than she, he had also said firmly that if pressed he was going to own to one of the Home Office jobs to which members of the Metropolitan Police Force were from time to time seconded. Duncan Mackintosh, apart from one single doubtful glance at McLeish's breadth of shoulder, did not seem inclined to press further and at that moment they were distracted by a noisy group arriving at the other end of the bar.

'There's Alan Fraser. I thought they'd have kept him in Oban a bit longer.' Duncan Mackintosh sounded thoroughly startled, and they all looked down the bar to where Alan Fraser, face very swollen and both hands heavily bandaged, was calling for four beers. He accepted a hand to get his anorak off from a slight black-haired man, olive-skinned and as tall as he, but who looked pale and mildly unhealthy beside his glowing colouring. McLeish, considering Fraser, noticed again the air of authority and the look of one accustomed to being recognized as he nodded in greeting to the group next to him. Someone drew his attention to McLeish, and he looked over, unhurriedly, picked up his drink, and made towards him, a space clearing round him as he moved.

McLeish was momentarily distracted by Francesca who had returned to his side and was pressed close to him, half hidden by his shoulder. 'That's Alan Fraser,' she said, anxiously, only increasing his puzzlement since she normally had the unhesitating social confidence of the successful eldest child.

Before he could ask her what the matter was, Fraser had joined them and was thanking him, formally, for his services the day before. 'And Francesca — I hear I've to thank you for the helicopter. Duncan told me you'd not take no for an answer.'

Francesca, wholly uncharacteristically, mumbled something inaudible in reply, and McLeish took over the conversation, asking Fraser how his various injuries were settling down. As they talked he found more details of Fraser's career assembling themselves. This lad, twenty-seven or so (younger than Francesca which made her obvious embarrassment with him the more surprising), was one of the new young tigers who were pioneering climbing in the Himalayas without oxygen at heights of 20,000 feet and above. What was he doing in this part of the world?

'Is your granny still living here, Alan?' Francesca had finally recovered her voice, and was sounding exaggeratedly BBC standard against the soft Highland accents in the bar. McLeish realized she was still not at ease.

'Aye, and still doing the bed and breakfast.' Fraser's accent had, by contrast, thickened. 'And what are you doing with yourself these days? Are you done with all that education?' His glance just flicked over McLeish, and Francesca, looking particularly severe, scowled back at him. She nodded, unamused, and turned to McLeish.

'I made an idiot of myself ten years ago nagging Alan here to stay at school and do the Highers, as if he were one of the boys, and as if it were my business,' she said doggedly, flushed red over her cheekbones. 'He has evidently not forgotten.' She swung on Fraser, her natural force of personality fully engaged. 'Could we start again, do you think, Alan? When I was a child I spoke as a child. Plainly you were right about what you should have been doing. And I bought your book in hardback — what more can I say?'

She spread her hands in appeal, watching him anxiously, and after a slow couple of seconds he grinned at her, and leant over to kiss her cheek. McLeish who would have been perfectly prepared to hit him, bruises or no, had he not responded to Francesca's apology, wondered momentarily if this old quarrel had been fuelled by some sexual attraction between them, but decided, seconds later, that he need not worry. These two had quarrelled, whatever the ostensible cause, strictly because they were too like each other: able, proud, used to leading in any situation, rotten at taking advice and difficult to deflect from any path, however ill chosen. Neither of them was the slightest attracted to the other now, and wouldn't have been as a teenager.

'I'll forgive you. You saved my life, anyway, you and the boyfriend here.' It was said straightforwardly, with due acknowledgement but no particular gratitude, and McLeish reflected that members of climbing teams attempting the most dangerous ascents must owe each other their lives many times over. 'You've taken to the hills, then, Fran?'

'Under pressure,' she said demurely, slanting her eyes at McLeish, and Fraser transferred his attention.

'You work for the Home Office, I'm hearing?'

'Yes.'

Fraser considered the monosyllable, and glanced thoughtfully, as Duncan Mackintosh had, at McLeish's broad shoulders. He decided, visibly, to leave his enquiry for the moment and turned to greet a dark, stocky, middle-aged man with hair cut very short who had been waiting patiently at the edge of the group.

'I hear you were up the hill, too, the day, Alec? Alec McKinnon here is the police force for the glen, Mr McLeish.'

'Aye I was.' McKinnon shook hands punctiliously with McLeish. 'In borrowed boots, so I've blisters everywhere. I was catching up in the office, and I'd taken my boots out of the car that morning. It was a fatality reported, and I'd to get up there fast. The Fiscal has decided in his wisdom that an officer has to inspect all fatalities on site.'

McLeish nodded in professional recognition. A slight silence ensued, broken by Fraser saying that the Vernons were back, had Francesca met them when she was here before?

'I never met any of them, but Robert Vernon was a business friend of my father's. He very kindly organized me a holiday job on one of his sites when I was at Cambridge. The year after I was last here, in fact.'

Her audience blinked — including McLeish, accustomed as he was to Francesca's network of contacts.

'What were you doing on a building site, the typing?' Alan Fraser enquired unwarily.

'I was hired as an assistant to the engineers, but I found it boring. So I helped out in the labour office — hiring people, sorting out minor things, negotiating bonuses. You learn a lot about a site that way. In fact, I ended up as the deputy to the labour relations man after his assistant was carted off with DTs.'

Her audience considered her respectfully.

'Did you get on all right with the men?' Alec McKinnon asked.

'Of course I did. The Irishmen are shy of women, anyway, but everyone was incredibly gentlemanly. It's a lot rougher being a woman in HM Government service, I can tell you.'

'It's a huge firm now, Vernon Engineering, isn't it?' McLeish asked, deciding that he would sort out this bit of Francesca's chequered career with her at a later stage.

'Oh, yes. It's a big construction company — two of the biggest sites in London, as well as five or six engineering companies in the Midlands.'

She stopped as the group's attention was distracted by a blonde girl in the ubiquitous jeans greeting Alan Fraser.

'Hello there, Sally,' he said, rather over-heartily, and McLeish considered her. She was extremely striking, with fine blonde, newly washed, straight hair falling limply to her shoulders, and a long fringe covering a bumpy forehead. He smiled at her, taking in the elegant, beautifully fitting T-shirt and immaculate navy-blue jeans. Very sexy, he thought, admiring the slim waist emphasized by a heavy leather belt. Huge brown eyes looked seriously back at him as they were introduced, and he waited to hear her speak to discover whether she was local or one of the fishing set.

'How do you do?' she enquired politely, and that particular question was answered. She sounded like Francesca, so she was a tourist — Sally Vernon? He remembered Duncan Mackintosh pulling off the road two days before to let through the blue Range Rover. Daughter, then, to Robert Vernon and Vernon Engineering. He turned to refuse his fourth drink of the evening, civilly offered by McKinnon, and found when he turned back that Francesca and Sally had edged out of the group and were establishing each other's origins, and answering some of the questions in his mind.

'I met a Bill Vernon in the shop yesterday. Is he your brother?' Francesca was asking.

'Oh, Billy. He's my half-brother. Good bit older than me.' Sally Vernon made it clear she would willingly have denied even that kinship.

Not as much of a sexpot as all that, McLeish thought, with that small, firmly closed mouth and the considering attention she was giving Francesca.

'I work for Dad's company on the Western Underpass at the moment.' This pretty, soft blonde girl, so carefully presented, was quite as authoritative as Francesca, he realized. 'I'm just finishing the civil engineering exams — I've done the practical. My mum made me do it. She was Dad's secretary, and she says she had to marry the boss to get where she is. She wants me to get there on my own.'

Francesca laughed in recognition. 'I've got one of those mothers. Mine shovelled me into the Administrative Civil Service so that I could have a training at my back when I was left a widow with five children under eleven.' She frowned at McLeish and he moved hastily away to join Alan Fraser who was watching the girls from further up the bar.

'He's rather a dish, your boyfriend,' Sally observed, watching him go.

'I suppose so,' Francesca sounded surprised. 'Broken nose, of course — rugger players being like that. The real looker is Alan Fraser — cocky creature that he always was.'

'I like him very much,' Sally Vernon said stiffly, and Francesca said hastily that indeed he was very attractive.

'That's my father over there, just came in.' Sally nodded to the end of the bar where a grey-haired, stocky man was getting instant service.

'How are you after your adventures, then, Alan?' he was saying, his tone absolutely assured and just this side of patronage, rather like a Chief Superintendent asking after the welfare of a newly joined constable. McLeish wondered about the man who felt able to address this local celebrity in quite that way.

'Ah, Mr Vernon. You've not met John McLeish, who is a visitor like yourself and who rescued me yesterday. John, this is Mr Vernon, Sally's father.'

Robert Vernon put neatly back in his box, McLeish thought, shaking hands, with the reminder that here he was just a visitor and father to a pretty girl. The man himself, however, was unconscious of the by-play, and was calling authoritatively for drinks. He had the same bumpy forehead and high cheekbones as his daughter but, unrelieved by the fine blonde hair and huge brown eyes, the effect was totally different. This face glared out of boardroom portraits of Our Founder, or belonged on a senior Commander of the Met, the one who could be promoted no further because he was just too rough, however effective. He was in his sixties, probably, but had lost none of his edge or drive.

'Alan here works as a scaffolder when he's not climbing,' Robert Vernon explained briskly to McLeish. 'He's been on one of my sites and I hope he's coming back to another of them.' The voice was authoritative, but odd in some way, with the vowel sounds very carefully produced.

'It would depend on the bonus, Mr Vernon.' Alan Fraser was giving away no points. 'I work with Mickey — down the bar there — and we pick up another pair to make the gang. I'm due to meet them in London next week.'

A scaffolding gang, McLeish reflected, could probably command their own price in this year when all London and much of the south-east seemed to have become a giant building site. Alan Fraser placidly accepted a drink — a malt whisky — and nodded to two men in their late thirties, both unmistakably tourists and fishermen in thornproof tweed plus-fours. Robert Vernon turned from the bar and greeted them, then introduced them to McLeish.

'Mr McLeish, my son Billy — and Nigel Makin, who is Sally's fiancé.'

Billy must have thrown to his mother's side, McLeish decided, being a long drooping chap with thick dark hair, smooth-faced, blue-eyed, wide-mouthed, and with none of his father's or sister's attack. Nigel Makin, on the other hand, was a tougher proposition, a light 5' 10" or so, with the look of an athlete, smooth mouse-coloured hair cut very short, rather small blue eyes, long nose, thin mouth with the corners tucked firmly in. A hard man, McLeish thought, and was in no way surprised to discover that this Nigel was the newly appointed managing director of the civil engineering side of Robert Vernon's firm.

'I don't believe it,' Makin said incredulously, peering down the bar. 'Is that not Francesca Wilson down there, talking to Sally? Tall, dark girl. She was a *great* success on the Abbey Road site, everyone wanted to watch her climb ladders.' He sounded patronizingly amused. 'What is she doing now?' he asked McLeish.

'She is on the industrial rescue side at the DTI. One of their highflyers.'

'Bit like being a well-respected employee of the National Coal Board.' Makin spoke with all the contempt of the industrialist for the civil servant.

Francesca caught the tone if not the full comment as she arrived. 'Ah, Nigel, how nice to see you. Did you pass those exams in the end? Yes? What a relief for you that must have been.' She smiled on him maliciously as he choked on his beer and turned to greet Bill Vernon, whose face lit with pleasure. Nothing there to worry about, however, McLeish thought, and saw that Robert Vernon had reached, regretfully, the same conclusion.

'Never mind talking to Billy, you've plenty of time for that, Francesca. Come and talk to me. My God, you've grown up like your dad. I could hear him then, as clear as if he were still with us, God rest him. What are you doing as a civil servant? Who's the boyfriend?'

By mutual consent the group moved hastily down the bar, leaving them to it.

'I'm a quantity surveyor,' Billy Vernon explained to McLeish, clearly ruffled by his father's interruption.

Nigel Makin, on his left, was being just a shade too civil to the black-haired man who had arrived with Alan Fraser. 'All you climbers are the same, aren't you, Mickey? Alan here is going back on the hill tomorrow, battered as he is; and you've been back too, I hear, despite your arm.'

'My partner, Mickey Hamilton,' Fraser explained to McLeish in introduction. 'Had a bit of bad luck two months ago and broke his arm in two places. Give you trouble today, Mick?'

'Good as new,' Mickey said firmly, but he was holding his drink awkwardly and his right shoulder was hunched defensively. McLeish said something conciliatory about these things always taking time, and asked how it had happened, noticing as he listened that this was a Scot, but not a local boy. He was from Edinburgh, it emerged, and educated at an English boarding-school. Plainly finding something reassuring about McLeish, he explained that he too was going south with Alan to earn some cash as a scaffolder. He had started to train as a doctor, but had found that the only thing he wanted to do was climb. A conventional Edinburgh family, reacting much as one might expect, had refused to support this ambition financially, and so, like Alan, he worked for cash where he could, sometimes as instructor in a mountaineering school and sometimes, with self-taught skill, as a scaffolder.

'Of course, with two months off I'll need to earn a bit, and fast,' he was saying, the pale face anxious and strained. 'I did a bit of examination marking, but it doesn't pay well.'

McLeish unostentatiously got their drinks refilled, and kept to himself the thought that scaffolding was hardly the recipe for curing a still-unhealed broken arm. Employed virtually from the day he had left Reading University, when he had gone straight into the Met as a graduate entrant, he reflected that he had never had to consider the problem of keeping body and soul together when one's earning capacity was entirely tied up with one's physical fitness, and when the thing one most wanted to do was physically dangerous. How did these top climbers manage?

'I wish now I'd finished a medical training — you're always welcome on expeditions, and if you break anything, well, you can still see patients,' Mickey observed in partial answer to McLeish's unspoken query. 'Or you can find a rich wife. Or you can write, like Alan. Not that he does most of it, but he's well known enough for them to provide a ghost writer. Oh, good evening, Mrs Vernon.'

He stood back from the bar to let a pleasant-looking, smartly dressed, older woman come through. 'Can I get you a drink?'

'Thank you, Michael, Robert was getting me one but I see he has been waylaid.' She regarded her husband, still locked in conversation with Francesca, with untroubled benignity and accepted a very small whisky. She looked enquiringly at McLeish who introduced himself. 'Ah, yes. The young man who rescued Alan Fraser a couple of days ago.'

McLeish hastily gave Francesca the credit for having seen Alan fall, and got an approving look in return. He considered her as they talked; clear, pale-blue eyes, slightly protuberant, excellent pink-and-white skin, carefully made up, with her daughter's pale blonde hair, faded and discreetly restored. A little younger than her husband, he judged, and a force in her own right. Nor was she bothering to disguise the flattened Midlands vowels. McLeish, whose Scots teacher-parents exiled to Leicester had fought a long battle against the accent, particularly resenting their children saying 'wan' for 'one', decided she probably came from within twenty miles of where he had been brought up. She was chatting easily to Mickey Hamilton about the Western Underpass site, and he realized with respect that she knew a great deal about the negotiations surrounding the contract.

Francesca joined them just then, grinning from her chat with Robert Vernon, and Alan Fraser came over. 'You want to come climbing with us tomorrow?' he said innocently, to Francesca.

'Absolutely not,' she said, appalled, then blushed as he and Mickey burst out laughing. 'But you are kind to ask me,' she added, belatedly. She covered her confusion by introducing herself to Mrs Vernon.

'What about you, John? You done any climbing?' Alan Fraser asked, grinning.

'A bit,' McLeish admitted before he had realized what he was going to say, and Mickey and Alan regarded him with interest.

'Come with us tomorrow? We'll be going gently, crippled as we are. That is, if you can leave Francesca? I daresay she'll find something to do — clean the house, maybe? We're doing the Grant stretch on the Coire Dubh — graded Medium to Severe.'

'I ought to be able to get up that,' McLeish said longingly, and looked down at Francesca, who laughed at him.

'You go, darling. I really would hate it, and I'd hold you all up. I'll do the shopping and read, and mess around — I need a day off.'

'Just you stay away from boats, there's a good girl,' Fraser said evilly, silencing her as they made plans to meet and to find some extra rope for McLeish, who was confessing to having rock boots and basic kit with him.

'I hope you're not too out of practice for that lot,' Francesca said with amusement, as they made their good-nights and came out into the grey light that passes for darkness in the Highlands in August, the hills grey humps against the loch.

'I used to spend every moment I could at it. They'd both be far too strong for me normally, but Fraser's got two ribs strapped and his hands scratched, and Mickey's arm is giving him hell. I ought to manage.'

'Alan meant it for a thank you, of course,' she observed. 'That's why I'm not coming — I'd not be any fun if I was as miserable as I was when you brought me down the edge of the Coire last week. Though I suppose I'll have to learn one day, if you are keen.'

McLeish hugged her to him, cheered as always by any suggestion that she accepted their relationship as permanent. He had known her for seven months, and had asked her to marry him within three weeks of meeting her, but a bad first marriage had broken her confidence and she shied away from any thought of a second.

'Maybe you can play with that Nigel while I'm off up the hill?'

'Sally Vernon might have something to say to that, given that she is engaged to him. Actually that *is* odd because it is Alan Fraser she fancies.'

McLeish considered her doubtfully, since she was notoriously unobservant in matters sexual.

'I'm not doing it by observation,' she protested, reading his mind. 'Sally more or less told me. Her father doesn't approve, because he desperately wants Nigel to stay on and be the next chief executive, next year. I'm not guessing about that either: Robert told me.'

McLeish enquired severely whether Robert Vernon had been making advances to her, or indeed she to him?

'It's not that. He worked a lot with Dad, and we were talking about him. He thinks I'm like him.' She was sparkling with happiness, and McLeish realized how much it meant to her to have talked to someone who had known and appreciated her long-dead father. He kept a protective arm round her as she chattered all the way home, high with excitement and pleasure, under the barely darkened sky.

CHAPTER 3

McLeish woke slowly at six-thirty the next morning with the alarm making its peculiarly irritating electronic noise. He forced his eyes open, remembering why he had set it. He had to meet Alan Fraser and Mickey Hamilton at eight a.m. at the foot of the cliff in the Coire Dubh. He gazed blearily at Francesca who was roaming round the room clad in decent white cotton knickers and a pair of purple and yellow football socks. She stopped in front of the mirror, thoughtfully holding a purple and yellow football shirt against her.

'No,' he protested, half awake but clear in his mind. 'It looks terrible on you. Where did you get it?'

'Tristram. It looked terrible on him, too, which is probably why it is hardly worn. He was only at Grantchester a year, and of course none of the others were at the same school.'

'I should throw it away,' he said, crawling out of bed, opening a drawer and looking with pleasure at the pile of ironed and mended shirts which Francesca had created out of the chaotic pile of dirty and buttonless laundry he had shamefacedly brought with him. He had been much touched by this unexpected piece of domesticity on the part of the fierce Francesca, and had taken it as a major compliment to himself. As she bent to pull up one of the awful socks, revealing a large name-tape indicating that the sock was the property of T. M. W. Wilson, he suddenly realized that there might be an alternative hypothesis which better fitted the observed facts.

'Francesca, did you do all the sewing for the boys when they were at school?'

'Mum did a lot. But getting four trunks organized at the beginning of every term needed all hands to the bucket. Why?'

McLeish, reluctantly confirmed in his suspicion that, so far from being treated with proper feminine deference, he had merely received the same matter-of-fact treatment as any brother bringing home a school trunk full of torn and dirty clothes, did not enlighten her. He relieved his feelings by vetoing both football shirt and socks. She gave him a thoughtful sideways look, but put on another shirt and white socks.

'Why are you up so early?' he asked, sorting kit into a rucksack, and she grinned at him.

'I'm seeing you on your way with a good breakfast in you, same like it says in all the books. What about a cuddle?' She walked into his arms and he held her, listening to her breathe.

'Pity I decided to go climbing today.'

'You'll like it when you get there. Don't let them bully you into going faster than you meant.'

* * *

An hour and a half later he was at the foot of the main climb, uneasily conscious of the weight of his rucksack and the stiffness of his back. He turned a corner and came on Alan and Mickey, sitting on a rock, warming themselves in the sun. Alan looked him over professionally, and told him to empty his rucksack so they could check his kit. Much to McLeish's relief, Alan threw out some of the heavier stuff, providing substitutes from his own kit and observing that it was very interesting to be reminded what people had climbed with ten years ago.

'I'll lead, you in the middle, and Mickey can be last up, all right? Just you shout if I go too fast — I don't know how strong you are so I'll just set off nice and easy.' There was no discernible trace of patronage in the matter-of-fact statement, but McLeish braced himself to do his best.

He wasn't, of course, in this class, he decided 500 feet up, fingers jammed in a narrow cleft, his left foot pressed into a minute indentation in the rock as he felt with his right foot for the invisible ledge that had supported Alan Fraser at this point, but he was doing all right, climbing with borrowed skill behind this superb leader. Fraser looked like a dancer on the rock as he went up, cursing his bruised ribs, and McLeish felt clumsy and earthbound behind such elegance. But sheer strength also has a place in climbing, and McLeish, despite being a good thirty pounds heavier than either of the other two, held his place, and did not feel, at the top of the second pitch, that he had much delayed them. He arrived, panting but pleased with himself, on the narrow ledge which already contained Alan Fraser, who appeared to be hardly breathed but whose bandaged right hand was bleeding again, slowly soaking through the layers covering it. It was clear that sympathy, or even comment, would be unwelcome, so McLeish belayed himself on a rock spike and peered out and down to where Mickey was crawling round a tricky overhang. Making a bit of a meal of it, he thought, then gripped the rope and braced himself back against the rock as he saw Mickey's right hand come off and his shoulder swing away from the rock. The steadying pull on the rope brought Mickey back in, and he managed to get a secure grip, but he moved both feet and his left arm quickly to avoid the pressure on his right shoulder.

'Which arm was it Mickey broke?' McLeish asked, *sotto voce*, over his shoulder.

'That one.' Alan Fraser close beside him with a hand on the rope sounded sardonically amused. 'I'd not ask him about it, though; he's trying to get right to be in the running for K6.' He peered round McLeish and advised Mickey to take his time, which had the effect of galvanizing the other man into activity. 'Of course, we're all wanting to go to K6.'

A scuffle as loose stones shifted on the rock beneath told them Mickey was just below them, and Alan said he would move on since there was not room for three on this ledge — or not when one was the size of McLeish. He set off up a long sideways fissure in the rock, moving easily, not bothering with pitons though McLeish felt one or two might not come amiss if he was going that way. On the heels of this thought, Mickey hauled himself on to the ledge, obviously in pain, sweating and greenish-white. McLeish wordlessly offered him half a Mars Bar which he took gratefully and ate in two bites, hunched over his sore shoulder.

'You're going well,' he said civilly to McLeish, swallowing the second mouthful. 'So's that bugger up there. You'd never know he half killed himself two days ago. It was a bad fall, wasn't it?'

McLeish confirmed that he had expected to find a corpse rather than a climber so lightly injured that he would be on the hill again two days later.

'He's a bloody fool to have been climbing alone in that mist.' Mickey glanced up to where Fraser was just disappearing round a bend. 'He'll tie off there, so you'd better go.'

McLeish nodded, unhurriedly refastening his rucksack. 'I understand you and Alan are going to the Himalayas?'

'We hope so. We may have to buy our way in.'

'Can you do that?' McLeish asked, startled.

'These days, yes. There's a couple of American multimillionaires — they're both not bad climbers — and they just put up enough money to buy an extra team of porters or a few more young climbers to carry loads, and that way they give the expedition leaders a better chance of getting people on to the summit. And the millionaires get to go along, too. It's fair enough — I just wish I had the cash.'

McLeish nodded, and tucked this information away. He moved out on to the rock, and felt his left foot slip. Cursing, he recovered it, and shut out every consideration from his mind other than getting across that perilous pitch without disgracing himself. A difficult twenty minutes later he was once more beside Fraser on a narrow ledge, breathing rather too hard. Fraser waited courteously until he had his breath, then indicated with a downward jerk of his head three small figures spread out about fifty feet up from the bottom of the cliff opposite, a very much easier proposition than the side of the Coire on which they were engaged.

'That's the nursery slopes over there,' he said, grinning at some private joke. 'Hamish McDonald, who has the hotel is instructing,' he added informatively. McLeish looked down to see what was amusing Fraser, and his eyes focused on a familiar splash of colour: the banned purple and yellow socks, separated from the vetoed purple and yellow shirt by a long expanse of leg and a very short, bunchy pair of purple rugger shorts, the whole spread-eagled hopelessly on a piece of cliff.

'Francesca,' he confirmed grimly, as the small figure struggled to unglue her right foot, being just audibly shouted at by Hamish for her pains.

'She's planning to surprise us. Decided to sneak off with old Hamish and learn to climb.'

'*You* don't need to feel rejected, Alan. The first walk she took with me, I'd no idea she'd never really walked anywhere, so I ran her off her feet. She got cold and wet and furious. She just isn't going to let that happen again.' He considered the distant purple and yellow figure broodingly.

'I'll tell you something just as funny.' Mickey had managed the last pitch very much better, and was clearly feeling happier with himself. 'The other girl is Sally Vernon — see, just now, coming round that buttress? You offered to teach her, didn't you Alan? *She's* decided to go for Hamish.'

A little sharp, thought McLeish, studiously watching the climbers on the other side and wincing as Francesca banged her knee on an awkward corner. Had she had the grace to consult him, he would have told her that shorts were not the most sensible wear for a beginner — a decent pair of sweat pants would have saved her a lot of grief. And she would boil in that football shirt of Tristram's, serve her right.

'So it is Sally,' Alan Fraser said evenly. He looked sideways at McLeish and observed that the answer was maybe for them to collect some other women who would like to be taught how to climb, or taught anything else for that matter.

'We're wasting ourselves on that pair,' McLeish agreed equably.

'Oh, Alan's not going to give Sally up,' Mickey said, swiftly. 'She has a rich Daddy, which is what all us poor climbers need.'

Fraser continued to gaze across at the other side. 'She's engaged to be married to Mr Makin there, managing director and heir to Mr Vernon. She's a nice girl.'

'Too nice for you,' Mickey said. It should have been a joke but suddenly it wasn't and the air crackled with hostility. McLeish, who was watching Francesca make a nonsense of a comparatively simple stretch of rock, decided to take a hand.

'Dear, oh dear,' he observed mournfully, 'Fran'll be off in a minute.' Both his companions, with some relief, peered across the gorge.

'Sally's not going too well, either,' Fraser pointed out. 'See Hamish trying to split himself between the both of them. He'll be a weary man tonight, and him well north of fifty. Look at that!' He raised his voice to a bellow: 'Dirty old man!' The unfortunate Hamish could clearly be seen to have taken a firm grip on the back of Francesca's shorts, supporting her while she reclaimed her right leg. He abandoned her with a brisk pat on the bottom and slithered down to disentangle Sally, studiously ignoring the catcalls from the other side.

'Good as a play.' Mickey had recovered his equanimity. 'Why, may I ask, is Francesca wearing Grantchester games strip?'

McLeish explained, tight-lipped.

'Oh, Tristram Wilson — is she his sister? I was at Grantchester, in my last year, when he arrived with an enormous reputation as a treble. But his voice was breaking when he got there and so of course I never heard him sing. Is he any good now?'

McLeish, who was only musical to a limited degree, said that Tristram had turned out to be a tenor. The family view was that Perry's voice was the better of the two, but that Tristram was the better musician.

'If he is even spoken of in the same breath as Perry, he is good.' Mickey sounded edgy, and Fraser suggested lazily that they might all go and assist poor Hamish in his thankless task.

'She'd never forgive me,' McLeish said placidly, and both younger men eyed him with something between pity and wonder.

'Right, then.' Fraser collected his thoughts. 'We'll go on up along there and try the pillars by the Black Lochan, if you're still fresh, John? It's a couple of miles along the ridge here, another Medium to Severe when you get there.'

McLeish, winding in rope and packing it in his rucksack, realized that they would pass just above the spot where Fraser had fallen three days ago, but decided not to mention it since the man himself appeared to be treating the whole incident as a mere social solecism. They took the narrow grass-covered ridge at a fast walk, then Fraser broke into a run as the ridge broadened out and sloped down for a few hundred yards.

'Careful now, Alan,' Mickey said, cheerfully, jog-trotting along easily. 'You'd not want to trip over, would you?'

'I just want to look and see what came loose.' They trotted on, Fraser in the lead, all of them looking down at the smooth, worn, green surface, nibbled flat by the sheep who grazed nonchalantly on the edge of the cliffs. Mickey stopped to look at a rock, and Fraser slowed to let McLeish catch up.

'Loose rock flaked off here?'

Mickey had come up with them.

'Yes. Well, I suppose it happens.' Fraser leant over the edge to look at the long scrape that marked his fall, stretching a hand back to McLeish to brace himself with the physical ease of a man who regularly trusts his life to others. McLeish slid his hand further up Fraser's arm to avoid the scratched and swollen wrists, leaning back against his weight.

'Jesus Christ but I was lucky.' Fraser straightened up, the clear skin pale in the bright sun. 'Well for me you and Francesca were there too — it would have taken the lads all their time to find me.' He peered down again, braced by McLeish's supporting hand.

'Careful,' Mickey said abruptly, and McLeish said calmly that he had him all right, and glanced over, surprising a look of wretched misery and pain on Mickey's face. He looked back at the back of Fraser's head, sharply adjusting his view of Mickey Hamilton. The poor chap was not only jealous of Alan Fraser as a rival climber, but he had complicated his life by loving him as well, to the point where he was agonizingly jealous of anyone who came near Alan Fraser, man or girl.

They moved on quickly to the foot of the pinnacle and Fraser considered it.

'Do you want to lead?'

McLeish, fully conscious of the honour that was being done him, considered the pitch carefully. Though it looked straightforward enough, it was ten years since he had climbed seriously. It was irresistible, he decided; never mind these careful calculations.

Twenty minutes later they were at the top, and McLeish was out of breath but deliriously happy. He felt twelve feet tall, and well capable of running up the next pitch if need be. Fraser looking amused, said gently that he thought he'd better lead on the next one, since there was a difficult corner, but he would hand over on the final pitch. McLeish followed him up, visited suddenly with the strength of ten, and took over the last pitch with barely a rest, arriving at the top in a state of ecstasy. He waited for Alan Fraser to arrive, neat, contained and graceful as ever, blood seeping through the bandages on both hands but otherwise showing no signs of wear, and confided in him that Francesca would have to learn how to do this, or be prepared to sit by while he did, because having found climbing again he could not give it up.

'You're all right there,' Fraser observed, amused. 'She's decided to learn — it'll have been her, not Sally, who got Hamish away from the bar to teach them.'

'Is Sally not well able to get her own way?'

'Oh yes. Her parents wanted her in the business, but she held out, and did what she wanted at University. Then she trained in another firm. She's now going into the family firm, but on her own terms, as a qualified engineer.'

McLeish was impressed and said so, and, feeling at ease with and deeply grateful to his companion, he added apologetically that despite Francesca he couldn't get used to having girls doing men's work, and making nothing of it.

'No more can I. I'm used to wee girls who work in typing pools in Glasgow, and are easy impressed by the great climber, you know? I still feel they ought all to be in the kitchen.'

'Barefoot and pregnant,' McLeish agreed heretically, stretching long legs into the heather, blissfully happy in the bright day. How shocked Francesca would be, he thought smugly. As a man happy and fulfilled in his chosen career, he was not threatened by her ability and attack, and indeed rested secure in the knowledge that his attraction for her was precisely that he was engaged in the real world of action rather than the shadow world of political advice. But Fraser, now, without formal qualifications, without steady earnings, whose chosen way of life could be disrupted utterly by illness or accident, might well feel differently about a girl with a degree and a professional qualification, daughter of one of the country's richest men.

'I don't want to marry,' Fraser said to the sky. 'I don't want to do anything else but climb. Never have, and I don't think I ever will.' He sat up with a jerk, embarrassed. 'Where's Mickey? We need to rescue poor Hamish from those women.'

Mickey was climbing slowly, so McLeish and Fraser stood and cheered him on, feeling comfortably superior. It had been a wonderful day, McLeish thought, shouting insults across the intervening distance like a teenager. They gave Mickey a rest at the top, then they all abseiled down, making a race of it, and McLeish hit the ground at the bottom, and fell over because his legs had suddenly lost all strength.

'Timber!' Mickey shouted joyfully, and as they hauled him to his feet McLeish would have willingly forsworn his promising career as a detective for ever.

They trotted down the path, Fraser leading, apparently completely fresh, though cursing his strapped ribs. McLeish, jog-trotting just behind him, tried between gasps to express something of his joy in being helped to recover a much-loved skill, but Fraser brushed off all thanks, and they dropped out of the high valley, still running, breathless and scarlet with the sun and the day.

CHAPTER 4

John McLeish woke to the sound of wind and rain; no point at all in getting up this early, he thought luxuriously, and looked speculatively across to the other bed in the room where nothing of Francesca was visible but the top of her head. He thought of getting into her bed and waking her up but fell asleep on the thought and by the time he woke again, two hours later, she was up and eating breakfast in the living-room of their small cottage, with a coal fire blazing to counteract the damp that crept out of the old, thick walls in wet weather. Not the least of the incompatibilities between them, he thought, sleepily accepting a cup of tea, was the difference in their body clocks: Francesca was at her best in the mornings, while he was always wide awake and ready for another day's work at nine in the evening.

'Come back to bed?' he suggested.

'Certainly,' she said, obligingly. 'But later I must find a piano.'

Later the day had, if anything, worsened and he waved Francesca off to the hotel, dressed up to the eyes in bulky waterproof clothing, promising to follow her in due course. He had intended to sit down quietly with a lot of unpaid bills and unanswered letters but found himself restless and soon followed her over to the hotel, through steady, persistent rain. The hotel lounge was full of people sitting heavily in the deep, uncomfortable armchairs, reading year-old magazines and day-old papers with unfamiliar names. He added his dripping jacket and overtrousers to the overloaded coathooks and walked across to the bar and recreation room, an ugly single-storey extension jutting out from the edge of the hotel's formidable Scots baronial exterior.

The sole recreational facilities appeared to consist of a slightly warped table-tennis table, and a piano at the far end on which Francesca was playing a minor scale, over and over, at increasing speed. Sally and Bill Vernon were playing in bad-tempered partnership against their father and Nigel Makin. It was clear that Robert Vernon was the only person really trying, and he was arguing every point in an increasingly exasperated fashion. The four gratefully stopped play as they saw him.

'Get Francesca to play something with a tune to it, young man, can you?' Robert Vernon said irritably. 'She's been playing that same scale for the last hour.'

McLeish, who knew that Francesca was unlikely to have realized there was anyone else in the room, nor, if she had, would have thought anyone would mind listening to scales, said he would try. He advanced on her with the intention of reminding her of her obligations to society, but she stopped playing as he came up and lifted her face for a kiss.

'I'm done,' she said, cheerfully. 'I was terribly stiff, and my hands were sore from climbing, but it was better towards the end. I must find Hamish and apologize for yesterday.'

'You weren't that bad, surely? He's used to beginners.'

'No, it's not that. I had dreadful hay-fever yesterday, it just came on me, and I couldn't stop sneezing and weeping, so when we stopped for lunch I took two of my antihistamine pills. I didn't tell you, but when we started again after lunch I suddenly felt dizzy, and everything went round me, and I clung on and screamed for Hamish, who steamed across to grab me just before I fell. I got down, on a rope, with Hamish placing all my hands and feet, and I went home and slept for three hours until you got back. It didn't occur to me until I was in the middle of G minor just now that it must have been the pills. What a stupid thing to do, and really very unfair to Hamish!' She grinned companionably at Sally Vernon who had drifted up with the rest of the table-tennis four. 'I was terrible.'

'So was I,' Sally agreed, with fervour. 'Worse than you.'

McLeish opined, dead-pan, that from his vantage point there had been little to choose between the two of them, but on the whole he thought Francesca had been a shade the worse.

'Only with the assistance of hay-fever,' she pointed out reproachfully, amusing him as always by her innate competitiveness. She then had to explain what had happened to the rest of the group, now augmented by Alan Fraser, Mickey Hamilton and the long-suffering Hamish, revealed as a fading but still remarkably good-looking blond man in his late fifties.

'I should have noticed you were taking something,' he said, the Highland courtesy to the idiot tourist very marked, but Francesca rightly would have none of it, and said it had been particularly stupid of her, since the bottle clearly stated that the pills could cause dizziness.

'My only excuse is that I am usually sitting at a desk when I take them, and I don't seem to get very dizzy doing that. Anyway, sorry, and thank you for preventing me falling off.'

'Will you play something for us, then?' Hamish asked, sensibly changing the subject, and McLeish, possessed of an indifferent baritone and no real desire to expose it, faded quietly away towards the hotel lounge to find some coffee, leaving the group hunting through the piano stool for music. He got his coffee, placed himself in one of the less uncomfortable chairs, and was just reaching for a six-month-old *Illustrated London News* when he realized that Alec McKinnon, the local police force, was placing himself in the next-door chair. He offered him a cup of coffee, and waited to see what he wanted.

'It was good of you to go so quickly to young Fraser's aid,' McKinnon started formally, then elaborately found himself milk, sugar and a biscuit while McLeish waited patiently. McKinnon sighed. 'Ye work at the Home Office, I think ye said?'

The question was courteous but carefully phrased, and McLeish, under cover of the general noise from the bar, explained promptly who and what he was. 'I have my warrant card, of course.'

'No, no.' McKinnon waved the suggestion away, embarrassed but, as McLeish realized, in no way surprised.

'Did the Wilson cousins tell you Francesca had a copper for a boyfriend?'

'No. We'd a message from your people in London.' McLeish blinked at him, taken aback. 'You're young for your rank,' McKinnon observed, ungrudgingly. 'It's customary for forces to let each other know when someone of your seniority is going to be in their part of the world for any length of time.'

McLeish nodded, mildly alarmed. He was used to being recognized everywhere in the Met area, it was part of the family atmosphere; but it was a new thought that he was now going to be known wherever he went, at least to senior people in the local force. He realized that McKinnon was waiting for the answer to some unspoken question, and said that, strange as it was that someone of Fraser's experience should have fallen from a climb he knew like the back of his own hand, there had been nothing to suggest it was not an accident.

'Miss Wilson — Francesca — said to me that she had seen another person up on the ridge in a yellow anorak?'

'Yes, that's right, she mentioned it to me at the time; but when I looked the mist was down. She has long sight, and it was she who saw Fraser fall, and where he fell, too.'

McKinnon sipped at his coffee, then put the cup tidily aside. 'I wondered, you see. That lad had a lot of luck. He fell 200 feet down a cliff, and he was only knocked out. And you two had seen him — all right, Miss Wilson had seen him — and you then got to where he was lying very quickly indeed, by all accounts.' He paused, and finished his biscuit, and gave McLeish a quick sideways look. 'Before anyone could have climbed down to him, if there was anyone up there who had wished him harm enough to have dropped something on him in the first place.'

McLeish stared at the steady, unexcitable, square-shouldered fifty-year-old, now placidly munching on a sugar lump, and felt the curious sensation of having missed a step in the dark.

'Of course, I may be having a wee flight of fancy and trying to make life more interesting for myself and the boys up here,' McKinnon suggested, peacefully. No one, McLeish thought grimly, could possibly be less excitable.

'No evidence,' he said a minute later, having reviewed the events of the day.

'No. If the lad had been killed, as by all accounts he should have been, we'd not even know what he thought. And the damage would have been just the same whether he had fallen or been pushed in some way.'

Or, indeed, if someone had finished him off as he lay there on the hillside, McLeish thought silently. Nor would it have taken much to kill him, semi-conscious as he had been.

'What is Fraser's family?' he asked, to give himself time to think.

'His father was a seaman, lost off his ship when Alan was only a wee boy. His mother came back here — she was a local girl — and she and the grandmother brought him up in that butt and ben you see on the hill there.'

That's it, McLeish thought, enlightened; that's why he is like Francesca. It's another fatherless child, that same pride and driving competence, and the same carefully concealed need to be loved that informed Francesca's life. He came back doggedly to the main issue.

'Who would want to lay for young Fraser?'

'More than one father in this district. But no one I'd point to, and no one I think would feel badly enough to do it. Well, never mind, the lad's alive and well, thanks to you and your young lady. Indeed, I'm sorry to worry you with it on your holiday but I thought I ought to have a word. If ye think of anything now, ye'll find me at Carrbrae tomorrow and the day after.'

McLeish agreed to ring if anything at all occurred to him, and as he walked with McKinnon to the hotel door, he found himself glad that Carrbrae was fifteen miles away. It was difficult not to resent the intrusion into his and Francesca's longed-for holiday, particularly when, thinking about it calmly, he could not see how anyone could have dropped anything on Fraser. He settled down again in his chair, drifted off into sleep, and was woken half an hour later by two middle-aged ladies tripping over his feet.

'Who is that singing in there, just now, do you know?' The plumper of the two, having apologized, was listening, entranced and he listened too. Someone was singing 'Ye banks and braes o' Bonnie Doon' in a clear high tenor, perfectly produced, every word audible. Two lines later, McLeish sat up, incredulous, and sweeping the two ladies aside, marched grimly over to the door of the recreation room and pushed it open.

A crowd of about thirty were assembled, mostly climbers, uniformly square and sunburnt, huge mugs of beer clasped in large brown hands, but also a sprinkling of children and teenagers, plus Sally Vernon, Bill Vernon, Alan Fraser and Mickey Hamilton. There too, infuriatingly, was Francesca's brother Peregrine, who should have been safely immured in a recording studio in West London. He was standing by his sister at the piano, not a hair out of place, looking as usual like something out of a film, singing to the silent crowd. Francesca was playing for him, a tricky running accompaniment to the simple melodic line, chewing the inside of her cheeks as she did when concentrating. Perry was totally concentrated, apparently making no attempt at dramatic presentation and letting the words speak for themselves, but his audience was frozen in place by the grief and the sense of loss he was communicating.

Ye banks and braes o' Bonnie Doon,
How can ye bloom sae fresh and fair?

How can ye chant, ye little birds,
And I sae weary, full o' care?

The golden tenor voice sang on, and you could see the roses bloom, and feel the warmth of the wind that could make no headway against the cold of loss and misery. How did Perry, grown to a dazzling adult from a gilded child, who had been secure in this extraordinary gift since his childhood, understand anything about loss and rejection, McLeish wondered.

Perry reached the last line, every word clear. '*Departed never to return*,' he sang, drawing out the two repeated notes on 'return'. He let the last note fade, biting off the final 'n', and after a measured few seconds turned and smiled at his sister at the piano. She put her hands in her lap, and smiled back at him in perfect accord, and McLeish stayed by the door while the audience came out of its trance and applauded vigorously.

'John, look who's here!' Francesca appealed to him, radiant and perfectly confident that he would share her pleasure in having one of her brothers turn up in the middle of his holiday.

'Just passing, were you Perry?' McLeish asked grimly.

'Yes, actually,' Perry said, meticulously shaking hands. 'Sheena is another hour away from here, up the coast.'

McLeish, the wind taken from his sails, asked what on earth Perry's staggeringly elegant model girlfriend was doing in this part of the world?

'The Pollock Calendar. Michael Valentine is doing the shoot just up the coast from here. She doesn't want me there until six because it's a shooting day, so I thought I'd stop off and see you both.' He smiled on them, confident of his welcome, and turned aside politely to sign his name for the wide-eyed teenage daughter of a stolid English family who plainly could not believe her luck.

'But Perry,' Francesca obviously had not absorbed the ostensible reason for his presence, 'the Pollock Calendar? I didn't know Sheena did that sort of modelling. Isn't she, well, a bit thin for it?'

'This year, the Calendar is going to be an artistic triumph, Fran.'

'Ah. You mean they are all going to wear clothes? Like last year when everyone was dressed in tiny little overalls, sheltering behind giant wrenches or cuddling up to lengths of downpipe? She'll freeze in this climate.'

'*No*, darling, she and the others are being Scottish ladies in scenes from Scottish history, dressed to the eyebrows in historical clothing.'

'How is anyone to know it is the Pollock Calendar then?' Francesca who disliked Perry's dazzling girlfriend, was enjoying herself. 'In what portion of the historical clothing is the plumber's wrench to be disposed? I'm sorry, Perry, I don't seem to have grasped this at all. The one thing I do understand is why you have come rushing up here. Michael Valentine always looks very fanciable in his photographs — rather Sheena's sort of thing, I would have thought.'

'Bitch,' her brother observed, entirely justifiably. 'But yes, you have a point, I thought I'd better visit. Biff is driving for me — the Car is out there — and I thought we could have lunch and then go on slowly.'

The weather remaining unbrokenly terrible, the party drifted back towards the lounge. McLeish looked hopefully towards Francesca but she had settled down next to Perry who obviously had something to ask her. He watched the two faces, so alike, but yet so different from each other in overall effect. On Francesca, the high cheekbones, deep-set blue eyes and long straight noise looked austere, and serious; on Peregrine the same bones were changed and relieved by the fact that his eyes were less deep-set and were set off by very long black eyelashes, and that he had his dead father's clear olive skin and some curl in the thick dark hair. Francesca would always look interesting but, off her day, could look downright plain. Perry, on or off his day, was always dazzling.

Perry, seeing him watching, waved to him to join them. 'Who is the dark chap, John?' he said, indicating Mickey Hamilton. 'I've seen him before somewhere. I just can't place him.'

'Mickey Hamilton — he was at Grantchester ahead of Tristram,' Francesca said.

'Oh, *that's* where I've seen him. He's gay, then?'

'Perry! Just because he was at Grantchester. You mustn't say that sort of thing!'

McLeish, despite having his own reasons for thinking that Perry was right in this case, supported her. Perry smiled at him ungrudgingly, and turned to greet Alan Fraser with real pleasure, while McLeish watched, wondering idly how the relationship between Fraser and Hamilton worked. Fraser being evidently about as homosexual as the average tomcat, there must be stresses.

'How are you, mate?' Perry was asking cheerfully.

'Goodness, how you've grown.' Both young men fell about in recognition of what was obviously an old joke.

'Do you want to have lunch? Then I must away and see the girlfriend up the way here.'

'In the wee brown car?' Fraser asked, grinning. 'What is it? A stretched Rolls?'

'Something like that. I read your book, mate, loved it. What are you doing here? What's the talent like?'

John McLeish, watching this encounter benevolently, noticed that Francesca was looking just a little green-eyed at having her favourite brother monopolized and suggested everyone might have lunch, hastily including Sally Vernon and Nigel Makin in the invitation. Sally accepted at once and managed to sit herself next to Fraser. Nigel Makin sat down firmly at her other side, putting his hand over hers when asking her what she wanted to drink, and she blushed and looked annoyed.

'So how many of these women are there up the way, then?' Fraser was asking.

'Four principal models, and one's mine, mate. Then the usual hangers-on — make-up girls, stylists, wardrobe people.'

'I've never been able to imagine what *those* do, given that up to this year no one has worn any clothes worth mentioning,' Francesca observed.

'Would I be in the way if I took a lift in the wee car with you? I've an auntie living up there and I could sleep at her house,' Fraser asked.

'Just so long as you remember which of the girls is mine, you're welcome. Be nice to have company.'

McLeish had been watching Sally Vernon, who was by now looking furious rather than wretched. Francesca had been right, there was something there. He considered Nigel Makin who was stolidly eating roast beef and three vegetables and ignoring the conversation, and asked him a civil question about his job, getting an immediately sensible answer. They talked decorously through the meal, McLeish tucking away the facts about the Vernon Engineering empire, so that Makin warmed to him and started to talk about himself.

'I came from the house-building side, but I took over civil engineering as well six months ago. It's mostly a control problem — costs and materials — but the profit margins are much thinner in civils. We have a land bank so we can make a bigger margin on houses. Civils is project work, you have to make the money by being bloody well organized.'

They were interrupted by the party breaking up, Perry telling Fraser to hurry, bidding punctilious farewells, and kissing his sister.

'The week after next in London, then. Goodbye, John, very good to see you.'

'Nice of him to stop by, wasn't it?' Francesca said, smiling as she waved to the car.

'I take it he wanted something.' McLeish had no illusions about Perry.

'He did, in fact,' she admitted, fair-mindedly.

'He nearly always has something he wants when he comes to see you.' McLeish was aware that he was pushing his luck, and was less than surprised to get a very reproachful look. He laughed and kissed her, and ushered her back into the lighted hotel lounge, out of the grey afternoon. Sally and Nigel Makin had vanished so he was able to bundle her into her weatherproof gear and take her back to the cottage.

CHAPTER 5

Two days later on a bright Tuesday morning Sally Vernon, sitting at her father's right at breakfast in the hotel lounge, was well aware that she was courting difficulty.

'Dad.'

'Mmm.'

'You and Nigel are fishing today, aren't you? I don't really want to spend all day there, but I'll come at lunchtime. Is that all right?'

'Whatever you like.' Robert Vernon, who liked to read his newspaper uninterruptedly at breakfast, turned over a page definitively, but Sally persevered.

'Nigel wants me to be there all day, but you know I'm bored by a whole day. Please Dad, just help.'

Her father looked at her over the paper in exasperation.

'Just tell him you don't want to come till lunchtime. Have you had words?'

'That's right,' she said, thankful for the formula. 'I just want to go back to bed and get some sleep, then I'll turn up in a better mood. Please Dad, just tell him.'

'Your mother won't let me do this sort of thing for you when you're married, you know.'

'Thanks, Dad. I'm going back to bed. Tell Nigel I'll meet you at lunch.' She finished her cup of tea hastily, kissed her father and walked away. Her father watched her thoughtfully, from behind his paper, noticing sardonically that every man of his own generation in the dining-room was watching her hips more or less covertly as she swung through the room, elegant in designer jeans and a T-shirt.

* * *

In her bedroom Sally undressed and put on a black silk nightdress cut like a petticoat but stopping at mid-thigh, and considered herself carefully in the mirror on the inside of the wardrobe. Typical of Scotland that the only mirror should be too small to see yourself at full length and placed on the inside of a wardrobe door which swung closed unless you held it open. She smiled at her reflection, brushing her hair so that it fell almost to her shoulders, liking the contrast of the pale blonde hair with the exiguous black nightie and her fair skin.

She checked her watch, then looked carefully out of the window through a gap in the curtain and smiled to herself as she saw her father, her step-brother and Nigel loading fishing gear into the Range Rover, Nigel looking rather sullen. He glanced up towards her window and she stepped back involuntarily, although she could not have been seen. She waited until the car left, then pulled on a dressing-gown, made a phone call, and settled down with a magazine to wait.

Twenty minutes later there was a knock on the door and she slid out of bed to open it to Alan Fraser.

'We've got ages,' she said as he pulled her into his arms.

'Christ, my ribs. Ye'll have to be gentle with me Sally.'

'Take that sweater off, it's scratching me.' She helped him ease off the heavy Arran sweater, hand-knitted she observed jealously, and started on the buttons of his shirt. He held her breasts through the silk, feeling for the nipples, watching with pleasure as she breathed short.

'I left off my vest,' he said, grinning as she ran her hands gently over his ribs and she giggled.

'Well, a string vest isn't very sexy.'

'There are some that fancy it,' he observed, watching her go pink. 'Ouch! Stop that or I'll not be able.' He kicked off his shoes and pulled off jeans, underpants and socks in one and reached for her, pulling her on to the bed. He wouldn't let her take control, despite the fact that his ribs were obviously hurting, and she forgot in her pleasure to worry about it. He asked whether it had been all right for her afterwards but then he hardly needed to, she thought; he must have known that it worked. She turned over gently, so she could look into his face and was stricken to see how pale he was.

'Is it your ribs?'

'Worth it.'

'Why didn't you let me try?'

'I will next time,' he promised, eyes still closed, and she stroked the swollen cheek.

'How were the Calendar girls?'

'Delicious. All four of them.' His eyes remained stubbornly shut and she dug him sharply in the ribs.

'Stop it, Sal. How long have we got?'

'Till lunch. I promised to meet Dad then.' And Nigel, she added silently, but the quirk of Alan's mouth told her that he too had made that deduction.

'What are you doing this afternoon?' she asked hastily.

'Taking John McLeish up the hill.'

'Will you be able to climb?' she asked jealously.

'With my ribs you mean?' It took her a few seconds to realize she was being teased and she pulled his bright hair. 'Oh yes, he's not bad, but he's not in training and he's older, too. He went well on Saturday, and yesterday but he'll be stiff the day. And he and Francesca are likely doing the same thing as us this morning.'

She lay beside him considering the bruised profile. 'When are you going to London?'

'Next week some time. I'll get the best paying job I can. I don't mind trying your site if the bonus is right, but I've got to get the money — I've only just so much time. Or don't you want me there? Will I be in the way with you and Nigel?'

'I'm not sure I want to go on with Nigel.'

Alan sighed and squinted down at her as she lay against his shoulder. 'I'm going to K6 in September, Sal. Climbing is the only thing I want to do. I'll get out of the way now, if that's what you want.'

She lay still, having elicited precisely the response that she had feared.

'Sal.' His arm tightened round her. 'I'm not a marrying man. The married lads, they're always torn in two between the climbing and the wives. Look at Bonington — he promised the wife not to go to Everest. I could never do that.'

He moved out of her arms, swung his legs out of bed and winced as he bent to pick up his shirt. She reached urgently for him and stroked his back, laying her face against his shoulders.

'At least we have till September.' She felt him relax against her. 'Come back to bed. I'll make us some tea — they give you kettles here.'

She pulled on her dressing-gown and plugged in the kettle, thinking hard. If she wanted this man — and she did, with a passion that none of the other men she had been sleeping with since she was sixteen had ever aroused — she would have to go carefully. She made the tea, knowing that he took pleasure in watching her doing domestic tasks and took it over to him.

'It seems odd that I've known you five years and never been to bed with you till this summer,' she said conversationally, as they finished drinking. 'I suppose you were always otherwise occupied? Or didn't you fancy me?'

'Ah, Christ.' He put his cup down and reached out for her. 'Come here and we'll try it your way this time.'

* * *

The fishing party had arrived at intervals at the side of the river just above the falls. The day was cloudy but brightening so that the sun came through the clouds at intervals. Nigel Makin had arrived in a bad temper — justifiably, Robert Vernon conceded, in view of Sally's behaviour. He had, however, other things to do this morning and as he dispatched Nigel briskly upriver he called to his son to stay by him for a minute. He sighed inwardly as Bill backed clumsily out of the Range Rover, and thought bitterly of his first wife Susan, Bill's mother. That spoilt daughter of the County had been outraged when, furious at her barely concealed affair with a noted trainer, he had divorced her and married Dorothy. To add to his offence he had refused, absolutely, to meet her exorbitant demands for financial support. She had retaliated by keeping his son away from him for the best part of ten years by every means known to lawyers, and when she had belatedly realized the unwisdom of this strategy, had nagged him ever after to give Bill and her more money.

It was, of course, difficult to judge how much Bill had been behind this change of strategy. God knows he showed no other signs of any business ability. He had taken an extra two years to qualify as a quantity surveyor and had not shown any particular promise either on sites or in head office; he was pleasant enough but without the drive or the persistence needed to carry through a difficult contract. Robert Vernon sighed inwardly as his son dropped two rugs and a rod and turned anxiously to face him.

'Sorry, Robert.'

Being called Robert rather than Dad annoyed him too, but unreasonably; it had been Susan not the child of eight that Bill had then been who had insisted on eliminating any acknowledgement of the biological relationship between them.

'Doesn't matter. I wanted to talk before we started fishing.'

The look of anxious apprehension deepened, and Robert Vernon gritted his teeth. He reined himself back, hearing his wife Dorothy telling him forthrightly that he handled Bill badly.

'Bill, look,' he started awkwardly. 'When your mother divorced me she got a bloody good settlement for herself and a separate one for you.' He paused, cursing himself. Dorothy had told him not to start with a recital of the benefits Bill had already received, and one look at the shuttered, sullen face in front of him reminded him how sound her judgement had been. 'Be that as it may,' he plunged on, resolutely, 'the business is ten times the size it was then, and although it bloody well pinched me at the time, the cash you got doesn't look that much to me now. So, I'm going to give you enough to make it up to the same as Sally's getting next week when she's twenty-five. You'll get 200,000 shares in Vernon Construction, which allows for what you got before. They're yours absolutely, no trusts, and there may be more when I go, of course; but, as I said to Sally, there won't be much more until then unless it's for grandchildren.'

He stopped and reviewed the speech, pleased with himself. Vernon Construction's shares stood at over £10 and the gift he had just made put Bill into the millionaire class. He looked at him with the affection any donor feels for the object of his generosity and realized with horror that his son was chalk white and leaning against the big Range Rover. Had he been such a lousy father that this cash, which Bill must have known represented only about two per cent of his own holdings, caused the lad to pass out?

'Sorry, Robert, 200,000 shares? That's two million pounds. Oh God, I never expected anything like it. I can buy something up here.'

'Course you can. Make a nice holiday home.'

'No, that's not what I meant. I'm no good in your business — you know that. I can buy a farm — I've been saving for one and now I can do it. You don't mind, do you?'

Robert Vernon gazed at him, taken aback. 'What sort of farm?'

'A sheep farm in the Borders. This bit is beautiful all right,' a dismissive gesture wrote off the West Highlands, 'but the land's no good.'

'How much have you got already?' Robert Vernon sat down on the tailboard of the Range Rover, motioning his son to join him.

'About a hundred thousand, and the flat, of course, but I've got a mortgage . . .'

'You've done well — I thought you'd spent most of what I settled before, when you were at the university.'

'Oh well, I had some lucky investments as well.' Bill Vernon looked away, leaving his father to decide that he might have been too quick to dismiss this son of his as a financial fool. He knew the settlement he had made had been worth only £25,000 when Bill had reached twenty-five, ten years before. Somehow he had parlayed this into £100,000 plus a London house in Chelsea worth an easy £300,000.

'How much were you trying for?'

'I wanted £500,000, but £2 million-odd means I can buy a big enough farm to be sure I can make a decent living. I don't know yet what I'll buy now — this just changes everything. Thanks Robert, thanks a million. Thanks *two* million!' He snorted, somewhere between laughter and tears and blew his nose.

Robert Vernon put a hand on his shoulder. 'Don't think it had anything to do with your mother,' he said, resolutely ignoring Dorothy's warning voice inside his head. 'It was Dorothy who said it was only right to do the same for both of my children.'

The shoulder on which his hand rested stiffened. 'Sorry, forget that. Your mother's all right; it's just that she tried to bleed me white when I didn't have the cash.'

'I do know. She gets worried about being poor and old.'

'She'll not be poor, Bill, not while I live. We may not agree on what constitutes poverty but she'll not want.'

'Thanks, Dad.'

Ah, thought Robert Vernon in a flash of insight, that's what a father is to him, it's someone who looks after his mother — that's why I'm Dad all of a sudden. I maybe should have given the bitch a bit more cash all these years, and maybe I will give her a bit to go on with, same as Dorothy is suggesting.

'You've just not found your place in Vernon Engineering, Bill,' he said, judiciously, warmed by the acknowledgement, 'but that's not to say you've failed. You've always tried hard and, what's important, you've always been straight, not tried to bend the rules or gone in for anything not quite right with customers. That matters to me more than anything, you know; to deal with people I know are straight. I'm not one of the people who needs a son to follow me.'

He smiled benevolently on his son who looked at his feet and went perceptibly red.

'So let's go fishing, eh? I've told the lawyers to get on with it — it has to be done carefully because neither of us wants to pay tax we don't have to, but the shares will be yours in about six weeks.'

He dispatched Bill to his fishing, thinking that he was unlikely to be concentrating well enough to catch anything, and sauntered upriver to see how Nigel Makin was getting on. Makin had evidently got over his bad temper, and was casting steadily.

'Something over there in the pool under that bank. I think he knows I'm here,' he said quietly. 'I'll leave him a while. Any luck yourself?'

'I haven't been trying. I've been having a chat with Bill.' He watched the younger man for a minute: at thirty-six, he was the youngest MD of a major construction company in the UK. He had turned out to be one of the people who knew how to squeeze every ounce of profit out of a project. His immediate priority after the holiday would be the Western Underpass; even in the first flush of triumph at snatching this prestige job from larger firms, Robert Vernon never lost sight of his objectives.

'I was thinking about the Underpass,' he offered in explanation and without apology for letting business intrude. For Nigel Makin, as for him, business was the real world and holidays an interruption.

'Be interesting, that. I'm really looking forward to being there.'

'You can't give it all your time, of course.'

'No need. I can manage it by going there one day a week.'

This was offered in the flat North London accent with absolute confidence, and Robert Vernon nodded. Makin was a formidably hard worker and had sorted out the notoriously difficult Barbican site over the six months by a rigidly organized system of financial control. After a few furious rows — in which Robert Vernon had not been called upon to assist — the system had worked perfectly. As a resentful member of the production control staff had put it, nothing moved or breathed on site without being recorded by Nigel Makin's computer.

'What I have been meaning to say is that it's going to be worth lighting the Underpass site at night,' Makin commented. 'I know you aren't happy about the cost but without lights things will walk. We'll lose materials and people.'

'I know that. It was the client I was angry with, not being prepared to pay for decent security. There's some of our profit gone for a start.'

'We'll get it back.' Nigel Makin spoke with complete certainty and Robert Vernon looked at him with affection. Getting back expenses imposed by the clients is at the heart of successful civil engineering, and this man had a real relish for the job. 'We lost thousands — I reckon over £300,000 — in three months on the Barbican. Even the big RSJs grew legs and walked away overnight.' Nigel Makin was not amused by his own joke, his eyes were narrowed and he looked even more like a well-cared-for ferret. From a business point of view his obsession was entirely reasonable; a situation in which lorry loads of twenty-foot reinforced steel joists vanished into the surrounding streets in one night was well out of control.

'That was a bugger, that site,' Vernon observed companionably. 'And you and your team did well to get us out of there with something in our pockets. Of course it's worth lighting the Western Underpass. And getting some decent blokes. Young Fraser and his partner may be there — if the bonus is good enough, he told me, cheeky bugger.'

'Fraser and Hamilton were at the Barbican, of course.'

'Were they now?' Robert Vernon mentally came to attention. He scowled at the surrounding heather while Makin discreetly contemplated the middle distance.

'Fraser involved at all?' he finally, reluctantly, asked.

'Don't know, but several loads of steel went walkabout one night during the time when he and his gang were around. We asked them, of course, but they never saw a thing.'

Robert Vernon squinted into the sun, wondering whether it would not save trouble all round to have Fraser kept off Western Underpass, when suddenly the sun went behind a cloud and he could see what the bright dazzle had hidden — his daughter and Alan Fraser swinging down the road towards them. He watched them thoughtfully. Fraser, his red-blond hair like fire against the heather, waved a casual farewell to Sally and turned uphill towards a cliff, at the top of which Francesca and John McLeish could just be seen, sitting and eating lunch. Sally came towards the fishing party, smiling and sure of her welcome.

'Hello, I needed that. I'd got very tired. I came down with Alan because he is taking Francesca's boyfriend climbing this afternoon.'

'He's got a name you know,' Robert Vernon observed drily. 'Why does everyone call him Francesca's boyfriend?'

'I suppose because he's the strong and silent type.' Sally was unabashed. 'I can't even find out what he does for a living. Alan doesn't know either.'

They summoned Bill and sat at lunch, watching Fraser go easily up the cliff.

'We've got wine today,' Bill who was unpacking the hamper observed.

'Yes.' Robert Vernon waited until all four glasses were filled and, after checking that Sally and Nigel were still looking up at Fraser on the cliff, raised his glass to his son, wordlessly. Bill smiled in return, his face relaxed with pleasure.

Alan Fraser hauled himself over the top of the cliff, and Sally and Nigel turned away to take their glasses. Robert Vernon, warmed by his son's smile, raised his glass generally to the party and they all toasted each other as the fitful sun shone warmly.

CHAPTER 6

The last afternoon John McLeish spent in bed with Francesca. They got up in a leisurely way, and packed and had supper, McLeish firmly taking over the task of getting clothes into suitcases, having noticed with some pleasure that his admirable Francesca was an impatient packer. Someone else must actually have packed the school trunks he observed, laughing at her as she sat, pink and cross, in the middle of their clothes.

'All the schools insisted on trunks in which, if necessary, you could have put the boy as well as all his kit. One just dropped the stuff in. I don't want to go back to the grindstone. I'm afraid I'll never see you, it'll be like it was before we came up.'

McLeish winced, remembering the ten days before his holiday had started when he had worked virtually without a break and had seen Francesca for precisely eight hours, six of which he had been asleep. 'I've got an idea,' he said carefully, not looking at her. 'We could get married. We'd see more of each other that way.'

Francesca, sitting amid piles of clothes, climbing boots and towels, did not look at him either. 'I do love you, John,' she said to a pile of socks. 'I just don't want to get married again yet.' She sneaked a look at him and finding him still contemplating the inside of a suitcase, watched him helplessly, knowing that she was wounding him. He looked over at her, unsmiling, very large in the small room.

'Darling John, I'm getting there. Bear with me.' Seeing him still looking tired and angry, she dumped the socks and went over to him, pulling him to her.

'Don't leave it too long,' he said, unyielding, 'I might go off with someone else, you know.'

'I do know.' It was her turn to feel angry and rejected, but she knew this was unreasonable and bit her lip.

'Come on, I'll finish this and we'll go across to the hotel, get that over.'

Francesca, feeling herself too much in the wrong to object to this anti-social approach, meekly handed him clothes and kit and they finished the packing in an uncompanionable silence. Both of them felt better as McLeish closed the big suitcases and slung them into the car, leaving only the overnight case that would go with them on the Inverness/London train the next night. She slid a hand into his as they headed for the hotel, and was relieved to feel a small answering pressure. She looked sideways at his determined heavy jaw and checked her stride. 'John. Bit of a cuddle?'

He stopped and looked down at her sternly, but yielded as she had known he would. Not a man to bear a grudge, she thought thankfully; a good man and a kind one.

'Come on, I'll buy you a drink.'

He abandoned her with her drink in the hotel bar, looking for Alan Fraser. Well, the holiday had brought him that; the pleasure of an old skill revived and a superb teacher. Whatever Alan's motives — gratitude, a general hospitality to tourists, or indeed simple liking — he had given John a marvellous time and taken a lot of trouble with him. Francesca watched with affection as, failing to find Alan, he stopped to talk to Sally Vernon. She herself greeted Sally's father who was standing with Mickey Hamilton. 'Seen young Fraser?' he asked. 'I'm supposed to be buying him a drink.'

Alan arrived at that moment, lifting a hand to John McLeish, but making his way towards Robert Vernon. Heads turned as he walked down the bar, nodding to friends and acquaintances, apologizing gracefully but without any expectation that he would not be forgiven. The worst of his bruises and scratches had faded and the remainder were gone; and the red-gold hair above the sunburnt face showed very bright against the light as he accepted a drink. He had obviously been drinking for some time before joining the party; he was a little flushed and stumbling very slightly on his words. Mickey Hamilton observed, just audibly, that he was putting it away fast enough, and Fraser swung on him, eyes slightly narrowed. 'So would you be. I just heard some bad news.'

'What?'

'The New Zealanders have called off their Everest expedition — not enough sponsorship — and have offered to transfer the cash they do have in return for three places on K6 for Bryant, Woolley and Connor. Michaelson's going to take them; he says he's sorry but he's still short of cash. He may still be able to fit one of us in, but he isn't promising even that.'

He was looking steadily at Mickey, and it occurred to at least two of the observers that it would have been better if he had given the bad news privately rather than telling the whole bar. McLeish found himself again reluctantly reminded of Perry Wilson who, privileged and fêted for his gifts from early childhood, always tended to take the easy way out of a difficult situation. Mickey had turned white, the dark-brown eyes looking larger and more deep-set than ever.

'Can somebody buy his way in like that?' Robert Vernon asked, bluntly, taking the view that the subject, once introduced, was open to general discussion.

'Oh yes, they can,' said Fraser, 'but it'll take more than either of us can earn by September, even if my fucking agent gets off his backside and gets me a decent advance on the next book. And my ribs are giving me gyp.' He glared across at Mickey, who stared back, and then swung on Francesca.

'Now if I'd had the Highers, it might have been different, mightn't it?'

McLeish moved automatically to protect her, but she was in no need of assistance.

'No, you cuckoo, it's hard cash or sponsorship, not education they want. They'll take you both if they can, surely? I mean, I've seen pictures of those New Zealanders, sweet Charlie Bryant, well over forty with a face like a road map, and the other two look like ferrets. The sponsors will need something nice-looking to beam at the general public out of a tent, or round a mouthful of pemmican, or whatever.'

The brisk common sense of this approach, combined with the unkind dismissal of the New Zealand group, stopped Fraser in his tracks. 'Which of us are they going to take then, Francesca?' he asked, maliciously, but she gave the question careful consideration.

'Which of you is the better climber in K6 conditions?'

That was the sort of question, McLeish thought, mentally cowering under the bar, that would only be asked by someone out of a family like the Wilsons, where they all knew, beyond possibility of argument, which of them was the better musician in what circumstances.

'I am better on rock. Mickey has more snow and ice experience.'

Alan Fraser, just like a Wilson, had no problem being dispassionate about his considerable qualities.

'You, on the other hand, are more photogenic,' Francesca offered in exactly the same spirit, and Alan Fraser, reluctantly smiling, nodded to her in acknowledgement.

McLeish glanced down at Sally Vernon, who was watching Francesca with something between horror and admiration. Fraser came over to join them and he and McLeish fell easily into conversation. 'Will you be alright to work on a site?' McLeish asked.

'The ribs are still a bit sore, but I think I can handle steel. I won't work if I'm having difficulty — scaffolding's not a job to cut corners on, any more than climbing.'

The pride in his own capacity was very clear and McLeish was interested. This was not just something he did to earn money.

'It's a skilled trade. A good scaffold makes the rest of the work go faster. A bad one — not properly tied in, a sloppy job — slows up the site as well as being bloody dangerous. I've seen blokes killed because they were worn out by working on a bad piece of scaffolding.' He looked slightly embarrassed at his own intensity and changed the subject by drawing McLeish's attention to where Francesca and Robert Vernon had withdrawn to a small table and were locked in serious conversation.

'Old Vernon trying to seduce Francesca, is he?'

'No.' John McLeish spoke with complete certainty. 'That's what she looks like when she's fixing something.'

Francesca had realized that Robert Vernon was trying to ask a question which he either could not or would not formulate, and she set out to encourage him to go on speaking without contributing herself.

'I sometimes wonder you know how the government thinks it can run the country, just with a lot of civil servants,' he was saying, the carefully reorganized vowels very conspicuous. 'Without offence to yourself, Francesca, none of you can have any business experience.'

'That is quite true.'

'I suppose they consult some leading businessmen. I mean, through the CBI or some organization like that.'

This suggestion caused Francesca to abandon her vow of silence immediately. 'No point at all asking the CBI anything. No two of their members agree on any economic measure, so all the wretched chairman is able to say is that lower taxes or lower interest rates would be a "good thing". Which hardly ranks as an authoritative contribution to Government thinking.'

'Well, who does advise them? Who do they ask? *I* could tell them a few things. I built up this business from nothing, I put up my first three houses with money borrowed from my Ma's brother. All we had in the world, that was.'

'Robert, are you telling me you'd be prepared to take one of the government advisory jobs? When can you start?'

'I did have someone from Housing suggest I might like to advise on Ancient Monuments,' he said, pleased but doubtful.

'Please do not waste yourself on that useless lot at Environment — excuse me, my good colleagues in other less favoured departments. My own department needs about six people now for real jobs. For instance, the Industrial Development Advisory Board is two short: you could do that. Or if you fancied Chairman of British Engineering, which is three days a week, you could join a very short list indeed.'

'Do any of these jobs pay?'

'Not so's you'd notice, no. You don't need the cash, do you?'

Robert Vernon disclaimed matter-of-factly any pressing financial need and she sat tight, with an effort, while she watched him move cautiously to the next point. 'You might have to put up with getting a gong,' she offered, picking her moment. 'It starts at MBE and works up. Chairman of one of the big things gets lumbered with a knighthood or near offer.'

'What are the big things?'

Gotcha, she thought, joyfully. 'They're mostly full-time. But people who serve part-time in several things get Ks — sorry, knighthoods — as well. There's a crude points system. Chairman of a Quango, if difficult enough, rates a K.'

They both looked up, disconcerted, as a barman asked them whether they wanted another drink as it was close to time.

'Something else? No? Francesca, we'll have lunch in London with some of your friends. Invite who you like.'

'It doesn't work like that. *You'll* get invited for disgusting sherry with some very senior chaps. Can I say you might be available for part-time things?'

'Yes. Yes, you can.' He patted her hand and beamed at McLeish who was hovering hopefully.

'Sorry to keep her to myself, young man, but we'd things to discuss. Is your department like hers?'

McLeish replied placidly that it was in fact very different, and he wondered if it were not time to go?

'I heard you making a date,' he said, as they walked up the path to their cottage, companionably intertwined under the pale grey sky.

'It's business,' she assured him. 'I may have found a new useful man who wants to do things for government.'

'Just you keep it to that,' he said, warningly, for form's sake, wholly unworried.

* * *

Thirty-six hours later they were standing side by side in the corridor of the train gazing out at the suburbs of North London, which looked grey and small and cramped after the brilliant clear light and wide horizons of the Highlands.

'That was the best holiday I've ever had,' McLeish said, sadly.

'Because Alan took you climbing,' Francesca said, laughing at him. 'You'll have to tell him you're a copper.'

'Yes, of course. Oh God, I don't want to go back to the office.'

'We've got the weekend,' Francesca pointed out.

'Your family vultures are gathering. I wouldn't put it past Perry to meet the train.'

Francesca looked at him reproachfully but could not prevent herself peering anxiously down the platform as they arrived at Euston. He burst out laughing, delighted to have been able to rattle her so easily. She pulled her head in suddenly, looking smug.

'It is not my family but yours on the platform.'

'What?' McLeish, whose parents lived in Leicester and came to London only reluctantly for a day's shopping, was incredulous. He pulled her unceremoniously out of the way as the train stopped with one final jerk. Standing at the head of the train was Detective Sergeant Bruce Davidson, one of his key staff at CI, looking haggard and a good deal older than his twenty-nine years. He was leaning against a police car, complete with siren and insignia, parked square across the platform, its uniformed driver asleep at the wheel.

'Oh Christ,' McLeish said with foreboding. Francesca dropped on to the platform and to Davidson's obvious surprise and pleasure greeted him with a kiss. McLeish, descending behind her, understood immediately why Davidson had been so honoured: the windows of the train were lined with passengers, craning to see the daring criminal for whom the police presence had been assembled.

'Chief Inspector!' Davidson, who had also woken up to the public interest in his presence, greeted him resoundingly. 'Did you have a good holiday? You're looking well, the both of you.' He cast a sideways glance at disappointed passengers filing past them and lowered his voice to normal conversational tones. 'I'm sorry to do this to you, but Commander Pryce wants you, now. I mean, he'd have liked to have you the day before yesterday but we persuaded him, nae bother, that it would take twenty-four hours to contact you and get you back and it wouldna be worth it. So I'm to take you back with me to the Yard, in what you stand up in, and we'll send the driver on to your flat for some clothes.' He spread his hands deprecatingly, an extremely good-looking black-haired Scot from Ayr, running slightly to fat at the middle.

'I'm not doing that,' McLeish stated, furious that his holiday should be cut short in this way. 'I'm not due in till Monday.'

Davidson looked uneasy, and pointed out that there was a conference in an hour's time on the particular case for which he was wanted. McLeish, grittily refusing to have his timetable dictated, found himself being undermined by Francesca who was saying anxiously that he must go, of course. McLeish, exasperated, told her to shut up but the damage was done.

'I'll leave the driver with Francesca then, John,' Davidson offered. 'He can drive her home, then make his way back to the Yard.'

This offer had the expected effect on Francesca, a fellow civil servant, who scouted promptly any suggestion that public resources should be squandered in this way. McLeish, furious with both of them, was opening his mouth to utter some contrary direction when he observed that Francesca was near tears.

'I'll be with you, in a minute,' he said quellingly to Davidson, handing him his rucksack, and gathered her to him, unconcerned with his audience. 'I'll come back with you. They can bloody wait.'

'No, that's silly, and they've taken a lot of trouble to find you. Do go, darling, I'm going to cry and I don't have a handkerchief.'

'You never have a handkerchief,' he said tenderly. 'Here.' He dug one out from a pocket.

'Do go, John.'

'I'm going. Look after yourself. I'll ring you.' He let go of her reluctantly and headed for the police car to which Davidson had tactfully retreated, halting abruptly as he saw Alan Fraser and Mickey Hamilton, rucksacks at their feet.

'What's this then, John?' Alan Fraser was looking particularly wide awake, red-headed and amused. 'Will we look after Francesca while you are away for the next twenty years?'

'I was going to find you this morning and tell you where I worked. I haven't got a card but I'm at New Scotland Yard in CI. And would you look after Francesca, right now? Buy her a coffee and see she gets the car off all right? Sorry, I must go.'

He turned and waved to Francesca, indicating Alan and Mickey, and she waved back, head slightly tipped back in order, as he realized, not to cry. For a moment he was utterly outraged at having to leave her there, but the long habit of responsibility took over and swept him into the car beside the driver who had woken refreshed from sleep and whisked them through the thick London traffic going as fast as he could without using the siren.

* * *

Alan and Mickey arrived at Francesca's side and took her and her overnight bag away for coffee, observing that it had been very fly of the pair of them to have concealed the fact that she had a copper for a boyfriend.

'It's like being a doctor on holiday,' she said apologetically, blowing her nose. 'If you admit to it, you'll get to be consulted on everything.'

'He must be pretty senior for them to send a man and a driver like that,' Mickey Hamilton said. 'What is he?'

'A Detective Chief Inspector, and he works in CI which deals with murder. Not all murders, since most are dealt with where they happen. But CI gets the murders which are difficult for one reason or another — either they involve important people or they may be linked to another murder. They have a full-time man with a computer who does nothing but consider all murders wherever committed, in order to decide whether CI ought to call in a particular case.' The coffee and talking about McLeish were combining to keep tears at bay. 'But they are short-handed, and he's very good.'

'Done well for yourself there, Fran,' Fraser agreed. 'He likes it, doesn't he?'

'Oh yes. Loves it. Which is why I knew he'd have to go this morning. Ah, the cars.' She blew her nose, finally and definitively. 'Where are you two off to?'

'We're staying with a climbing mate for a couple of days till we get fixed up on a site. We'll be in a caravan if we end up on the Western Underpass.'

'Let us know, Alan. We could give you supper if you get tired of fry-ups.'

She set off to fetch her own car but Alan took her keys, drove it off for her, and made sure all her kit was loaded in, which she received placidly as a tribute to John McLeish.

CHAPTER 7

'I'm enquiring about a Mr Patrick O'Connor, please, admitted last night. My name's Stewart and I'm his guv'nor from the Western Underpass site, Vernon Construction . . . Yes, I'll wait.'

The speaker hooked the phone between his shoulder and his ear, indicating economically to the mini-skirted girl who appeared in the doorway that a cup of coffee would be welcome. He pulled a tray of papers towards him and started work. 'He's holding his own, is he?' Stewart listened, wincing, to a weary voice at the other end delivering a dispassionate recitation of the injuries sustained by Mr O'Connor on falling fifty feet from the scaffolding which he had been engaged in erecting. 'I thought he'd make it — he fell soft, hit the sand and missed the reinforced steel we had waiting by maybe six feet,' he observed to the unseen voice at the other end. 'Was he pissed, doc?' The voice grew wary and Stewart sighed. 'All right, all right, I'll let the insurance company sort that out. Thank you for your trouble.'

He shook his head, made a note, picked up his coffee and walked over to the window and stood watching the site outside. He was standing in what had been the living-room of a substantial Victorian villa, its proportions destroyed by a desk placed across the fireplace facing out into the room, by telephone and light wires crudely draped around its once elegant marble. Crowded into the rest of the room was a dining-table large enough to seat ten, surrounded by ten unmatching chairs.

The bright September sun lit the whole disheartening scene, revealing the layer of fine dust that drifted in even through closed windows and despite the half-hearted efforts of the elderly general labourer who was dabbing at the furniture with a filthy duster. The villa itself, surrounded by a fringe of Portakabins, sat facing out over a hundred-yard-wide stretch of scarred clay, reaching further than the eye could see right out into the West London suburbs. The villa looked ridiculous and forlorn, but Jimmy Stewart had seen only a viable building which would save the expense of buying more Portakabins.

As he watched, one of the big pile-driving machines started up, the noise very clear even through a closed window. The eight o'clock hooter went off, and men scattered on the site, all helmeted, Vernon Construction employees in yellow, Vernon Construction engineers in green, and the client's consulting engineers in blue. He reached for his own helmet, which uncompromisingly stated him to be site agent, and made towards the door, banging into one of the ten chairs and cursing as he did every morning. He walked into the villa's dining-room, uncomfortably full of men in working clothes, his eye skimming them automatically to see if any of them looked useful.

Today being Saturday, men came sightseeing from other sites to find out if the bonus was better than where they were. You could pick up some useful labour on a Saturday, and he just hoped the lad who had been wished on him by Head Office as industrial relations officer and site personnel man knew how to do that. He pushed his way into a small boarded-up section of the room, and both men occupying the tiny partitioned segment of the room visibly jumped. Stewart raised his eyebrows at the man he knew, Douglas Allen, a young personnel trainee who looked permanently a bit too pleased with himself for Stewart's taste and who was at that moment looking particularly self-satisfied.

'Mr Stewart, this is Alan Fraser who has a team of three men working with him. I'm just going to take him out to the foreman scaffolder on Section I.'

'I'm a foreman scaffolder, myself, and I'll see the general foreman,' said the bright-haired man.

Jimmy Stewart's eyebrows went up and he took a long, unhurried look at this cocky customer. A glamour boy, with red-blond hair that shone in the dusty, tired room, and blue eyes; tall and light, but with heavy powerful shoulders; young for a foreman scaffolder, who are part of a site's aristocracy, but recognizable anywhere as a scaffolder, even without the distinctive scaffolder's tools carried slung from his belt. It was something about the slight swagger with which all scaffolders strode around the site, the heavy keys dragging their belts off their hips, like cowboys in a Western.

'What's your problem, lad?' he asked, pleasantly.

'Not my problem. I hear your scaffolders are a load of dossers, but I know your general foreman on that section and he's all right. I hear you're a foreman short since yesterday, too.'

This statement, addressed as to an equal, caused Stewart to raise another eyebrow. A foreman scaffolder, however conscious of his market position, usually demonstrated some deference to a senior site agent. A fellow Scot, of course, West Coast; but there was something about the man that was more than the Scots lack of deference to authority.

'Will I do instead of the GF?' he asked with interest.

'Why not? The gang is in there.' He jabbed a finger at the waiting room. 'We'll stand up some steel for you.'

Jimmy Stewart belatedly glanced at Douglas Allen who said, stiffly, that in the particular case of a scaffolder this was probably a sensible procedure.

'Where's he come from?' Stewart asked, watching out of the awkwardly placed window as Fraser marched his group over to a stack of scaffolding poles.

'His home address is given as Culdaig. He's on subsistence, living on the caravan site,' Douglas Allen reported efficiently, 'and his mate is Michael Hamilton, home address in Edinburgh. The other two are brothers — Irish, addresses in Cork.'

Stewart nodded, and stood quietly beside Douglas Allen and watched. Alan Fraser had been joined by a dark man — as tall as he but slighter, pale-faced with deep-set brown eyes, and by two heavy-set Irishmen, recognizable anywhere by the way they walked, as if pulling booted feet from Irish mud. Their shoulders were hunched and their arms held slightly away from their bodies as if to balance themselves. All of them took off their jackets, in a leisurely way, revealing the scaffolders' tools dangling from their belts, and moved towards the pile of eighteen-foot scaffolders' tubes. Hamilton rolled an eighteen-foot length of tube off the pile, grabbed it by the middle, heaved it vertically into the air and dropped it on to the spike, not a movement wasted. Fraser's red-blond mop of hair flashed in the sun as he stood up another eighteen-foot length. One of the stocky men wordlessly put out a hand and took the tube as the younger man bolted on a crossbar. The other Irish brother moved in to help, and as Stewart watched appreciatively the makings of a scaffolding tower appeared under their hands. After ten minutes Fraser casually checked the bolts and nodded to his group. 'All right,' Stewart called, 'you're on.'

'How's the bonus? I've done £200 a week where I am, but we're getting buggered around by the engineers.'

'You got a certificate?'

'Oh, yes. We're a company.'

Jimmy Stewart nodded. No one on a building site who could possibly help it was on a PAYE system. They all had a certificate under the Act that enabled them to be paid gross of tax, on the basis that they would be responsible for the earnings of everyone they employed. God alone knew what actually happened to the tax.

He continued to watch Fraser. There was something about him which compelled attention; he had just that faint air of being used to the limelight. He had stopped, hands on hips, and was looking up at a scaffolding tower erected ready to enable the shuttering carpenters to put in the framework into which reinforcing steel would be fixed and concrete poured to make one of the myriad pillars which were going to support the roadway. He said something to the dark chap and was up the scaffold in a flash, thirty feet above the ground in seconds, leaning out to tighten a bolt. He went over three bolts, then shouted down to his oppo, who swarmed up towards him carrying a length of steel as casually as if it was a hammer. Fraser took it, bolted it in, shook the structure, and climbed down, jumping the last six feet.

Jimmy Stewart, curiosity thoroughly aroused, intercepted the two men as they came past the villa.

'Find a bit loose then?'

'Should have been bolted in again above thirty feet. It was a bad job. It would be worth going over all that lot in this section. Don't mind checking them for you this afternoon, if you like.'

'That'd be useful. Travelling man are you?'

'That's right. I need a place on the caravan site, and I need every penny I can earn.'

'What are you doing with it? Getting married?'

'Get away.' The man laughed. 'I'm a climber. I'm hoping to get on a Himalayan expedition in October.'

'Ah.' Well, that explained it, thought Jimmy Stewart resignedly. He loathed working in London because of the vagaries of London labour, and here he was with a good foreman scaffolder who was only doing it as a hobby. Typical.

'This is Mickey Hamilton — he's a climber, too.'

'How do you do.'

Jimmy Stewart blinked at the clear Edinburgh accent. 'Just a hobby for you lads, is it?'

'No, I'm trained, I've been on sites since I was sixteen. Mickey here used to work on sites in vacation from his university and I trained him. He's alright, but he'll not make a foreman.' Fraser was laughing at him. 'You ask the general foreman on Section I, he'll tell you. Any steel I put up won't wave in the breeze like that mess there.'

They had stopped by the office door and were idly watching a police car whisk across the tangle of roads by the fence and nose its way through the gate.

'Can't keep those buggers off the site,' Jimmy Stewart observed, and stood his ground as a stocky man got out of the back and headed into the office. 'You lads get away to your dinner. You're on to check these towers this afternoon, OK? That copper will be wanting me to fill up forms about the lad who fell off yesterday.'

Alan and Mickey waved a farewell to the Doolan brothers who constituted the rest of the gang, and walked across the road to the pub, dodging traffic. The dusty room was shabby; the pub itself had been long overdue for renovation before the urban motorway contract had been placed, and the owners had decided there was little point replacing the dirty plush curtains or shabby carpet during the three years the construction contract was expected to last. These were men who understood their business, however, and they had put substantial money into creating one bar running the whole length of the big room and the latest and most efficient cellarage and beer delivery system. Eight people, including a hand-picked Irish tenant and his wife, worked flat out behind the bar every hour of licensing hours. It was probably the most popular pub in London, with a turnover which gave credence to the popular view that the whole building site was administered from the pub: Jimmy Stewart, as a known customer, would find a gin and tonic placed automatically before him, unless he indicated otherwise as he walked in, and all the major subcontractors could depend on having their particular tipple put out for them at the lift of a finger.

Alan Fraser and Mickey Hamilton, moderate drinkers both, smiled at the prettiest of the barmaids, Deirdre Kelly, a cousin to the tenant and imported from Dublin, and asked for a pint of beer each and two pint glasses of water.

'Sally Vernon is over there,' Mickey Hamilton said, with an edge to his voice, 'attempting to attract your attention.'

Fraser looked round in a leisurely way and raised his glass to a corner table, indicating that he would be along to join them in his own time.

Deirdre glanced at him with interest. 'Boss's daughter, isn't she?' she enquired, putting four pints neatly in front of a silent quartet who had just arrived and who were indicating wordlessly that she should not hesitate to pull the next four. She did so, watching Fraser, and placed them just as the quartet arrived at the end of their first pint. Building labourers are always thirsty; hard work and dust and the heat of the sun dehydrate the human system very quickly, and on a hot September day most of the customers were sinking two pints or more of liquid before they could even taste it.

'Yes, she's a trainee engineer.'

'Well for some.' The barmaid, pink and pretty, with clear fresh skin, black hair and black eyelashes, was the object of much attention and could have had her pick of the site. She looked curiously at the slight blonde girl whose long, fine, fair hair was sticking to her scalp where she had taken off her site helmet. 'She'll be worth a few bob.'

'She's not as beautiful as you.' Mickey Hamilton raised his glass to Deirdre but she was unimpressed, watching appreciatively the way Alan Fraser's wide shoulders moved as he fished for money to pay for their drinks.

'Give me another one, please, I'll take it over there. And for my friend here.' He picked up the drinks and walked over to the corner, the barmaid's eyes following him.

'Do you want to sit outside, Sally?' Fraser said, and she smiled lazily and rose in one movement, indicating to the rest of the group that they should stay where they were.

'I'll see you, Mickey,' Fraser said. He walked out with Sally into the pub garden, a tiny, crowded terrace, sheltered by a London plane grey with the fine cement dust that covered everything within a hundred yards of the motorway site.

She smiled at him. 'Not pleased to see me?'

'Of course I am, I just wasn't expecting you, you've come back early.'

'Oh, well. It was a bit dull up there with you gone, so I came back with Bill and Nigel. Mum and Dad are coming back in a couple of days as well.'

'Nigel's here, too, is he?'

'Yes, but I've told him I'm busy tonight.' She touched the back of Alan's hand in open invitation. 'You could come round to my flat.'

He considered her soberly. 'We'd need to be careful.'

'No need. Everyone knows I know you from Scotland.' She gave him a provocative sidelong look over her beer, and he relaxed.

'I'm still staying with friends.'

'My flat is about ten minutes away.'

'I'll come later — I've promised to tie in some of that scaffold — they've had some useless buggers on that site and I don't want anyone working off those towers until I've checked them.' He sounded as he did when wanting to go and climb, and she, realizing he was immovable, agreed to meet him later.

* * *

Three miles away in the Department of Trade and Industry's headquarters Francesca was sitting in the office of her immediate superior, Rajiv Sengupta. She smiled at him, admiring the cool look of him in his immaculate suit, and the way his black hair shone, tidy above his expensive shirt. She had known him for ten years, since he had supervised her in Jurisprudence in her second year as an undergraduate at Cambridge. He was, she observed with interest, uncharacteristically in a fuss, picking through the papers on his desk, talking obsessively.

'So, Fran, what we need to establish — damn, I did think I had replied to that particular Treasury idiocy in a way that meant it would not recur — is whether you can manage without me, or whether I should cancel and start all over again. My mother will be furious, two uncles will be disappointed, and my father will probably disinherit me, but all this has to be considered against the needs of the Department.'

'Rajiv, nothing should be allowed to get in the way of your annual return to India. How are they to manage the harvest without you, or the annual sacrifice?'

Rajiv, scion of a Brahmin family, son of one of the richest men in modern India and nephew to the Permanent Secretaries of two major Departments of State in the Indian civil service, grinned at her across the table and loosened his Hermès tie.

'I knew you would see the problem in proportion, dear Francesca. The point is that we really are short-handed here. We have eight rescue cases, all major, under consideration, of which about four are serious. The other four, which are hopeless, will take even more time to deal with.'

Francesca nodded; for the size of the unit which she and Rajiv operated, and which was charged with giving assistance to firms in difficulty where this would preserve employment in the Assisted Areas, four active cases constituted a solid workload. Eight was a serious overload, particularly since, as Rajiv observed, persuading Ministers to refuse assistance and dealing with the subsequent outcry from all interested parties took even more time and effort than actually rescuing a sick company.

'Three out of four of the current cases are textiles — well, they were all running when you went on leave. Jennifer Freeman in Chemicals and Textiles has mumps, and so has Andrew Michaels, who is the accounting case-officer for two of these.'

'How very odd,' Francesca observed. 'Mumps is not particularly infectious — I mean you usually only get it from people with whom you are in very close contact.'

'Frannie, dear, could we, do you think, not make that observation publicly, much as I admire the breadth of your general knowledge?'

Francesca gazed at him, disconcerted. 'But they are both married. To other people.'

'Darling, that sounds a little odd, coming from you.'

'*Not* very nice to go on about it.'

Ten months previously, Francesca had been brought home rather early from a posting to Washington, in the middle of her much publicized affair with the married junior senator for West Virginia. The fact that this had followed the painful break-up of her first marriage when she was only twenty-seven was generally held to be a justification. Rajiv, however, having known her since she was nineteen, was not going to let her get away with taking a moral stance on the subject of adultery.

They eyed each other across the table until she blushed and looked away.

'Moreover,' he went on severely, 'Peter is in hospital, as you know. If I now go on leave and there is a crisis, there is no one for the next three weeks between you and the Permanent Secretary.'

'The colonel is dead, I take it, and the gatling jammed also?'

'Oh yes, all of that. The dreaded Paul Tucker will be in charge, since David Llewellyn is busy in his constituency and is off on a freebie to Turkey.'

'You mean a fact-finding mission. How can he do such a thing and leave us with the awful Tucker?'

'I suppose he feels that with the House not sitting there are limits to the damage Tucker can inflict.'

Francesca opined that this was doubtful reasoning, and that their normally popular and reliable Minister for Industry must have suffered a brainstorm to feel it safe to leave the conduct of the Department's business in the hands of a blatantly incompetent and lazy Parliamentary Under-Secretary of State.

Rajiv agreed that her strictures were probably justified and watched her thoughtfully as she pulled his in-tray towards her and riffled efficiently through it. She looked across at him. 'Go Rajiv. It's no good cancelling leave, there is never a good moment to take it again. *I'm* here, I've had a good holiday, and nothing here is too dreadful, so far as I can see. I have nothing better to do: John was snatched off the train to do that rape and murder case in Croydon — I saw him for an hour on Sunday and I'll be lucky to see him again before next weekend.'

Rajiv stood up decisively on the other side of the desk. 'You have persuaded me, Fran. Your first job, before you do anything irrelevant like reading the files or starting any work, is to take part in a delightful discussion organized by Sir Jim. He has decided that we ought, as a Department, to be developing a list of people suitable for appointment to government jobs.'

'We have one. Has he never seen it?'

'No, no, Fran. A *different* list with lots of new names on it. He is convinced apparently that out there, somewhere, are many top-flight industrialists longing to be appointed to the various delectable government jobs available. Our failure to serve them up is viewed as Unhelpful.'

'I see.' Francesca considered her mentor of ten years' standing and decided calmly not to tell him she had found a major contribution to any such list. 'Well, I dare say I can weather that. Go on, you'll need to pack, and I have to catch up before this meeting.'

CHAPTER 8

Three weeks later, on a Tuesday morning, the ten o'clock hooter echoed, and all over the site men dropped down off scaffolding, put down shovels, turned off machinery, and made for the site canteen. An engineers' meeting on Section I was kept going by the force of character of the man who had called it, but most of the staff were also stopping work for coffee, or breakfast. Bill Vernon and Nigel Makin, shut away in a tiny, cramped office in the Portakabin adjoining the villa, decided that they both needed a proper breakfast.

'Give it twenty minutes,' Nigel advised, glancing out of the window. 'Let them get the lads fed.'

Since morning break on a building site lasts thirty minutes, this warning was sensible; the canteen staff, struggling to get food on to the plates of a regular clientele of 400 men within fifteen minutes, would give irregular visitors to the canteen very short shrift.

'Have you seen Sally this morning?' Bill asked, with some malice. Nigel Makin had been nitpicking his way through the ground preparation costs on Section I, which seemed likely to be twice those allowed for in the estimate and two and a half times the price which Bill Vernon had finally agreed in last-minute negotiations with the Department of Transport.

'No.' The monosyllable was inexpressive and Nigel Makin did not seem inclined to be deflected. 'I'm seriously bothered by those costs, Bill. Not only did we need almost twice the depth you people originally estimated — that's 70 per cent more square yards of muck — but I can't see how all that steel got used. Even given the extra 70 per cent we've used close on 2,000 tons of rebar and rewire more than we ought to. That's a lot of steel. It's been growing legs and walking off the site. It's another one like the Barbican, and I've got to stop it. We lost 2,000 tons there in February, before the production controllers could sort out what was happening and organize an investigation. Now it's been happening here recently, when we had sickness and holidays among my people here. Bastards. They watch you all the time.'

He was moving restlessly, watching the site from the window, scowling at the bristling steel edifices, boxed around with scaffolding, that were beginning to emerge from the ground and marking out the line of the flyover which would take one set of traffic away to the south-western suburbs and the old road through Southall.

'It's the same pattern,' he said, the pale-blue eyes narrowed as he watched a lone scaffolder picking over steel. 'Nothing much goes adrift for weeks, even while we're still fencing the site; they wait till we start really building up materials, then 2,000 tons disappear in three days. What I ought to do is to start matching records to find if we've got any of the same people here as were on the Barbican in February, but I just don't have the time.'

Bill Vernon shifted. 'Don't we always lose materials?'

'Not 300,000 quids' worth we bloody don't, Bill.'

'Who are they selling it to?'

'There's half a dozen sites around here that won't be too particular about where their materials come from. We'd never be able to identify it — it's bog standard material.'

Bill Vernon found himself remembering a film about the Spanish Inquisition in which the camera, for reasons either of censorship or economy, had remained focused on the face of the inquisitor rather than the horrendous injuries being done to his victim. In the film the inquisitor had been a thin dark man with burning eyes, but in real life of course an inquisitor was just as likely to have been a lightweight of less than six feet with mousy-brown hair and pale-blue eyes. Nigel Makin's methods would necessarily be different, society having moved on a bit from the sixteenth century, but he was inspired by the same moral force.

Bill suggested that they might now go across to the canteen, and they both jammed helmets on as they left the Portakabin offices. They walked into the canteen and joined the tail end of the queue. Two hundred men were seated at the crowded tables, and the windows were misted with steam, not one of them open despite the fact that it was a warm September day. The whole smelled strongly of grease and baked beans. Possessed of healthy appetites, the two men were undeterred by their surroundings and both emerged at the end of the line with two fried eggs, bacon, sausage, canned mushrooms, tomatoes and baked beans plus a generous helping of chips. They edged their way towards a table whose occupants looked up momentarily from the task of shovelling in food. From long practice, Bill Vernon just managed not to wince at the smell of stale sweat; site labourers are travelling men living away from their families and wear the same ancient trousers and shirt during a whole week's work. They throw the lot away at the end of the week and buy another pair of trousers and a shirt from Oxfam or a second-hand-clothes stall after their Saturday lunch-time session in the pub. Since it was now Thursday, the smell was ripening and the atmosphere in the canteen was distinctly polluted.

'Didn't know you ate here, Bill, with the real workers?'

Bill Vernon, mouth full of egg and baked beans, nodded wordlessly to Alan Fraser at the next table. He was sitting with his team, all of them leaning back in the uncomfortable battered steel chairs, drinking tea. Fraser, Bill observed, though dressed in ancient, torn jeans, heavy working boots and an old shirt, covered with cement dust, still somehow looked as if he were dressed for a film, as if make-up girls hovered not too far in the background, prepared to renew the smudge on his forehead where he had pushed that bright red-blond hair back under his helmet. Mickey was also too elegant for his surroundings, and both of them looked like greyhounds against the thick-set, pale-skinned pair of Irishmen who were running to fat, their heavy belts with the scaffolders' keys sitting uncomfortably under the convex curve of their bellies.

Just at that moment Sally Vernon walked in and stopped at the counter. Every man in the room watched her with interest. The handful of girls working on the site mostly found the canteen too squalid and uncomfortable, so she was an unusual sight. She hooked her pale blonde hair back behind her ears, picked up her cup of tea and turned to look round the canteen, making no attempt to conceal that there was one only person she was looking for. She smiled widely and happily as she saw Alan, and walked over to join him, the smile fading only briefly as she took in Bill and Nigel also.

'I was told I would find you here,' she said smoothly to them all. 'I usually come in for a cup of tea around this time, anyway.' She smiled confidently at the two Irish members of the team who were showing every sign of alarm, asked for the sugar, and sat back.

'Glad you're here, Sally. I wanted to check what time we are due tonight.' Nigel Makin sounded strained, and watched her steadily as Fraser gazed thoughtfully out of the window.

'Not till eight o'clock.'

'I'll pick you up then.'

'All right. You're not really going to eat all those baked beans, are you?'

Nigel Makin, successfully distracted, started to explain about the necessity for a good breakfast while Fraser got unhurriedly to his feet, collecting his gang. He looked down momentarily at Sally. She looked back at him, unsmiling, and Bill Vernon found himself holding his breath. He slid a glance sideways at Nigel Makin and saw that none of it had been lost on him either; he was pale and his mouth was set in an ugly, dead straight line.

'Have you heard any more about K6?' he said hastily to Alan Fraser, and realized as he spoke that this was also an inflammatory issue.

Fraser stopped, and looked over Bill's head at Mickey, who replied for him. 'There's room for one of us. The sponsors are seeing us both tomorrow. They already know Alan; they don't know me.' This, dispassionately offered, chilled the group into silence.

Fraser lifted a hand in farewell, and swung on to the scaffold, looking, Bill thought enviously, quite different from anyone else. He clambered upward, scowling slightly, alongside Mickey Hamilton.

'How's the arm, Mick?'

'Will you stop asking about it? I don't ask about your ribs.'

The furious response took Fraser by surprise. 'Sorry, Mick. Pair of crocks, the both of us; we just need to keep it from the competition. The sponsors will never know.'

'These sponsors — it's a Quaker company isn't it?'

'Old man Shackleton is, yes; I read it somewhere. He's chairman. What's the worry, Mick — do you think he'll be prejudiced against Piskies?'

Mickey Hamilton, reared as an Episcopalian in Edinburgh, laughed unwillingly. 'No. I just wondered what they were like about people who had a spot of bother in the past.'

Both men considered the point, and Fraser said, reluctantly, that he thought old man Shackleton was unlikely to be tolerant of misdemeanour of any sort, despite his Quaker persuasion.

'Hardly anyone knew about my problems anyway — it was nine years ago. You must be one of the few around, Alan.'

'That's right. And I'd forgotten about it till you reminded me. No one's going to go back nine years to catch up with you. Stop worrying, Mick.' He passed a length of steel.

Mickey Hamilton nodded, taking it from him smoothly and putting on a clip. Handing the clip awkwardly, he drew breath sharply at the pain in his arm. He glanced sideways to check whether Fraser had noticed, and was reassured to see him totally engrossed in advising the Doolans on the placing of the next section.

* * *

Over at the Department of Trade and Industry, Francesca was eating an early lunch in the canteen, a room which, while six times the size of the Western Underpass Section I canteen, also smelled of stale fat and baked beans. She was at a big table at one side, sitting with eight men older than herself. One of them, her godfather Bill Westland, a Deputy Secretary responsible for six of the Department's most difficult divisions, was holding forth to his entire table about the difficulties of finding any half-way respectable businessmen to take on any of the advisory, non-executive posts for which Ministers in their wisdom had seen fit to provide.

'It's no good Jim going on at us. We know we badly need some decent commercial judgement on the Board of British Engineering, and what am I being offered by my colleagues? Peter Rawlings, who retired from the Treasury last year and has never seen a factory, I shouldn't think. Angus Macfarlane — admirable chap, must be over seventy now.'

'You could have Fred Jennings,' the other Deputy Secretary present volunteered. 'He's just turned us down for the insurance regulation jobs because he wants something more active.'

'We don't seem to know anybody new,' Bill Westland said sadly. 'It's just the same old weary stage army we pass on to each other.' He gazed at his baked beans and decided that they were too nasty to go on with. 'I suppose I'd better take poor Rawlings; no one else is going to.'

'*I've* got an idea for someone for you,' Francesca said smugly.

'Who?'

'Robert Vernon. Chairman and Chief Executive of Vernon Construction. He's got six engineering subsidiaries, with a £500-million turnover between them, as well as the construction side which is about £1 billion. He's sixty-three.'

'I've seen pictures. Would he be interested?' Bill Westland had stopped eating and was leaning forward.

'He put it to me that he felt the time had come to give something back to the community.'

'He wants a K,' three people said, in unison.

'Yes,' Francesca agreed happily, 'so I indicated that I might be able to introduce him to senior people in this Department.'

'Where did you find him?'

'On holiday, with his family. We got talking.'

'Would he do British Engineering as a non-executive?' Bill Westland asked.

Francesca opined that he probably would.

'Well done, Frannie.' Westland heaved himself to his feet and beamed at her. 'Do you want me to ring him? No? All right, fix it with Mrs McPherson and wheel him in. This afternoon would not be too soon.'

'Can I be there, too? It's me he knows.'

'I daresay I can live with that for once.'

'Sir.' She grinned at him.

'How's young John then?' her godfather enquired paternally.

'Just coming out of that Croydon murder — I mean a man has helped police with their enquiries and will appear in court tomorrow, and so that's that. We've only spoken on the phone for the last week — I was going to take another lover if this went on.'

Bill Westland told her firmly that men must work and women must weep and that she was not to distract a good man, highly thought of in his field. 'Time you married him and had some children,' he added severely, cutting no ice at all with Francesca, who told him briskly that he was out of date: nobody got married these days, and if he checked with Establishment Division he would find that no distinction was made when it came to maternity leave, pension provision, and so on.

'You're not going to do that to us?' her godfather said, appalled, while the rest of the table listened, fascinated.

'No, but people are not to nag.'

* * *

Four miles away and four hours later, in her flat near the Western Underpass, Sally Vernon and Nigel Makin were having a conversation along something of the same lines. Nigel had deliberately turned up early to pick her up for dinner, and without fuss had taken her to bed. He was good, she thought, lying back half asleep while he efficiently showered and shaved, even though it had been Alan Fraser she had wanted that day.

'Sally, it's time we got married. I want children, so do you, you're qualified now, what are we waiting for?'

She considered his face reflected in the shaving mirror, which she could see through the bathroom door. 'I'd like to wait a bit longer, Nigel. Why such a hurry? Are you afraid I'll spend all my money?'

'No.' He was unoffended as she knew he would be. 'It's yours, you do what you like with it, though you'd do better to let me invest it for you. You can put some into a house, or put up with what I can do on my pay — it's your choice.'

She felt as she had before, both admiring and resentful. Nigel's rock-solid belief in his capacity to rise to the top of Vernon Engineering and his genuine lack of interest in the substantial fortune her father had settled on her ought to have been attractive. But she felt in some part of her being that the possession of that kind of money should get more respect than Nigel was according it.

'Some men would be pleased to have a rich wife,' she said, and he turned to look at her through the open door.

'Some men would know how to spend it for you, too,' he said, deliberately, and watched while she looked away.

'Your dad wants me to go to Riyadh for the power-station negotiations in the New Year. We need to get married before then. What about it, Sal?'

He came back into the bedroom, a towel knotted round his hips, and flipped open his briefcase to look for a clean shirt, apparently confident. But Sally knew that a crisis had been reached, and that he would not come back if she sent him away now. She hesitated, furious with him and herself. He looked up from his briefcase and smiled at her, wryly but not unkindly.

'I don't want to be pushed,' she said.

He walked over to the bed, unsmiling now. 'And I don't want to be messed around.' He sat down on the bed and turned her to face him. 'We've been engaged for six months, and I don't want to get married in a scramble and have everyone think you're in the club.'

She pulled herself free of his hands and sat up straight in the middle of the bed, thinking that the whole conversation was about Alan Fraser but neither of them was prepared to mention his name.

'I just want some time to think.'

He looked exasperated to the point of fury and she was momentarily frightened but he had himself in hand.

'Give us a kiss,' he suggested and, disarmed and relieved, she moved into his arms. He started to make love to her, holding her down uncomfortably, ignoring her complaints, and she finally responded with equal ferocity.

'You'll have to have another shower. We're going to be very late.'

'They'll forgive us. You can have a shower first.'

Neither of them spoke again of the issue lying between them as they hurried into clothes, but as he held open the door of the flat for her, he put his arm round her. 'It'll be all right, Sal. You've just got cold feet.'

* * *

Robert Vernon had begun to be irritable about his daughter's late arrival, and was making his son uncomfortable by fidgeting round the brightly lit room, fiddling with the various ornaments and objects which covered every surface. It was a large room and in its original shape had been generously proportioned. The addition of a substantial bar, with shelves containing every drink known to the Western world and flanked by four bar stools, had gone a long way to destroying the proportions, and the inclusion of a vast wall-fixture which held a large TV and banks of equipment for reproducing music had completed the job. Thousands of pounds' worth of the latest hi-fidelity equipment was being deployed in playing extracts from the current revival of *South Pacific*.

Bill remembered his mother observing maliciously to friends that her ex-husband was the only really rich man she knew whose house contained not one single object that she would want to steal. He mentally conceded the justice of this statement as he watched his father pick up and regard with pride a massive phallic *objet d'art* covered, regardless equally of expense and the dictates of artistic taste, in silver gilt. Of course, he reminded himself, it wasn't meant to be art; it was a duplicate of the object presented to the relevant sheik in commemoration of the Raj al Oued sewage works. Nor had his stepmother been of the smallest assistance; herself the daughter of a small shopkeeper, her taste ran to Victorian painting and was represented in this room by a substantial oil, even more substantially framed, of a large spaniel gazing slightly cross-eyed at a small puppy, the whole entitled 'Motherhood'.

He stood up as his stepmother came into the room and kissed her, realizing that, while he had been brought up to see her as the person who had robbed his mother of all that she wanted, this was a pleasant, infinitely capable woman who wished him well, and who indeed had insisted that he be treated the same as her own daughter. It probably made no difference to Dorothy Vernon what he himself thought: she had stepped only once outside the canons of her sound Methodist upbringing to take the one man she had ever wanted, and then only when she was convinced that his wife had forfeited every right to him. The fact that he himself was not successful in the business mattered not at all — he was Robert's son and he was treated as such, unless of course he transgressed her standards of behaviour.

She turned towards him now, her pale, grey-blonde hair freshly set in a perm of the style favoured by the Queen, her wide, slightly popping, blue eyes, matched by her sapphire-and-diamond earrings and necklace.

'We'll not need all that lemon. I must speak to Luigi.'

Bill watched, amused, as she jabbed at the bell, rings flashing on the stubby, beautifully manicured hands. He removed himself tactfully to the other side of the room as she complained to the Italian who ran her household, a complaint which he received with both seriousness and respect. Neither of them obviously saw anything incongruous in the wife of the chairman of one of the UK's largest companies, concerning herself with wasteful use of lemon.

'You'll have to watch all that, Bill, if you want to run a business of your own, or they'll rob you blind. It's not dishonesty with Luigi, of course; he'd not be with me if he wasn't as honest as the day is long. But he's careless. He likes things to look nice but you can do that without waste.'

'What happened to the chap you used to have? Norman?'

'Oh, him.' Dorothy Vernon put her glass down with a snap. 'Did Robert never tell you? I caught him taking wine home with him. He left that day.'

'We've never got anyone as good as him since, though.' Robert Vernon had come back from his telephone call. 'For fifteen years the house and the farm ran like clockwork.' He put an arm round his wife's shoulders. 'I wanted to give him hell, promise him jail the next time round, and keep him, but Dorothy wouldn't have it.'

She looked at him with impatience; it was obviously an old argument. 'He'd have done it again. If you knew the trouble my father had with people stealing from his shop — grown men and women — you'd not speak like that, Robert. People either respect other people's property or they don't, and there's no half-way. If you find you've got one who doesn't know what's right, you've to get rid of him.' She twitched a cushion straight, irritation in every line of her body, and both men were relieved when the bell rang and Luigi could be heard admitting Nigel and Sally.

'I'm sorry, Mum, I was late off site and needed a bath.'

Dorothy Vernon kissed her and Nigel, observing drily that it hadn't mattered to her but her father had got in a twitch. Robert Vernon rose above this.

'You want to hear where I've been invited?' he asked, generally, as Luigi dealt with drinks.

'Buckingham Palace?' his daughter asked, pertly.

'I've been asked to come and have a talk with a Mr Westland in the Department of Trade and Industry.'

'Why, Dad?'

'Well, I'd mentioned — to young Francesca Wilson, in fact — that I was concerned about where the government was getting its advice on industry, and she mentioned that they need people to advise on engineering. I'll tell you something else, too. You know that boyfriend of hers — big chap, went climbing with Fraser? Well, he's a copper.'

'A *what*?' It was Nigel Makin, who asked.

'A policeman. A Chief Inspector no less, at New Scotland Yard.'

'A detective or uniformed branch?' Bill Vernon asked.

'Oh, a detective. Francesca says they never tell anyone what he does when he's on holiday because everyone wants to talk about his job, so they just say he's Home Office. She told *me*, she said, because senior people in her Department know and she wouldn't want to put me at a disadvantage.'

'I knew about him,' Sally said, and instantly wished she hadn't, as Nigel looked sharply at her.

'Francesca tell you?' Her father sounded disappointed.

'No, no,' she hurried to reassure him, trying to ignore Nigel. 'Alan Fraser and Mickey Hamilton were on the same train as them, coming back to London, and apparently a police car was waiting to pick him up. So John McLeish had to tell them then, and Alan mentioned it to me.' She looked sideways at Nigel and was not at all reassured to see him looking dead-pan.

'We'd maybe better ask him to see if he can find out where the steel went to off the Barbican and the Western Underpass?' he said to Robert Vernon.

'Scotland Yard won't be interested in that,' Bill Vernon objected. 'You'll have to settle for the local flatfeet if you are serious about trying to catch up with the losses at the Barbican. But you're joking, aren't you? That steel will be well away by now.'

'If you let people get away with theft, Bill, you might as well give your business away and have done with it.'

'And they'll do it to you again somewhere else.' Dorothy Vernon refilled Nigel's drink.

'Oh, they've tried,' he assured her. 'We lost a bit at the Underpass while I was elsewhere. I'll see it doesn't happen again.'

Bill Vernon got up and ostentatiously took Sally over to the other side of the room. 'Got a bit of a bee in his bonnet, hasn't he? Why isn't he busy getting married?'

She looked at him surprised; they had never been particularly close and he did not usually ask her personal questions.

'I'm not sure I want to,' she said. 'I'm not sure what I want.' She glanced back into the room. 'Dad says you're going to buy a farm in Scotland? Perhaps I'll do that too, or something like that.'

'You can't — you're the heiress to the business!' Bill was amused and scandalized. 'Alan Fraser won't be any good to you,' he said, suddenly. 'Too much of a rover. Look, Sal, he's got another girl, you know.'

He watched, not unsympathetically, as tears filled her eyes.

'Who is she?'

'A model. He met her in Scotland. Sorry, Sally. I'd rather not have told you, but I thought you ought to know.'

She nodded and stared out of the window, fingering the enormously expensive, pale-red, heavily padded silk curtains which Dorothy Vernon always bought. Her step-brother stayed by her side to give her time to compose herself.

'Sal,' he said, cautiously, 'look, he goes to K6 in a few weeks, doesn't he, whatever any of us want? Why ruin your chances for — what — six weeks?'

'You don't understand.' She was no longer tearful but mildly contemptuous. She turned back definitively to the rest of the group, deployed on the heavy leather chairs and chesterfield sofas which Robert Vernon had bought twelve years ago when Vernon Engineering reached a £500-million turnover for the first time, and went round to the bar to fetch herself a second large drink.

CHAPTER 9

John McLeish, with the aid of a secretary, was clearing his desk at New Scotland Yard of its accumulated piles of paper, files, and odd messages written on scraps of paper.

'Oh, God,' he said gloomily as his secretary bore in a further pile and hesitated as they both contemplated two already toppling in-trays. 'Just put it down by the side, Jenny, I'll get through it. Most of it's rubbish isn't it?' he asked hopefully.

'A lot of it is,' his secretary confirmed. 'There are three things marked "Addressee's eyes only", which are about your pension — I rang up and asked in case there was a deadline for reply.'

'Mm.' A good secretary was beyond price and McLeish roused himself to say so, conscious that he had barely addressed a word to her that was not an order over the last two weeks. He sat down with coffee and started through the in-tray, wastepaper basket at his right hand ready to receive most of the offerings being circulated. He arrived at the communiqué about his pension rights and realized after a third reading that he was none the wiser. It was clear that a decision of some sort was required of him and that its consequences, in what he felt was the improbable event of his actually reaching the age of sixty-five in the employ of the Metropolitan

Police, might be far-reaching. Or might, on the other hand, not matter at all. He had no idea which. He looked at the papers irresolutely, then remembered that he had available to him an excellent source of advice on all matters connected with a public service bureaucracy.

He had reached for the telephone before he recalled that Francesca was on her way up to see a machine-tool manufacturer in Doncaster whose cash flow was unlikely to permit him to meet the next month's wages bill unless the DTI helped. He sighed, and tried to read the communiqué again. He had got to the second paragraph when the internal phone rang smartly.

'I have a Sergeant McKinnon calling you from Carrbrae, in Scotland.'

McLeish stared at the phone, his mind switching slowly to the hotel in Culdaig with Alec McKinnon gently but persistently picking at the details of Alan Fraser's fall. He listened, frowning slightly, to the soft Highland voice courteously hoping he had a good journey home and enquiring after Francesca, and remembered his manners enough to ask after mutual acquaintances in Scotland.

'Well, it was Duncan Mackintosh that was there, you see.' Alec McKinnon sounded relieved to have found an opening. 'He was away up the hill, looking for a student who had sprained her ankle, and he had Roddy Moffat with him — I don't think you met him, but he's often here, he's a plumber in Strathclyde — and it was Roddy who saw the jacket.'

'The jacket?'

'You remember, Francesca saw someone in a yellow jacket on the ridge the day Alan Fraser fell? Well, Roddy saw a patch of yellow on the hill yesterday and he went to look in case it was the student, and he found this jacket tucked under a rock. The wind had caught it and a sleeve was flapping. Well, he knew the jacket, it was his own and he'd lost it from the hotel the day young Fraser was hurt. It was an old one, but it was patched on the side.'

McLeish managed with an effort to remember that this chatty Highlander was not a member of his staff and waited patiently for the essential parts of the story to ensue. Roddy Moffat, it transpired, had expressed great pleasure at getting back a favourite jacket and had to be prevented from speculating publicly about the motivation of a person who would take the wrong jacket and abandon it on the hillside when he realized his mistake.

Duncan Mackintosh had brought Mr Moffat and the jacket straight to the police at Carrbrae, where he had been sworn to silence and the jacket bagged and labelled. Would the Chief Inspector not agree that it did look as if someone had been laying for Alan Fraser that day? Someone who, realizing he or she had been seen by Francesca, had abandoned the only item of clothing that would have been identified at that distance?

McLeish, who had got the point three sentences earlier, agreed that it was a circumstance suspicious in itself but not conclusive.

'I know it's difficult to believe that a body would cause Fraser to fall, because he might have been killed,' the Highland voice said apologetically. 'But I thought you ought to know.'

'What's your next step?' McLeish decided the Scots could do their own thinking on this one instead of trying to shift the mess on to his overloaded plate.

'I ought to be on the next plane down to have a wee word with Fraser and warn him that there may be someone laying for him. He's working as a scaffolder on the big Western Underpass site.' The voice was as unhurried as ever, but all trace of diffidence had gone. 'Then when I got back here, I'd start finding out who was here the day. But I'd warn Fraser first.'

Yes, indeed, McLeish thought, digging his pencil irritably into the blotter.

'I don't think I could just have a word on the telephone, even if I could find him to speak to,' Alec McKinnon offered when the silence became unbearable.

'No, no, you couldn't.' McLeish accepted the inevitable. 'It's a day and a half of your time, though, isn't it? Would it be helpful if I had a word with him — I know where he is, and he knows now I'm in the Force. I can go down and buy him a drink, tell him what you've told me, and get him to ring you. I'll also put him in touch with the local station near the site — it's Edgware Road, my last posting — and they can keep an eye out.'

He listened grimly to McKinnon's thanks. 'Then it's over to you to see what you can find up there,' he pointed out, firmly. 'I'm just a friendly messenger.'

They said goodbye; McLeish summoned his secretary and asked her to get a message to one Alan Fraser on the Western Underpass site, inviting him for a drink at the King's Head at six p.m., without disclosing that McLeish worked at Scotland Yard or indeed was connected in any way with the police force. He buried himself again in his work, and had disposed of one and a half trays by the time his secretary, flushed and exasperated, returned to him. Bruce Davidson, looking amused, was with her.

'I'm sorry John,' said Jenny, 'but it's impossible. The site won't even say whether this Mr Fraser works there or not, and Vernon's Head Office says that only the site has the records. They say it is not the policy of the firm to confirm whether people work on their sites without the man's express consent, given in advance.'

McLeish looked at her blankly, but Davidson was laughing. 'It's a casual trade, John, all sorts of blokes are in it. They'll not want to be bothered with phone calls on site — they'd more likely be from bookies or debt collectors or women trying to catch up with blokes who'd left them with a baby. It's like that thing they had in the Middle Ages — sanctuary. Once you're in, no one can get at you. Like the army, too.'

McLeish gazed at him. 'I must be tired, I should have known that. Sorry, Jenny. Well, since we know he's there, I suppose I could just hang round the site at going-home time?'

Jenny and Davidson considered him doubtfully. 'There's probably more than one exit,' Jenny pointed out. 'It's a big site.'

'Where's he living?' Davidson asked sensibly.

'Ah. On the caravan site.'

All three of them contemplated the vision of John McLeish asking his way round the caravans attached to a major construction site.

'You'd probably end up boiled for soup,' Davidson advised, gloomily. 'And you'd stick out like a sore thumb.'

'This is ridiculous,' McLeish stated. His subordinates both fell silent, watching him think.

'Important, is it?' Davidson asked, casually. McLeish considered him irritably, and said that in fact it was important, he had agreed to do an errand for another force and he ought to do it today. 'In fact,' he said, arriving at a decision, 'get me the top man on the site — the manager — and I'll talk to him.'

In five minutes he found himself talking to Jimmy Stewart and explaining with some embarrassment that all he wanted was a drink on police business which in no way reflected discredit on Fraser, and that he had failed to get a message through any less exalted channel. Stewart agreed to pass a message as discreetly as possible to Alan Fraser, bidding him to drink with John McLeish at six p.m., and observed that he hoped Fraser would turn up. McLeish, realizing that there was no way of convincing this hard man that Fraser was not necessarily the suspected link man in the latest bullion robbery, got Jenny to telephone to Scotland to confirm that he had arranged to see Fraser, and plunged back into the in-tray, knowing that he was living on borrowed time. The Croydon murderer had been charged that morning and remanded to a prison hospital, this being the only available free space in the London system for the next two days. Inevitably, around lunchtime, someone in the overworked hierarchy above him would realize that his hands were free and find something to put in them.

* * *

Robert and Dorothy Vernon were working in neighbouring offices in the house in South Molton Street that housed the small Head Office operation of Vernon Construction and Engineering. The main power-centre of the empire was in Hounslow, a brand-new building, purpose-built by and for Vernon Construction and Engineering — open-plan, air-conditioned and uniform, with every desk and divider the same. The firm's founders worked in the West End, in high-ceilinged rooms, thickly carpeted, with graceful, curved windows framed by silk curtains, and large, expensive, Swedish desks. Framed photographs of Dorothy Vernon placing the first brick of a housing estate, and Robert Vernon turning the key of a power station, hung on the walls, but Dorothy's office was humanized by a large Lichfield photograph of Sally, which Dorothy was considering thoughtfully. Her daughter looked at her out of the frame, blonde hair falling round bare shoulders, the eyes very alert. The photograph had caught her character; you could see that this was a girl who had to be led, not driven — just like her father. She got up and walked into the next-door office and sat while her husband finished his phone call.

'You're going to the Western Underpass this afternoon, aren't you? Do you have to?' She stretched out a hand to take his and he looked back at her.

'I don't know what I'd do if I didn't have you, Dolly. Yes, I do have to. It's bad to cancel these things.'

'You're looking very tired. I don't want you getting ill. Shall I come with you?'

Robert Vernon pressed her hand. 'That'll be nice — I thought you had a committee?'

'I'll cancel it.' Dorothy Vernon was Deputy Chairman of Vernon, and the title was in no way honorary. Having worked for the firm for forty-two years, thirty of them with Robert Vernon, she knew more about its operations than most of its senior executives and deployed her formidable body of knowledge and her shrewd, hard head very effectively. She was responsible at Board level for all matters of personnel, public relations and employee relations and, as Robert Vernon acknowledged, could have run any department including finance, if he had not wanted to see her sometimes.

'Are you going to come round the site with me?'

'Mm. But I'd like to have a look at the canteen — were you doing that? No? Well, I'll come with you for some of your tour and then ask to be taken there.'

'I'll get Janet to tell Stewart — he's the agent,' Robert Vernon offered.

'Don't do that. Don't even tell him I'm coming. James Stewart has never taken site canteens seriously. If he's warned, he'll do just enough tidying to make it look all right, and I hear it's a disgrace.'

Robert Vernon grinned at her. 'You mean this is going to be a war? I thought you were coming to see after me?'

She nodded amused but resolute. 'So I am, but I'll just give Stewart a fright while I'm there. Sally will be around, of course.' She sighed. 'And Alan Fraser, I suppose; he's got his living to earn, whatever's happening. Nigel is supposed to be down there, too, going through the tender with Bill. Well, you don't have to meet Mr Fraser.'

'He'll be a hundred feet up a scaffold if he's doing his job,' Robert Vernon pointed out. 'I'm not going to avoid him.'

'He knows you are coming?'

'Well, Stewart knows, and he's a cunning devil. I told him it was informal and to make no special preparations. That means all the site will know. I'm due at three-thirty and the car's leaving here just after three. Let's have some lunch.'

* * *

On the Western Underpass site, general foremen on every section were hurrying labourers to tidy the site, as they had been doing for the last twenty-four years. A civil engineering site as cramped as the Western Underpass, which goes right through a crowded London borough, is particularly resistant to order, and every man had been pressed into service to help tidy up. On Section I, where everything else had been reduced to order, six labourers under the charge of their ganger marched up to the piles of tube awaiting erection and determinedly started to arrange them in neat piles.

Alan Fraser, forty feet up, watched them for a minute, then swarmed down to threaten vengeance on any man who touched his store of scaffolding tubes. He listened, disbelieving, to the ganger's explanation of his reasons and resignedly signalled his group to come off the scaffold and help arrange the tubes and the clips so that they looked more orderly, all four men working flat out and angrily. They usually reckoned to make their basic hourly rate again in bonus, and their rhythm had been disrupted and time lost. This sequence of event and emotion was being repeated all over the four-mile site, so that by the time Robert and Dorothy Vernon arrived at three-thirty the site looked like a textbook illustration, and the labour force, as Jimmy Stewart observed, was working like a set of one-armed paperhangers to catch up with the day's work.

It was an impressive combination which Robert Vernon read effortlessly. He forbore to comment, getting quite enough entertainment for the day from watching Stewart's alarm as he saw that Dorothy Vernon was also present and his subsequent furtive efforts to get a message out of the room.

'Will you have tea, Mrs Vernon?' Stewart was enquiring hopefully, secure in the knowledge that new cups and saucers and a respectable tray had been purchased that morning.

'I will, James, but later. I'd like to go and see Section I — that'll be the car-park end, furthest from here, won't it?'

She waited placidly for Stewart's driver and odd-jobman, pressed into clean clothes and a haircut for the occasion, to appear with the Land Rover, and hopped in beside him and Stewart. He had time only to glare at his secretary, but she was a resourceful girl and had wasted no time in getting a phone call to the section to warn them of the honour that was about to be theirs.

'I see it's a tea-break,' his visitor observed. 'I'd like to take tea in the canteen, if I may.'

Jimmy Stewart, who had decided to accompany her rather than Robert Vernon, started to explain, aghast, that this was an unscheduled tea-break as Section I would be working late and high tea had been laid on. 'The police are letting us close the road from six this evening till six tomorrow morning, so we're doing a ghoster,' he confided. 'I mean an overnight shift.'

Dorothy Vernon, who had known what a 'ghoster' was for forty years, thanked him for the explanation and asked if he would escort her to the canteen. He looked despairingly from her unyielding face to the streams of men making for the canteen door, and braced himself, summoning up his courage to offer her his arm over the potholes in the site. An overlooked piece of loose reinforcing wire lay snaked across their path and he broke into a sweat, but his red-headed Scots foreman scaffolder, dropping casually off the deck, scooped it up without breaking stride and dropped it on the newly constituted steel-scrap pile.

'Good afternoon, Alan,' his guest said pleasantly, and the scaffolder stopped in his tracks.

'Mrs Vernon,' he said, taking off his helmet in direct contravention of site rules, for which Stewart forgave him from the bottom of his heart.

'I am taking tea in the canteen.'

Young Fraser, Stewart was grimly pleased to notice, looked as appalled as he felt himself, but rallied and accompanied them down the path. One might have known, Stewart thought, mentally abandoning his career with Vernon Construction and relocating himself to the big Laing site in North London or the Wimpey site beyond Southall, that the canteen would be at its worst. It operated largely on a part-time staff of local women, many of whom had left to receive children from school at three-thirty; this particular meal was therefore being served by about half the regular staff. The September heat had compounded the problem by bringing every man off the site to get a drink of tea, and two canteen hands were struggling to meet that demand. A long queue had built up with only two as opposed to the usual five, good women serving the inevitable fried collection of chips, sausage, bacon, tinned mushrooms, tomatoes and eggs. Someone had put out a minor conflagration just before the tea service started, and a faint pall of yellow smoke and a strong smell of burning hung over the counter. It was the end of a long working week and the smell of working clothes sweated into for five days was almost palpable in the airless room.

'Will you get Mrs Vernon what she would like, Fraser, while I find us a table?' He favoured Fraser with a menacing glare and shot off to the other side of the room, clearing a table by sheer force of character and opening the nearest three windows as he went. He saw a familiar face and hailed it with relief.

'Nigel, will you watch this table? Mrs Vernon is here and she'll need somewhere to sit. And could you find some better chairs?'

Nigel Makin, appreciating the emergency, pushed aside the nearest disintegrating steel chairs, and commandeered two better ones. He cleaned off the table with a handkerchief, just as Bill Vernon arrived, grinning and armed with a mug of tea and a doughnut. 'I see Dorothy's here. That'll send the balloon up.'

'You're just boat happy — the rest of us have to live here. Sally around?'

'Haven't seen her.'

Dorothy Vernon's presence in the queue was beginning to attract attention as Stewart panted back to her. Fraser, who clearly had the makings, was suggesting that she might like to sit down and he would bring her tea and cakes.

'No, no, I like to see how the canteen is laid out. And how are you, Michael?'

One of the little mysteries he would sort out afterwards, Stewart thought resignedly, was how the wife of Vernon

Constructions' chairman knew his latest foreman-scaffolder and his oppo. He listened to the conversation, which appeared to be about mountain-climbing, observing sadly that Mrs Vernon was noting every detail of the canteen operation while she kept up her end of the conversation. He closed his eyes momentarily as one of his general labourers, press-ganged into helping out behind the counter, shovelled an errant couple of slices of bacon back on a plate with a thumb black with ingrained dirt before thumping the plate down on the glass counter. As he opened his eyes again he saw Sally Vernon, and dropped back in the queue to enquire savagely if she had known her mother had planned to honour the site today.

'She didn't — I saw them last night and only Dad was coming.'

He nodded, then considered her more carefully. 'You all right, Sally? You're looking a bit rough.'

'I'm all right, Jimmy, I think I've got a cold.'

'Your mother's seen what she came for,' Stewart said, resignedly. His gaze swept the battered chairs and the rickety tables with formica peeling off them, all unmatching and bought cheaply from three other sites. He squared his shoulders and shepherded Mrs Vernon and her daughter, together with his two scaffolders who were plainly trying to avoid joining the group, over to the window table.

Mrs Vernon refused a place looking out of the window and settled herself facing into the room. During the polite manoeuvring, the wad of filthy newspaper which had been placed under one leg of the table to make it stable, became dislodged, so everyone's tea slopped as they sat down. Dorothy Vernon's gaze rested on her half-filled saucer, and the way she looked away without comment struck a chill right through Jimmy Stewart. Bill Vernon hastily introduced a distraction by pointing out that the big crane was moving. This took Mrs Vernon's attention outside the canteen for a blessed minute while Stewart ducked under the table and got the leg wedged so no further disaster could take place.

'Will Phase I be finished by the time you need to go to K6?' Bill Vernon was enquiring, mysteriously, as Stewart surfaced.

'Mostly. There's only the one place on K6 at this moment anyway — Mickey and I are battling for it.' It was Fraser who replied.

Whatever this one place was, Stewart observed that Fraser expected to get it. He was just about to enquire quietly of Sally Vernon what all this was about when he realized that the others around them were staring at the canteen door.

'It's Dad,' Sally Vernon said, redundantly, as her father strode over towards the table. Behind them a young surveyor scrambled to fetch tea from the counter. Jimmy stood up to give Robert Vernon his chair. Fraser and Hamilton, he saw out the corner of one eye, had seized the opportunity to fill their thermoses from the pots of tea on the table and Fraser was hunting for sugar. They passed the pot up to the Doolans, who filled their thermoses and then passed it on to Bill Vernon and Nigel Makin who also had thermoses with them. Stewart looked round to introduce his scaffolders to Vernon, but found himself pre-empted.

'We've met.' It was a previous acquaintance which seemed to have given pleasure to neither party, Stewart observed: Mr Vernon was looking stony and Fraser embarrassed.

'I didn't know that,' Stewart said involuntarily, feeling aggrieved. Bad enough to have two Vernon children on site; at least you could see them and keep them a bit isolated from the site gossip. To find that the chairman of the company had acquaintance among the scaffolders, who are the heart of a site and privy to every plot and rumour, was a bit much. He anxiously searched his own conscience for things that were not going right, and had just identified enough problems to make him thoroughly uncomfortable when he became aware that the tea party was breaking up. He sprang to his feet, narrowly avoiding knocking the table over, and led the group towards the door.

As he waited to lead the senior Vernons to whatever shortcoming of his they next planned to uncover, he noticed that

Fraser had collected his thermos and was on his way, swiftly and economically, raising a hand in general farewell and sweeping his team with him. Stewart looked after them enviously as they escaped into the warm September evening, putting on their helmets as they went over to the tower they were erecting.

A long hour later the senior Vernons had retired to the main offices for another cup of tea. The site hooter wailed, drawing catcalls from the men who were not going off-shift but would be continuing overnight. John McLeish heard it as he wedged his car into the pub carpark and walked over to the site fence to watch the exodus; he realized that one section must be going on past the normal working-time. His eye fell on a little knot of uniformed policemen redirecting traffic, and he saw they were closing a road.

McLeish tilted his head back, shading his eyes against the setting sun as he located a pair of figures about eighty feet up on a bristling tower of scaffolding. He briefly switched his attention to the big crane lumbering infinitely slowly on its crawlers towards the site gates, now thrown wide to let it through, and then looked up again at the scaffolding tower. The two figures were descending. One of them was Fraser, unmistakable anywhere, if you had climbed with him. Suddenly he stopped, still too far away and too high up for any feature to be visible, and pulled himself in, clinging to the tower. McLeish started forward, hair prickling because the movement was so ragged and jerky and uncharacteristic. Fraser paused, then started to descend again, slowly and hesitantly. Then his feet slipped on a bar, his full weight being taken on his arms. The other figure started to scramble across to him, but, as McLeish watched helplessly one hand came off, then the other, and Fraser fell like a stone through the bright September evening.

* * *

John McLeish was through the gate and jumping piles of steel to get over to the bottom of the tower before he had realized he was moving.

'Keep back,' he shouted to the small group standing by the site offices and hurled himself over the rough ground to where Fraser lay, on his back, with his arms thrown up and one leg sticking at an unnatural angle. There could be no reprieve this time, McLeish thought dully, kneeling beside him; he had fallen across a small pile of reinforced steel joists, breaking his back and inflicting God alone knew what other injuries. The blue eyes were open and unfocused, but a pulse still beat in his neck.

'Alan,' John McLeish said, gently, and the eyes moved to the direction of his voice. 'It's John McLeish. Just lie still now and we'll get you shifted. Where does it hurt?' He realized he was babbling.

'It doesn't hurt.' It was a thread of a voice and John McLeish saw that Fraser was fighting for breath, gulping in air through an open mouth. The lungs would not be functioning, he remembered drearily, with a break high up on the spinal cord.

'You'll be all right, Alan. You just need some oxygen.' He looked sideways at a heavy, dark, older man who had arrived at his side; the man nodded and slid away to the offices.

'Can't move,' Alan Fraser said, between gulps. McLeish reached for his nearest hand, already clammy and chill, and held it in both of his for the ten minutes it took for Alan Fraser, totally unaware of the frenzied activity around him, to slip away into unconsciousness and die.

The site nurse and the ambulance arrived a moment later, together with the police car and crew that had been supervising the road closure, and Mickey Hamilton, out of breath and trembling after his descent from the tower.

'He's gone,' McLeish said, flatly. 'He's not to be moved.' He placed Alan's hand gently at his side.

'Sir?'

He recognized the young constable, neat in his shirt sleeves.

'Yes, Woolner. Put up a screen, don't let anyone move him or touch anything.'

‘What can I do?’ It was the site agent who was asking him. McLeish wordlessly showed him his warrant card. Mickey Hamilton was kneeling at his side, white-faced and dazed, and McLeish indicated to the site agent that he should be gently removed. He looked over to the small group he had shouted at, and slowly realized who they were. Robert Vernon was barking at the office staff to get back out of the way, and Dorothy Vernon was kneeling on the ground beside a huddled figure whose bright blonde hair fell forward over her shoulders. Nigel Makin was also kneeling by her. Bill Vernon, recognizably in a dither, was following his father about.

McLeish nodded to young Woolner, who was improvising an effective screen, and turned back, painfully, to the body from which Alan Fraser had already departed. The red-blond hair underneath the broken helmet moved in the evening breeze, giving a momentary illusion of life, but the face was already set in death.

‘Aah, Christ!’ he said aloud, in misery, feeling pressure behind his eyes. He found a handkerchief and blew his nose with trembling hands. He waited till he thought he could stand up without stumbling or crying with rage, then looked up into Woolner’s sympathetic, enquiring face.

‘Sir? We have two cars with radio here.’

‘I’m coming, give me a minute.’ He was still hardly able to speak or move. He felt as if a giant animal were pressing on his shoulders and back, too heavy to shift. He thought of Francesca, who was wheeling and dealing in Doncaster and must be told the news before she heard it elsewhere, drew in a deep breath and steadied himself. He looked again at the broken body, the back arched over the pile of joists, the helmet pushed down over the forehead by the impact of the fall and said goodbye silently. Then he got shakily to his feet and turned to the task of finding the person or persons, so far unknown, who had, this time, succeeded in effecting the murder of Alan Fraser.

CHAPTER 10

'Chief Inspector?' Jimmy Stewart had been standing in the doorway of his office watching the big, dark bloke behind the desk for a full minute before realizing the policeman was oblivious of his presence. 'Sorry to bother you, but I've a late shift on and I've to decide what to do with them, whether to keep them on or send them away. Do you want them kept?'

McLeish reluctantly stopped making notes. 'No, it doesn't make any odds if you send them home, provided we are sure we have everyone's address. I'd like you to stay, and everyone who is left in the canteen.'

'Young Michael Hamilton's away at St Mary's, you know. The nurse didn't like just to send him back to the caravan.'

'Yes, that's alright.'

Jimmy Stewart, interested, considered the bent head. 'You've talked to him, then?'

The dark head came up and Stewart wished he hadn't asked, although the bloke behind the desk was a good bit younger than him.

'Briefly, yes. And there is a man by his bed. I take it all the Vernons have gone home, too?'

'Aye. But Nigel Makin is still here if you want him — in his office in this building.'

'I thought we'd taken over all your offices?'

Stewart, feeling relief at this sign of humanity, said that Nigel Makin's office was no bigger than a broom-cupboard, so the assembled police forces had been good enough to spare it to them.

'Sorry, but I didn't want to let people disperse before we'd had at least a preliminary go round the course.'

Jimmy Stewart nodded, wondered whether to risk any of the questions in his mind and decided against it. The speed with which the investigation had got under way had been impressive. The bloke currently occupying his office, who had appeared from nowhere as Fraser fell, had assembled in the canteen all the visitors plus Fraser's scaffolding team, the canteen staff and the top management, and had stationed a uniformed policeman at the door. He had commandeered a site secretary and dispatched the rest of the site to continue work, with two uniformed policemen on the gate to dissuade anyone from leaving. Within about twenty minutes, so it seemed to Stewart, the site had been taken over by police: young, uniformed men, looking about sixteen apiece, and older tougher ones in plain clothes, some of whom he recognized as being from the Edgware Road CID. Within two hours the group in the canteen was down to six people, all the others having been interviewed by three separate teams who had taken over the site offices. No doubt about this chap, who looked enormous behind his cramped desk, being in charge of the lot. They all deferred to him, even the tall man in a good suit who had come to look at the body for half an hour or so before an ambulance had finally been allowed to take it away.

Stewart hesitated in the corridor of the Portakabin, the office door still open, and squinted up into the powerful lights which were cutting through the gathering darkness of this September night. He could just see the police group, helmeted and moving gingerly, as they crawled about the scaffolding platform from which Fraser had fallen. He looked down the site and under the light saw a small group of his staff, deprived of their offices, huddled with the resident engineers, blue helmets mixed with green. He pushed his own helmet back, deciding, reluctantly, that he would do better to call off this shift and send everyone home. With the offices full of police, his staff and the engineers had nowhere to operate from — control would inevitably be lost and papers would go astray. And he would lose half the site shortly, anyway, unless he got the canteen back into action: the men had been working for over three hours since the five-thirty break, and they should have another break at nine-thirty. He was already on borrowed time . . . but it would be difficult to arrange again for the road to be closed for twelve hours; you were looking at three weeks' delay there, and, bugger it, he had a job to do, too. He stepped back into his office and shut the door decisively.

'I need the canteen, you see, if I'm to keep the shift on.'

The big policeman looked back at him and you could see he was a careful bloke, for all he was young.

'Yes, I do see.' He pulled himself to his feet bumping his knee on the desk, and plunged past him down the corridor, knocked at the door of the next office and went in. He emerged a minute later, summoned Stewart to follow him, and walked over to the canteen. The staff were sitting in a closed, suspicious group at the end-table, the four men playing cards and the three women knitting. At another table sat the remaining two members of Fraser's gang, looking pinched and cold, slumped like sacks of potatoes.

'That's all right, I'll take these two with me and put them in an office to wait. You get the canteen open. Give everyone something to eat. We'll be through in the offices in an hour.' He nodded, collected the two Irishmen and walked out, leaving Stewart to jolly the canteen staff into action. The phone was ringing as McLeish walked back into the office and he snatched it up.

'Which of the boys is it, John, just tell me?'

He blinked at the phone and slowly remembered that he had left a message at the hotel in Doncaster for Francesca to phone him urgently. Of course she had thought first of her brothers.

'Sorry, darling, it's nothing to do with them. It's Alan Fraser. He's been killed in a fall on the Western Underpass.'

He listened to the shocked silence at the other end of the phone and realized he might have broken the news more gently if he had not, somewhere, resented the fact that her first thought had been for her brothers. 'I'm sorry. I was there, I saw it,' he said, in exculpation.

'Oh, darling. My poor John. I'll come back, I'll get the milk train from Doncaster.'

One of the advantages of a girl with four brothers, on the other hand, he thought, his head aching suddenly with unshed tears, was that she was unmoved by male macho behaviour. He would be wasting his time trying to tell her this death was all in a day's work.

'Don't come back,' he said. 'I'll be fully occupied tomorrow — I just didn't want you to see it in the papers.'

'I'm coming. Henry can cope here, now I've introduced him.' The clear voice was definite. 'What are you doing tomorrow, anyway? Is it Croydon again?'

'No. We're treating this one as murder, and it's mine to do.'

'Murder?'

'Better not talk on the phone.'

'Oh, Christ. Darling John, are you sure you haven't gone OTT because you loved him? People do fall off scaffolds.'

'The lads in Wester Ross found a yellow anorak hidden on the hill yesterday,' McLeish said, between his teeth, and waited out the silence on the phone.

'Ah. There *was* someone above Alan on the hill that day, then. And everyone else at your end has been asking you, a) are you sure about this? And b) if you are sure, ought you to be doing it because you are involved? I'm sorry, darling. Kind men have just looked up the milk train for me and it is impossible — I'll come down on the first train tomorrow, and at least I'll be in London.'

'I'd be glad to have you,' he conceded, cheered as always by her swiftness of comprehension.

'What are you going to do now?'

'Finish here — it'll take an hour or so — then go home, then start again from the Yard in the morning. I can't operate out of these offices permanently.'

'I know you don't want to talk on the phone, but how did he fall? Was he pushed?'

'No, he fell. The autopsy may tell me why.'

The silence at the other end of the line was eloquent in its distress for him. She broke it first. 'I agree, it's hopeless to talk on the phone. I'll brief Henry, get to bed, and I'll be on the seven o'clock train.'

* * *

An hour later John McLeish had done all he could. Everyone near Fraser on the scaffold, or who had seen the fall, had been interviewed briefly, as well as the group who had eaten tea with him. Fraser, it appeared, had been working rather slowly, but nothing untoward had happened until he had suddenly swayed on his feet, clasped at a bar, and before Mickey, working near him, could get close enough to grab him, he was gone. The two Irishmen, whom McLeish had interviewed personally — brothers, classically christened Patrick and Michael Doolan — had been working ten feet above. They had sworn, tearfully, that neither of them had dislodged anything which could have fallen on Fraser, pointing out that this was a recognized hazard for inexperienced scaffolders and just did not happen to people like themselves. There was not much to drop either, as Michael, the more intelligent of the two, had pointed out — really only a choice of a scaffolding key or a bolt, either of which would have bounced off Fraser's helmet; that was what a helmet was for.

'You'd want to drop a length of steel on your man to push him off,' he had said, sweating slightly with anxiety and conviction, 'and *that's* happened before, but no one dropped any steel today.'

Mickey Hamilton, trembling and clammy with shock, had not been all that clear as a witness, but he was certain he had not seen anything fall. Fraser had just handed up a length of steel to the Doolan brothers, told them that he was going off site for a bit and to cover for him — and had fallen a few seconds later. All three men had apparently been in such a state of shock that this evidence was not wholly dependable, but McLeish had his own reasons for thinking it unlikely that this had been an accident caused by a fellow scaffolder's careless move.

* * *

He was organizing papers into a set of envelopes when Jimmy Stewart put his head tentatively round the door. 'You can have your office back any minute, Mr Stewart. I'm sorry to have kept you out of it.'

'I'll be glad of it,' Stewart said drily, 'but it's not what I came for. There's a man at the gate asking for you, not one of yours — I mean, not police. The lad you have on there didn't feel he should leave the gate, or let him in, so he asked me to carry a message. He's called Perry Wilson — he says he knows you.'

McLeish looked at him blankly, then realized what had happened. Francesca, prevented from arriving instantly by the small matter of a 200-mile journey and no trains, had organized a substitute for herself. How old did she think he was? he wondered, torn between love and exasperation. He told Stewart he would come himself and walked out into the night with him.

He had been working with the window tightly shut and the noise seemed very loud as he emerged. The road that ran along the edge of the side and fed traffic into the main road had been closed; police barriers could be seen to left and to right, and the closed road was bridged by a giant crane, with men swarming round it. The whole scene was lit more brightly than the day by arc lights. As McLeish watched, alarm hooters sounded, the dozen men who had been clustered round some object on the other side of the road retreated, and all the bobbing helmets moved well clear, blue helmets grouped together, apart from the green. The crane engine whined, and infinitely slowly a huge concrete beam rose from the ground, steadied and started to move sideways, its progress barely perceptible across the road.

'That's the casting yard over there,' Stewart shouted in his ear. 'We cast those beams on site — they're too big to shift round the country — but there isn't room on this side of the road so we do it over there. Every three weeks we close that slip road and take the beams over. Blue helmets for resident engineers — look at them, we must have every one of Rickett's top brass here, waiting for us to drop one.'

'Would it break?'

'If it started to swing — see that now?' Stewart fell silent.

The beam had developed a very slight pendulum action and a man on the ground was semaphoring violently to the crane-driver perched high above the site, lit up in his cabin. The note of the crane changed and everyone waited, watching, while the pendulum stilled. When the beam was completely steady the crane started again in its infinitely delicate task.

'Let it get swinging, you see, and it'll break the chains and come off. It might not break itself, though likely it'll come off one end at a time and *would* break — but it'd break whatever it fell on. Or whoever; that's why you have everyone standing clear. Though it's not usually on jobs like this you get the accidents — it's the odd ones, like drivers backing into people on site.'

'Or people falling off scaffolds.' McLeish completed his thoughts for him, deciding that a man whose entire site had been disrupted while he was trying to do a job as delicate as this one deserved some minimal explanation. 'We had information that someone was laying for Fraser, that's why I'm not treating it as an accident.'

'Ah.' Stewart suddenly looked quite different, as if his whole perspective had changed.

'Keep that to yourself.'

'I will, yes. There's your visitor.' He pointed to the gate where two figures could be seen, chatting comfortably. They resolved themselves into young Woolner from Edgware Road, getting in a bit of overtime, and Peregrine, dark and tidy, propping a piece of paper on the gatepost as he wrote on it. As they arrived he handed the paper to Woolner, who could be seen thanking him.

'Making you sign a statement?' McLeish asked with interest.

'Not yet,' Perry said, amicably. 'How are you, John? I am sorry to hear about all this.'

Woolner, rather pink, was shoving the paper in his tunic and explaining that he had younger sisters for whom he had solicited Mr Wilson's autograph. McLeish led Peregrine firmly away.

'It's good of you to come, Perry, but I could probably have got home to bed by myself.'

The younger man considered him, unembarrassed. 'She didn't tell me to come, you know; she just rang me to make sure I'd heard, since I knew Alan too. I came to keep you company.'

Oh God, McLeish thought, both touched and embarrassed, I have become a Wilson brother. When I am thought to be in trouble or distress, one of this quartet will come lolloping through the snow with a keg of brandy round his neck. He decided he had never been sufficiently grateful for his own, more distant family relationships.

'I also came', the St Bernard by his side was saying earnestly, 'because I am worried about something and Frannie said I must tell you at once.'

Please God, not drugs, not now, McLeish prayed fervently.

'Mickey Hamilton. I met him briefly with you and Frannie in Scotland, remember? She ticked me off for saying, perfectly truthfully, that he was gay, and so indeed was half of Grantchester Coll. when he was there. He is here — I mean, he was scaffolding with Alan?'

'Yes, Perry. You do think he's gay?'

'Oh yes. I don't know if he always was or whether he got into it at school, but he was involved in a huge scandal during his last year at Grantchester. It was one of those rows that had everything: drugs, small boys — well thirteen-year-olds — a creepy local nobleman with a triple-barrelled surname, Saturday evening parties at his country house — the lot. It was kept quiet, of course, and I think no one was actually expelled, if only because most of the older boys involved were leaving anyway, so they just went home a bit earlier. The aristocratic poofter shot himself: *that* was public, of course. The name's escaped me since all this is nine years ago. Two masters got the push. And the Head retired early, three months later.'

'It does come back to me. I hadn't realized the school had been so much involved. How do you know all this, Perry? Oh, of course, Tristram's football shirt.'

Perry, always quick on the uptake, said he absolutely agreed that Frannie must be made to stop wearing up all their old clothes, their poverty-stricken, anxious youth being well past, and that he would willingly buy all her clothes for her if she would let him.

'The point is, however,' he went on firmly, 'and Charlie and I still congratulate ourselves on this, that Tristram had actually left the school when the scandal broke. He left after his first year there and went to Teversham — Charlie's school. He was having trouble at Grantchester — the place was an absolute hotbed, the Head was queer as the proverbial coot and that set the tone. So we fixed him up a place at Teversham — my own school not being considered quite adequate for one as clever as Tristram — and he moved there after his first year. Charlie had a word with his housemaster, too, at Grantchester, to make sure he came to no harm in the meantime.'

'How old was Charlie?'

'Oh, turned seventeen. That was why we thought he had better do it, rather than me.'

McLeish enquired, fascinated, where in all this the Wilsons' perfectly competent mother had been, and where indeed their older sister? Perry sighed. 'We told Mum some of it afterwards. She'd only have got rattled, poor old bat, she is one of four sisters, no brothers, and she didn't really understand about boys or boys' schools. And Frannie had just gone up to Cambridge and was lost to us for a bit. Anyway, we fixed it, I mean Teversham was very glad to get Tris, he's a very *good* tenor and did them proud. Got a minor scholarship to Magdalene, after all. But what I'm trying to tell you, John, is that although we heard about the whole thing from boys who had been in Tristram's year, *lots* of other people knew. The school had gone totally to pot, most of the older boys were involved. One of that particular sixth form, who is in Fran's Department, failed his positive vetting to work for the Secretary of State even eight years later.'

'Was she cross with you for not telling her all this at the time?' McLeish asked with interest.

'Now you mention it, yes, rather,' Perry said, amused. 'But she said at once that I must tell you, and it wasn't just raking up old gossip. Hamilton was in neck-and-neck competition with Alan for a place on the K6 expedition — anything, including an old scandal, might have made a difference. And he was on the tower with Alan when he fell.'

McLeish held open the door of the site office for Perry, thinking hard. 'Would Alan have known this history? He wasn't exactly in the public school net?'

'Well, they'd known each other for yonks, hadn't they? Mickey's parents were summer visitors. I don't mean Alan was gay — quite the reverse, let me tell you, he was having a thing with one of the girls who was with Sheena on the Calendar shoot — but they were close friends. Hamilton probably had told him. Or someone else might have — as I said, quite a lot of people knew about it nine years ago.'

McLeish decided that, as he had thought before, the siblings' view of Perry as the least clever of them was wrong. He might not be as academically able as the rest but he was much the most perceptive about human relations. It was all too possible to envisage a younger Hamilton, shaken by the whole incident, confiding in a friend from a different world. Might Alan Fraser have used that knowledge nine years later to give himself the edge in a competition for a coveted place on a climbing expedition?

'The thing about Alan is — was — that he was the sort of bloke people told things to.' Perry was sitting on the edge of Stewart's desk watching the crane. 'Just like making a film,' he observed with interest; 'endless men armed with clipboards standing around under huge arc lights while three blokes actually *do* something. Sorry, I got sidetracked. I well remember confiding in Alan myself that summer in Scotland when I was fifteen — I was in a state, my voice had gone, I wasn't sure I would ever sing again, and there were Tris and Jeremy making records, loved by all, piling up the cash. Talk about green-eyed.'

McLeish was listening, fascinated, having never before heard this golden star express any doubt at all about himself.

'So I wept all over Alan, who was only a couple of years older. I can't remember what he said to cheer me up but I felt a lot better afterwards.'

He paused, still not looking at McLeish. 'But if you think about what fifteen-year-old boys are like, John, it was fairly remarkable that I felt able to tell my troubles to anyone, never mind a contemporary. Alan was like that.'

Yes, indeed, McLeish thought, and remembered with pain how easily he had been able to talk to the dead man who had been some five years younger than him. So others must have felt like that: Alan Fraser was probably a walking repository of other people's secrets, as those detached personalities often were, and it was possible that he had been killed to eliminate the knowledge in his head.

'Thanks, Perry,' he said. 'I must look all that up — I'll have to talk to Hamilton again anyway.'

'He has no form, John, no one was charged. So somebody has to have told you. If you have to say it was me, then you have to.'

'It's more than likely Hamilton will tell me himself.'

'Unless he killed Alan?'

McLeish agreed this was a reasonable caveat, and said that he was now going to go home.

'Can I drive you? The Car and Biff are in some unsavoury back street around here — I left him fending off offers of Illegal Substances.'

'If you've brought that Rolls down here, sunshine, you'd better go and find it again. The local lads have probably got the wheels off by now. I've got my own car here, thanks.' He stepped back to let Perry through, momentarily anxious lest he kiss him as he invariably kissed his brothers, and saw Perry's eyebrows peak in amusement.

'Sleep well, John,' he advised, patting him on the shoulder. 'See you soon.'

* * *

By ten o'clock the next morning McLeish had survived an interview with his Chief Superintendent, who was uneasy, as he had been the day before, about leaving him in charge of the case because of his personal involvement. McLeish had sat tight, watching his superior work himself once more through the logical steps which in the end came down to a) it was plainly a case for CI, given the earlier history in Scotland; b) investigations must start quickly; and c) there was no one else at CI above the rank of detective sergeant who had any time at all. The Division, always under pressure, had been further hit by the defection of one of McLeish's fellow DCIs, a quiet ,well-liked chap in his fifties, who had come in the day before, looking like a ghost, and while assuring his secretary that he felt fine, had cried out and sunk to the floor in the throes of a major heart attack. He was now in intensive care. Even the Chief Superintendent, it was felt, would have to accept this, however reluctantly, as disqualifying him from taking on a new case.

'The fact that Robert Vernon and his wife were there makes it more difficult — you don't suspect them, I take it?'

'They were there, both in Scotland and at the site, sir,' McLeish said patiently. 'Six people were around both yesterday and in Scotland on the day that Fraser fell: Mr and Mrs Vernon, their daughter Sally, his son Bill, plus Nigel Makin, Sally's fiancé. And, of course, Mickey Hamilton, Fraser's oppo, who is in St Mary's.'

'Hamilton must be the best bet, surely?' The Chief was sounding hopeful.

'He's where I'm starting.'

His superior regarded him balefully. 'You just keep me in touch, John, you hear? *Yes*, Mary, I'm coming — I'll be somewhere in Devon the rest of today and the night, John. We've got that rapist, or the lads think we have, and it turns out he's one of the local bigwigs, wouldn't you know it? Right, I'm off.' He stood up, a square, round-headed tough, six inches shorter and fifteen years older than McLeish. 'Don't get yourself in a mess, John,' he advised. 'You find you're too close to it, tell me and we'll find someone else.' He bent a basilisk look on McLeish and dared him to wonder aloud precisely who else? 'Autopsy through yet? No? Idle buggers. All *right*, Mary.'

McLeish stood aside so as not to impede his headlong progress and watched as he marched down the corridor still giving instructions to his secretary who was running to keep up with him.

He went soberly back to his own office to find six telephone messages stuck to his blotter. The first was from Francesca and said simply that she would be in her office at the DTI by eleven. The next asked him to ring a colleague in Forensic; that would be the preliminary autopsy results and could wait for five minutes. The third sent his eyebrows right up — Sally Vernon was asking to see him, at any time today, and was at home waiting for his call. The fourth was from Dorothy Vernon, asking only that he would ring the same number. He looked at both those messages twice, uneasily, and decided to leave them for a few minutes too. The fifth was from Sergeant McKinnon at Carrbrae, offering his presence forthwith if required, giving a list of places where he would be reached that day, and confirming that he had been to see Fraser's mother and grandmother. The final message was from the man on duty at St Mary's: Mickey Hamilton had been passed, if not fit, at least as not needing a hospital bed, by the doctor on duty that morning and was wanting to discharge himself; would DCI McLeish please advise?

Of these, only the last one was urgent. Unless he was planning to issue a warrant for Hamilton's arrest, he had no power to cause him to be kept anywhere he did not want to be. A decision needed making quickly to spare the man on the spot embarrassment. McLeish got through to him and asked to speak to Hamilton.

'I don't have to stay here.' Hamilton sounded shaky and frightened.

'No, you don't,' McLeish agreed. 'You are one of the people I most need to talk to, since you and the Doolan brothers were closest to Fraser when he fell. I'm basing myself at Edgware Road; they've given me a room there. Could we meet there, say, in an hour and a half, and we'll try and get clear what happened?'

'I told you what happened last night.'

'Not really. You were too shocked to be making much sense, so I only spent about ten minutes with you. I need to go over the whole thing, if you are feeling well enough.' He listened to the silence at the other end.

'I must go back to the caravan and get some clothes.' The voice sounded strained, and McLeish sighed.

'You were sharing with Fraser, weren't you? You'll find that some of my blokes are there doing a search through his kit. They'll let you in to get your things.'

'Oh God.' Hamilton sounded daunted.

'Tell you what,' McLeish offered. 'Let me talk to the chap on duty outside your room. He can take you to the site, and bring you on to Edgware Road.'

'You're arresting me!'

'No, I'm not, I'm just trying to get you to Edgware Road in the easiest possible way. Do it how you like — only I need to talk to you today.'

The pause lengthened, and McLeish hooked the phone between his shoulder and his ear and shuffled the other five messages into order. If Hamilton decided not to accept the offer of an escort, he would nonetheless be followed and dissuaded from doing anything other than come straight to Edgware Road.

'All right, have it your way.' The voice was grudging but no longer so shaky. 'I'll call the copper outside the door, and you can tell him what to do.'

'Thank you,' and McLeish economically instructed Detective Constable Andersen, whom he knew from his time at Edgware Road.

The autopsy was clearly next in importance, so he rang through.

'You'll have it written by late this afternoon, John,' the voice assured him, cheerily. 'We might not have found it so quickly if you hadn't told us what happened before he fell. No wonder he turned giddy — he was full of antihistamine — quite a lot still in the stomach. You know, John, the stuff that people take for hay-fever. No, you can buy the pills over the counter, there are lots of proprietary brands. They're all a bit different, but we'll be able to tell you which later today. They all come labelled that they can cause dizziness or drowsiness and shouldn't be used if you are in charge of machinery — or if you are a hundred feet up, building a scaffolding tower, as they doubtless do not think to tell you. What? No, no, far too much for him to have taken in the ordinary way. He was given it, all right.'

McLeish thanked him and rang off, shaken, with an echo in his mind. He picked the last message off the bottom of his pack and got through immediately.

'Fran? Darling, nice to have you back, but just listen, will you? Get the mob out of your office.' He waited while Francesca cleared her office which, as he could hear, was as usual full of people. She had a bigger permanent staff than he did and she had been out of her office for twenty-four hours.

'You remember when you went climbing with Hamish and turned giddy because you took antihistamine? Who was there when you apologized to Hamish?'

'Is that what happened to Alan?'

'Seems so.'

'Oh God, oh God. Someone got the idea from me!'

'Frannie, stop. Whoever it was would have thought of something else.' He cursed himself for not having realized how far ahead he was in his thinking, and for not breaking the news more gently.

'Sorry to spring it on you,' he said, lamely. 'I'd just got the autopsy result you see.'

'It's OK.' She had herself in hand, and was back in the hotel's recreation room, the old piano beneath her hands. 'You were there; and Robert Vernon, Sally, Bill and Nigel Makin were playing table tennis. Then, later, when I apologized to Hamish, everyone was there — you remember it was wet — all the Strathclyde boys, Perry, Alan himself, Mickey . . . and Dorothy Vernon had come down by then. But it doesn't really matter who was and wasn't there. You know what the claque is like — by evening everyone in the hotel and doubtless away to Carrbrae would have known that a tourist had to be half-carried down off the rock because the fool had taken antihistamine tablets to clear her head.' She stopped, and McLeish heard her blow her nose.

'I'm sorry, darling,' he said, sadly.

'Can we have lunch?'

'I'm sorry again. I'm taking a statement from Mickey Hamilton. Ring up Peregrine.'

'He rang five minutes ago and offered, but I was waiting for you to call. I know he saw you last night.' She was fighting tears, he could hear, and his heart was wrung. 'I'll do that, though. I need him.'

It's not him you need, it's me, John McLeish thought furiously, and I'm not available and won't be till God knows when. What a bloody job this is.

CHAPTER 11

'Sally, your father and I would both rather we had Ted Hughes here.' Dorothy Vernon was sitting by the side of her daughter's bed, holding her hands. 'Now, stop crying, this is no time to give up. You rang up Francesca's boyfriend — I must stop calling him that, I mean Chief Inspector McLeish — but he hasn't rung you back. What are you going to say to him?'

She shook her head at Robert Vernon who was hovering in the doorway. 'Don't you go thinking you can treat him as a friend, my girl, he's a policeman. Ted Hughes says he's young to be a Chief Inspector, so he's good. What are you going to say to him?'

'What I told you the day before yesterday.' Sally's fine blonde hair was clinging wispily to her neck, and the clear skin was blotched and mottled so that she looked about fifteen years old, and plain with it. 'The second test was positive, so I'm pregnant. And I don't know who the father is.'

'There's no need to make yourself interesting.' Dorothy Vernon was pale with anger and distress, and had put on too much jewellery; bracelets like handcuffs flashed in the light as she reached to take away Sally's breakfast tray. 'There are only the two candidates, aren't there? And it's something that's happened to other women before.'

'It's more likely to be Alan's than Nigel's,' Sally said, tearfully.

'Did you tell Alan that? I know you told him you were pregnant, but did you tell him he was the likely father?'

'Yes, yesterday morning. Just before I told you. He said he didn't see it was any more likely to be his than Nigel's.' Sally sniffed and reached for her handkerchief. 'Then he said he was sorry, ignore that, but equally he couldn't marry me or anyone now, and he'd help me with the money to get rid of it, if I was sure that was what I wanted. And *then* he said that since it could be Nigel's maybe I would prefer just to marry Nigel and I need never worry that he'd say anything.' Tears of rage and distress started to pour down her face again and Dorothy Vernon called to her husband who she knew was still outside the door to get a wet flannel and come and help.

He mopped Sally's face tenderly for her, then sat back on the other side of the bed, looking wretched. '*And* he had someone else,' she said, seizing the flannel and scrubbing at her face.

'I could kill the bastard,' Robert Vernon said, and both women looked at him in horror. 'Jesus. I forgot. I'm sorry.'

Sally Vernon pulled herself together with an effort of will and gently released her hands from her parents'.

'I've got to talk to the police, and I don't mind talking to John McLeish; he was nice to me and he knew Alan. Then I've got to decide what to do.'

Her parents, both tough, competent, extremely successful people, looked back at her helplessly.

'If you weren't pregnant, would you now want to marry Nigel?' Dorothy Vernon, practical to the backbone, broke the silence to ask, and her daughter looked back at her with approval.

'The right question, Ma. I wouldn't marry anyone right now.'

Robert Vernon was looking explosive but his wife shook her head at him. 'You don't want a baby without a husband,' she stated kindly but firmly, and her daughter looked back at her resentfully.

'That isn't necessarily true, Mum. I know you waited five years to have me, till you and Dad could marry, but it's different now.'

'No, it isn't.' Dorothy Vernon spoke with the flat confidence of unshakeable moral standards. 'A baby needs two parents who have agreed to stick together in a proper legal arrangement.'

'It might have red hair,' Sally said, and started to cry again.

Dorothy Vernon raised her eyes to heaven and bustled her seething husband out of the room with instructions to ring up John McLeish and arrange for him to come round, and to get their personal solicitor, Ted Hughes, over. Robert Vernon agreed to call the Yard, but refused the solicitor. 'He can see her with you in the room, Dolly. I don't want even Ted Hughes in on this. She's done nothing wrong.'

Dorothy Vernon shut the bedroom door gently behind her and turned to face him.

'That young man turned her down flat the day before yesterday, and she's not used to that. It's my fault as much as yours, don't think I'm putting the responsibility on you, Robert, but she's not been crossed much. *And* she's pregnant, and you and I know that does funny things. I don't know how that lad fell off a scaffold with no one within ten feet of him, but there's something funny. The police aren't treating it as an accident either.'

Robert Vernon looked at her, then stopped to take her in his arms. She was very pale except for spots of red over her cheekbones and she was looking ten years older.

'Oh, Robert.'

'Don't worry, my lovey, we'll get through this, it's all right. Did she tell Nigel she was in the club?'

'No, she didn't. She just told him she didn't want to marry him and gave him back his ring.'

'Why didn't she tell him she was in the club?'

'Oh, Robert, it was Alan Fraser she wanted. We may not like it, but there you are.'

Robert Vernon nodded, slowly. 'She didn't tell him, and she doesn't seem to want him now — even though the favourite got scratched.'

'Robert! The boy is dead.'

'I've not forgotten. He wouldn't marry her.'

'Well, that was honest of him. She's a rich woman: he could have gone climbing for the rest of his life without worrying about where the cash was coming from, and he wouldn't do it.'

'Stiff-necked bugger,' her husband observed, as the phone rang. Robert Vernon picked it up and told his secretary he would take this one. 'Mr McLeish? Sorry, excuse me, Chief Inspector. Yes, I know Sally rang you. She's in bed, she's not well enough to see anyone. Is it urgent? Are you treating this as murder?'

He listened to John McLeish's succinct explanation of the autopsy results, unconsciously puffing out his cheeks as he did when he was bothered. 'Bit of a coincidence, your being there then?' he observed.

'No.' John McLeish had woken up that morning, clear that nothing would be gained by trying to suggest that his presence at the site was coincidental or on a friendly basis, and he now explained the reasons for his presence to Robert Vernon. He had been at the site of the murder as a policeman and it was appropriate to say so. Nor did this disclosure give the murderer an advantage. The fact that a link had been made in the official mind would put pressure on him, whoever he was.

'I would like to see Miss Vernon as soon as possible: I need to talk to everyone who was at that table in the canteen. I understand if she can't manage today.'

Robert Vernon grunted. 'You need to talk to me and Dorothy as well.'

'Yes.'

'You may as well come round, and do us all, including Sally, but I'm not letting you talk to her unless I or her mother are with her, you understand? She's not fit.'

'I've got two interviews to do about one-thirty — I could come later?'

They fixed for five o'clock, and Robert Vernon put the phone down, scowling. He looked across at his wife. 'I'm supposed to be at the DTI with that lad's girlfriend and her boss at three o'clock. I'd better tell them I can't do it.'

'No, you go to that, Rob. Whatever's coming, it won't be helped by us sitting here worrying. I'm not doing that meeting on the Vernon Trust. Peter can chair that. He knows they're not to decide who gets what today, anyway. I'll stay with Sally. I'll get her clothes sent over from her flat, and I'll keep her away from the phone. You'd better get yourself ready and have some lunch.'

He nodded and kissed her, and she watched him out of the room, then returned to her daughter to tell her about the arrangement.

'Was Dad still very angry?'

'Yes, he was. Not with you.'

'Alan didn't rape me, you know.'

'*I* know that, Sal. Your father still thinks you are his little girl. He has difficulty remembering you are twenty-six and have a life of your own.'

'Why did he not mind when I was going to marry Nigel?'

'Because he thinks he owns him.'

Sally Vernon, tears drying on her cheeks, stared at her mother who was tidying around the bed. Dorothy Vernon dropped a pile of Kleenex into the wastepaper basket and looked back at her. 'Your father is wrong about Nigel, who has a mind of his own. He'd look after you. You could still have him, Sally, if you wanted. He's a generous man, he'd take on the baby as well. You think on. Damn that phone . . .'

Dorothy Vernon vanished to answer it, leaving Sally Vernon wide-eyed with astonishment.

* * *

McLeish had a hasty lunch at his desk, still struggling with the perennial CI problem of 'forming a squad' or finding a team to work with. He had managed to drag Bruce Davidson away from another investigation that was just finishing; he had borrowed a room at Edgware Road; and he had persuaded them to release two detective constables to work with him, not of course full-time but along with everything else they were doing. It would be unreasonable to complain: two of Edgware Road's uniformed constables were also deployed, one accompanying Mickey Hamilton and the other helping a sergeant and Detective Constable Woolner search the caravan that Alan Fraser had shared with Hamilton.

He drove himself to Edgware Road, leaving the keys to the car with the sergeant on duty so that it could be moved round Edgware Road's inadequate carpark as necessary. The sergeant told him Hamilton and the escorting Constable Andersen had already arrived and had been given lunch. Hamilton had been agitated about the time and was apparently due at another appointment, of critical importance, at four p.m. It was now two-thirty and he was asking if he could be taken there by police car — would DCI McLeish believe it?

Bruce Davidson was also present, as McLeish had asked. 'Don't worry, I'll see what's to do. I know where he's going, it is important — to him, anyway.' A busy afternoon for Mr Hamilton, McLeish thought with interest, making a statement about Alan Fraser's death to the police, then the key interview with the K6 sponsors.

'Had you not better put off that interview?' he asked, briskly, greeting Mickey Hamilton.

'Why? So you can arrest me?' Hamilton was wired for sound, as Perry would have said, pacing round the small interview room where he had been placed, very pale, hands pushed into his pockets.

'You're not in much of a state to take the sponsors on, are you?'

Hamilton stopped pacing and looked at him properly. 'I didn't kill him.'

'You were there.' Davidson had managed to settle himself on a chair with a notebook but both McLeish and

Hamilton were still standing. All three listened to the echo of those monosyllables.

'Was he frightened, did you think?' Mickey asked painfully.

McLeish felt the aching pressure at the back of his neck again. 'Not at the end. His back was broken. He had all he could do just to breathe, I don't think he had time to be frightened.'

Mickey Hamilton stared at him, then sank into his chair and bent his head into his hands. McLeish recognized in his bones the weight that was pressing Mickey down. He sat down himself, shaken, and asked Davidson to organize some tea, remembering that Mickey had loved the dead man, even if it was not reciprocated.

'He was my best mate,' Hamilton said desperately, gulping for breath.

'Cancel that fucking interview, Mickey,' McLeish said involuntarily, feeling protective of the weeping man opposite him. Mickey pulled himself together with an enormous effort, then his face creased.

'Sorry,' he said, and put his head and arms on the desk and wept again. McLeish decided to sit it out, sending Davidson out again for sweet biscuits. As Mickey recovered, he urged the biscuits on him, waiting as he ate his way through the whole plateful.

'I *had* better ring up and say I can't see the committee today,' Mickey said, with a sigh that came from his boots. 'Can I use a phone? I'll talk to Charlie Hutchinson, he'll know by now about Alan, and he can explain.'

They let him go with a constable to find the phone, and when he came back he sank into his chair in the total relaxation that follows tears and the abandonment of all plans for action. McLeish took him gently through the background details: his age twenty-seven, the same as Alan Fraser, and four years older than Tristram who had been a new boy at Grantchester when Hamilton would have been one of the sixth-formers getting themselves into trouble. And after

Grantchester the University of Southampton, where he had read medicine but which he had left without a degree to go on an ill-starred Everest expedition from which three climbers had been lost. He had never gone back to complete his course and had made his living for the last six years doing some teaching and as a scaffolder.

McLeish, watching him carefully, explained that the autopsy result showed that Fraser had been drugged.

'Well, I knew there must be something wrong — he just fell, none of us were anywhere near him,' Mickey observed drearily, obviously exhausted. 'What was it, do you know?'

'Antihistamine — a huge dose.'

'But he takes that, anyway.' Mickey was apparently unaware of the implications.

'Not at this time of year, surely?' McLeish asked, familiar with Francesca's sufferings.

'Oh yes, September can be very bad if you have an allergy to mould — Alan often found himself weeping and sneezing. It was I who suggested he should see a doctor, and he found this allergy. I've known Alan since we were children, you see; my parents used to take me to Culdaig for holidays.'

'What did he take?'

'Trilumax. They don't make you so dopey — I mean, they've got a benzedrine substitute in as well. I found them for him.'

McLeish glanced at Davidson who nodded in confirmation that those were the pills that the caravan searchers had found. He made a note to tell Forensic to compare whatever Alan had been given with Trilumax. He then glanced up, to find Hamilton looking sick.

'I can read upside down,' he said, in explanation. 'All teachers can.'

'Sorry. Like civil servants.'

'What was the drug in?'

'I haven't had a full report yet. But he probably took it within a couple of hours of his death. You all ate your tea together, didn't you?'

Mickey's head came up and he stared at McLeish, wordlessly.

'Will you go through what happened for me? Who was there, who arrived when, what they ate, everything?'

Mickey sat still, watching him, the brown eyes very alert in the swollen face. 'The stuff comes as a pill and it tastes bitter, I do know that. But Alan takes — took — a lot of sugar in tea or coffee, he said it was how he got his energy. It must have been in the sugar.'

McLeish said that it was a possibility, but other people probably took sugar, too.

'He was perfectly all right for an hour at least after tea — we were going like the clappers. Then we stopped for a breather.' Mickey focused in the region of McLeish's tie, eyes narrowed as he remembered. '*Then* we started again, and Alan fell about twenty minutes later. Just before six.'

'That's right. I was meeting him then.'

'I just can't remember how long the stuff takes to work. It's quick if you take it with liquid.'

'It was a very substantial dose,' McLeish observed, then thought about it. If it were quick-acting, then it seemed unlikely that Alan Fraser had taken it with his meal. The gap would have been too long. 'Do you eat or drink anything except in the canteen?'

'We all have thermoses, and drink from those when we have a breather. We buy pots of tea in the canteen, and fill the thermoses from those.' Mickey's voice died away and they looked at each other.

'We've found a thermos,' McLeish said grimly.

'His is — was — blue and white. We all have different colours to save getting them mixed up. We all take different things in our tea — I mean milk and sugar, of course.'

'When did Alan finish his thermos, then — how long after tea?'

'He didn't drink it all. We don't — oh Christ, I mean we didn't. We have a stop every hour and we'd another two hours to go before the real canteen stop. So he wouldn't have finished it.'

'Did you actually see if he did?'

'No. No, I suppose he might have done, but then he wouldn't have had anything left for the real break. And Alan wouldn't have done that. He's a mountaineer — you don't finish all your rations when you can't easily get more.'

Now that has to be right, McLeish thought respectfully. The thermos had been picked up, practically empty and without its top, when the area had been searched. McLeish had assumed it had fallen with Fraser and lost its top.

'Did he screw the top back on?' he asked Hamilton.

'Well, he would normally. I didn't notice particularly.'

McLeish, for a brief moment, contemplated wearily the labour induced in sending members of the uniformed branch seventy feet up a scaffold to drop thermoses, their tops screwed on more or less thoroughly to see what would happen. More important for the moment was the question of how the lethal tea had got into the thermos. The murderer would have had to know Fraser's habits well; would have had to know that he would take a drink after an hour or so, at a time when he was high up on a scaffold. Moreover, he would have needed to know that Alan would then take only one cup, so a large amount of the drug would have to be put in. He felt the familiar momentary prickle of the scalp and considered Mickey Hamilton carefully. There was a good clear brain there; he had got very quickly to the actual poisoning method — unless of course he had known already, and with precision, how it was done.

'When did he fill his thermos?'

'When we all did. We get a pot of tea, a jug of boiling water and a jug of milk in the canteen. We help ourselves to what we want and we fill our thermoses at the end of tea. As you know, tea was a bit different yesterday because of the Royal Walkabout. There were two pots going, and I expect everything got a bit mixed up.'

McLeish looked at him thoughtfully, trying to envisage the scene, and did his best to extract an account of the thermos-filling activity. Two points were clear from Hamilton: that the four scaffolders, Bill Vernon and Nigel Makin had all filled their thermoses from the same pot of tea, and that later they had topped them up with boiling water.

'So it wasn't in the pot, or you would all have been affected,' McLeish suggested. 'Do you all take milk and sugar?' He watched as the bones in Hamilton's face tightened.

'I don't, but Alan did, and both the Doolans. We all take milk. The sugar is on the tables and there were two bowls on this one because it was a big table. I've no idea who used which bowl. We had a milk jug given to us, but we ran out, so Mrs Vernon passed their jug up and Alan topped up with that.'

Oh dearie me, McLeish thought, echoing, as he did when harassed, his good-tempered father, it's going to be one of those! The canteen had, of course, washed everything up after tea, well before Fraser had fallen from the tower. 'Do you fill your thermoses after every meal?'

'Yes. We rinse them under a tap to clean them if we remember, before filling them up again. It's pretty basic on a site, very like being on an expedition. You look after your feet and you eat enough and you don't let yourself get dehydrated, but you don't bother much with the niceties. I don't suppose Alan had rinsed his out since lunch — he just took the top off and let it air while we were having tea.'

'Where was it standing?'

'Oh, in the middle of the table, where all ours were.'

McLeish contemplated him, unspeaking, and Hamilton looked back, replaying his own words in his mind.

'Yes, I suppose anyone could have dropped something in.'

McLeish took him patiently through the events of yesterday's tea. Mickey was an excellent observer who had taken a real malicious pleasure in the site-management's discomfiture, but all that emerged was that in the general mêlée of anxious passing of plates and pouring of tea it would have been possible for anyone at that table who was well prepared to drop a dose of antihistamine into either the sugar, the jug of milk, or any of the four thermoses standing waiting to be filled.

The field, therefore, still contained all six people who had been in Scotland and at tea: Robert, Dorothy, Bill and Sally Vernon, Hamilton himself, and Nigel Makin. No obvious candidate having emerged from contemplation of the probable method, McLeish then returned to the question of motive. Mindful of his earliest mentor, who had said that once you'd got away from the murders committed by nutters where there were no rules, in ninety per cent of all other murder cases it was dead obvious from Day One who had done it. It was usually a member of the family or near offer, which was what you'd expect, given what family life was like. The remaining ten per cent were done by clever buggers who wanted something badly, and you had to work at who'd got what out of the murder and you'd find your man that way. McLeish had suspected then and confirmed subsequently that this thesis needed some expansion, that people wanted the damnedest things which you would never be able to guess. But it wasn't a bad way to start. What had Mickey Hamilton wanted that would be achieved by this death? He sat thinking for a minute, well aware that the younger man was becoming increasingly uneasy as the silence stretched.

'I could just as easily have been selected for K6 as Alan, you know,' Mickey said. 'I do have more experience on snow and ice. Alan himself said so to Francesca. You heard him, you were there.'

McLeish leant forward, alert. 'Alan was better known, though. Might have been more useful to the expedition in that sense, mightn't he?'

'He wasn't fit. His ribs were still giving trouble after that fall, although he was pretending he was all right.' The resentment in Mickey's tone was unmistakable.

'Your arm's not too good either, though, is it?' McLeish pointed out, and Mickey's involuntary, instantly checked movement to pull the shoulder back said it all.

McLeish watched him, trying to judge this man; it might be very important to know how concerned Mickey had been about the nine-year-old incidents at Grantchester.

Investigation had shown that they had been fully as lurid as Perry had suggested, and moreover that Mickey had been one of eight senior boys most heavily implicated. Had any of the parents of the younger boys involved been willing to have their children give evidence, indeed, he would have had a criminal record. The difficulty for the parents had been not only the potential publicity but the fact that, as the local force had duly remarked, it would have been difficult to suggest the boys had been in any way coerced. Would the sponsors of this trip mind that Mickey was gay, or did he have to conceal that, too? McLeish felt himself in a dilemma; but for his relationship with Francesca and Perry he would not have known of this incident in Mickey's past.

'Is there anything else you can think of that might be helpful?' he asked unhopefully, and watched as Mickey politely appeared to rack his brains without producing anything useful. He gave it up, and explained that Mickey's answers would be produced as a statement which he would be asked to sign.

'Are you going to talk to any of the K6 people?' Mickey asked abruptly, and McLeish saw a chance.

'Not yet. But, as you must see, if they say they would have taken Alan rather than you it does give you a motive.'

'I didn't kill him.'

'Then you have nothing to worry about.'

'You might upset the sponsors.'

'I'm not going to talk to them unless I have to.' McLeish watched Mickey bite his nails.

'They probably *would* have taken Alan if he was available and there was only one place, just because he is better known. I don't mind telling you that, if that's what you want to know. But I could have got on as well — I could have contributed a bit of my costs and they did — do — badly need one more climber.'

'So, unless there were some other reason for not taking you — like your arm for instance,' McLeish suggested, smoothly watching the flicker of alarm in the brown eyes, 'you would have reckoned your chances?'

'That's right.' Mickey was alert now, watching him carefully. 'But I'll agree that they are better with Alan gone.'

McLeish nodded. By agreeing that Alan had stood at least partially in his way, Hamilton had rendered it formally unnecessary and prejudicial for McLeish to talk to the K6 committee right now.

McLeish left him to wait while his statement was typed and decided to let Davidson cope: if Mickey had murdered Fraser to get his place on K6 then he wasn't going to flee the country, or not until the whole expedition left in three weeks' time. In the meantime, there were other people to interview.

CHAPTER 12

Robert Vernon, occupying himself with telephoning his managing directors while being driven to the Department of Trade and Industry, knew he was causing agitation. Anxious men all round the United Kingdom were being contacted in their cars and hauled out of their meetings. In one case, where disquieting rumours had been reaching Head Office, the earnest candour with which the secretary explained the difficulties attendant on getting her boss to a telephone had left Robert Vernon grimly convinced that Jarvis was even now being sought frenziedly through the afternoon drinking-clubs of Birmingham. He made a note, and looked up to find that his driver was parked on Victoria Street outside the DTI's glass frontage, carefully avoiding the eye of a traffic warden. Robert Vernon reluctantly decided that the errant managing director would have to be let off the hook this time; in the hour or so that he would be with these types at the DTI, that competent young woman would most certainly have found her wandering boss, dried him out, and provided him with a decent briefing. Time, however, to go and see that office without giving any notice.

He got heavily out of the car, aware that he had been distracting himself with work to avoid thinking about his daughter, and found himself explaining his business to a middle-aged uniformed messenger with an uncertain command of the English language.

'That one, there,' he said, exasperated, as he read his own name upside down on a pink slip of paper among a dozen laid out in a random pattern on the table-top inside the glass cubby-hole. The man looked at him in wild surmise and picked up a wholly different piece of paper. Robert Vernon sighed and suggested he ring Miss Francesca Wilson. The man's face cleared happily and three minutes later Francesca appeared, demurely grey-suited.

'Thank you, Charlie,' she said kindly to the messenger. 'Can I take the chitty?' She reached into the box, extracted the right slip and took Vernon across worn flooring and up the stairs to the central lifts. The whole operation, he thought, looked incredibly run down and shabby, and he was signally unimpressed by the company in the lift. Francesca was nicely turned out, though wearing much less make-up than the girls in his office, but the rest of this shower looked like a dole queue gone live; not a decently cleaned pair of shoes among them and two dirty collars. His gaze shifted to a smallish older man hunched into the far corner of the lift, whose grey hair had needed cutting for months and who had cigarette ash and what looked like mince down the front of his jacket.

'I want you Francesca,' this personage said malevolently. 'Your colleagues are producing for me great nonsense on these rescue cases.'

Robert Vernon gaped disbelievingly as Francesca courteously assured this aged derelict that she would attend upon him late that afternoon.

'Gerhard Bukowsky — Sir Gerhard — Chief Statistician,' she explained as they got out on the seventh floor.

'I thought you had to be British to work for the government,' was all Robert Vernon could find to say.

'For the Foreign Office or the Security Services it is a requirement that you be born a Brit, but not otherwise. It doesn't seem to do the FCO much good, I'd have to say.'

Robert Vernon, mentally reviewing the Foreign and Commonwealth's roll of British-born traitors, could only agree with her. They had arrived by then in an office where the people looked more what he expected. A brisk, conversant young man courteously offered him tea and apologized for the momentary delay, since Mr Westland was still on the telephone. Robert Vernon regarded him with suspicion, in case he sat down at a typewriter, but he showed no signs of doing so. A very large man, not tall but substantial, appeared at the door of the office and welcomed them in; must be carrying all of seventeen stone, Robert Vernon thought disapprovingly.

'Robert, this is Bill Westland. Mr Vernon, Mr Westland.'

'Very good of you to come. I've asked Francesca to join us, if that is all right?'

Francesca smiled at him serenely as Robert confirmed that this would be acceptable. He settled down prepared to give Bill Westland a hard time.

'Francesca — normally a reliable sort of girl — tells me you may be willing to help us with some of our major commercial problems, Mr Vernon? In a non-executive capacity.'

Clever bugger, Robert Vernon thought, admiring and disarmed, and allowed that this was true.

'You will understand of course that it is the Secretary of State who makes all these appointments, and we are trying to put together a short list for him.'

'A very short list,' Francesca observed, pouring tea, and totally missing the swift suppressive glare from her senior officer.

'Like that, is it?' Robert Vernon asked, grinning.

'You have to put up with being messed around,' Francesca said cheerfully. 'But we do need you.'

'I doubt if I could have put it any more clearly myself,' Bill Westland said, clipping his words and favouring her with a basilisk glare that silenced her. 'But perhaps we could discuss the areas of most interest to you?'

With Francesca effectively out of action, he and Robert Vernon sparred round each other, achieving understanding if not agreement, and parted amicably with protestations of mutual esteem after forty minutes. In the courteous flurry attendant on finding his briefcase, Francesca observed *sotto voce* to her godfather that the good Mr Vernon was angling for Chairman of British Engineering, had he not observed?

'Yes, of course, but I have to clear lines. Well, thank you again, Mr Vernon. Francesca, will you see Mr Vernon gets past the dragons all right on the way out?'

Francesca, relaxed now that she knew she had indeed brought off a major coup, trotted to the lift, moving fast to keep up with Robert Vernon who was noticing that this time the place was full of older women in brown cardigans looking like superannuated librarians. Having got the feel of the organization by now, he decided gloomily that they were probably all senior advisers of unimaginable distinction.

'You going to be working here when you're sixty, Francesca?' he enquired with interest, as they got out of the lift.

'I'd rather turn out like that than be locked up at home with two sets of twins,' she said, effortlessly following his line of thought, and he laughed aloud.

'Someone's got to have the babies — you're as bad as my Sally.' He scowled thinking of his Sally, and Francesca watching him covertly said how awful it had been about Alan Fraser; she herself had been told late last night, but she understood all the Vernons had actually been on the site.

'Yes,' Robert Vernon said heavily. 'I'm just off home to sit with Sally while she sees your young man.'

'You needn't,' Francesca said, bristling slightly. 'Sit with her I mean — John's very orthodox, and he wouldn't bully her.'

Robert Vernon did not comment, and they walked on in silence.

'I expect she's very upset?' Francesca ventured, and wished she hadn't, as he gave her a suspicious sideways glance. 'I mean, she'd known Alan for some years, hadn't she? And she was actually there — awful for anyone. John was very upset and he'd only met him this summer.'

Robert Vernon's face relaxed. 'That's true, right enough. Yes, it was a bad shock to her.' He paused and added carefully that she had found Alan Fraser particularly attractive.

'Indeed he was,' Francesca confirmed tranquilly.

'You didn't fancy him?' Robert Vernon asked with interest.

'No, I didn't. I was just wondering why. I guess it's mostly because he was younger than me and I have four younger brothers — I mean, I'm immune to anyone younger. Viewed objectively, not much of a bet as a boyfriend either — he'd have been half-way up a mountain whenever you wanted him, wouldn't he?'

'That's right. And a one for the girls, by all accounts.'

'I'm sure that's right. You remember, my brother Perry took him off to Ardnacraig to see the Pollock Calendar shoot? He was apparently a tremendous hit. Gail Smith — that dazzler who does the Levi ads — was very smitten. He'd been seeing her in London.'

She put out her hand to shake Robert Vernon's in farewell and he held it thoughtfully.

'Difficult bloke altogether.'

'If you mean bloody-minded, yes. That's why we quarrelled all those years ago — I knew he ought to go back to school for a year and get his Highers. Boys always get restless and want to leave school when they're sixteen, and you just have to jolly them along. No chance, no way, no one could make him, even though it would have been to his advantage.'

She was looking pink and annoyed even at the memory of this tussle, and Robert Vernon nodded. 'I found that with him myself,' he observed and Francesca looked at him enquiringly, but he was not willing to expand.

'I must go, Francesca. Thank you for arranging that,' he added as an afterthought. He wrung her hand and hastened out of the door, leaving her wondering what in the conversation had disconcerted him. She watched him go, remembering Alan in the bar after a climb with her John, both of them laughing, John pale with exhaustion but a deeply happy man, and felt ashamed of herself. Whatever her own reservations about Alan, he had been much loved.

* * *

John McLeish was also thinking about Alan Fraser as he and Bruce Davidson were eating their first Big Macs, a second round cooling in their boxes in the car. A bag of apples also awaited their attention, courtesy of Francesca, who had been so appalled by his description of the average detective's diet that she had taken to pressing health-giving supplements on him.

'Have an apple, Bruce. Fran says we'll get scurvy or rickets if we don't eat properly.'

'Ye're under her thumb, John. She'll be seeing ye have the school milk at break next.'

'What else has she given me?' McLeish decided to ignore that.

The bag turned out to contain a promising-looking crunchy bar which, in the event, was constructed from the sweepings from a threshing-floor stuck together with treacle. He ate an apple hastily to try and get rid of some of the grit but he was still picking bits of chaff from his teeth, with Davidson who had refused one, grinning smugly, as he arrived at the Vernon stronghold. A uniformed driver took his car away — still covered with the fine cement dust that hung everywhere in the air around the Western Underpass site — and another man showed him up.

They were received by Dorothy Vernon, nicely dressed in a suit he would have had difficulty describing, but with the usual flash of diamonds at her ears.

'Come in, Mr McLeish.' She had called him John in Scotland but made an easy transition to formality, and he introduced Davidson.

'You won't mind if Robert and I sit with you while you are talking to Sally? She's still very upset.'

'Certainly, if that is what she wants.'

Dorothy Vernon gave him the sharp look of one whose requests to men of his age did not usually receive qualified answers, and he smiled patiently back at her. She showed him into a smaller room where Sally, dressed, very pale and swollen-faced, was sitting in a large leather chair. Her father's study, McLeish realized, easing himself into another vast chair while Bruce Davidson established himself in a corner.

Dorothy Vernon made to sit, but Sally stopped her. 'I'm OK, Mum. I'd rather just do this myself. Honestly.' The bright brown eyes, so like her father's, glinted in the tear-stained face and Dorothy Vernon yielded, reluctantly.

'Would you like some tea?' she offered, clearly seeing a way in.

Sally refused promptly and McLeish murmured that he and Davidson had just had lunch, so Dorothy Vernon left. Formidable woman, McLeish thought; no sign of temper or being thwarted, though it probably didn't happen to her much these days.

He considered the girl before him, her blonde hair looking dull, unwashed and lifeless. 'You know why we are here?'

He got a nod.

'We are treating Alan Fraser's death as murder because the autopsy found a high concentration of antihistamine in his blood. In my terms, he would have had to have taken about thirty tablets, and it is not possible he did that by accident.'

'Did he fall in Scotland by accident the day you rescued him?'

'That must now also be open to question.'

He waited patiently to see if she had anything more to say, then explained that he would be wanting her to tell him as much as she could about the events of the day before. 'Do you always have tea in the canteen?'

'Only when the site is working late. It is disgusting, that canteen, all greasy food — but it is the only way of getting a meal without going off site. I'd gone to the pub for lunch, and I didn't want to do that again.'

'Did you know your parents would be there?'

'No. I knew Dad was visiting the site, we all did; everyone had been tidying up for days. Mum decided to come at the last minute. I suppose we might have guessed they would turn up in the canteen since it was the only one on the site, but I didn't think of it. Nor did anyone else, judging by the state of the place.' She looked at him, obviously remembering something. 'I knew you were meeting Alan, though.'

McLeish stared at her, feeling rather than hearing Davidson stop writing behind him. 'He told you?'

'No, Nigel did. He was passed the message and asked to get it to Alan — it was just a phone message you see — and he told me. Bill was with him — in fact, he took the message up to Alan.'

McLeish sat, feeling as if he had turned to stone. Fraser had been killed just before he was due to meet him, and three people who had been in Scotland at the time of the earlier attack knew of the meeting.

'You presumably knew I was a policeman — I mean, there's no secret about it when I'm not on holiday, and I know Francesca had told your father?'

'Nigel and Bill and I were there the night before last, when Dad mentioned it — I don't think they knew before that. But I did — Alan told me.'

A small silence fell and she blew her nose.

'It must have been a terrible shock for you,' John McLeish offered, using another of the stock phrases to oil an interrogation, and watched with pity as she started to cry.

'I'm pregnant,' she said, not looking at him, and McLeish waited helplessly, not liking to ask the obvious.

'I don't know who the father is either,' she said, weeping steadily and causing McLeish to glance anxiously towards the door. He waited, stolidly, out of long experience, while she got herself in hand. She looked round for a clean handkerchief and he passed her his own, reminded irresistibly of Francesca who never had a handkerchief, either.

'I mean it could be either Alan or Nigel; Alan more likely, given the timing. I don't know what to do.'

'Does your mum know?'

'Yes. And she told Dad.'

'When did you tell them?'

'Day before yesterday.'

'Did you tell them the full strength?' McLeish, thoroughly conscious of all the implications of what he was hearing, realized this had come out a little rough, but left it.

'Yes.'

'Wait a minute: did Alan know?'

'Yes. He asked if I was sure it was his. Then he offered to pay for an abortion.' She started to weep again. 'He didn't want to get married, you see. He wanted to be free to climb.'

McLeish, who very much wanted to get married but who could also well remember a time when he, too, had wished fervently and solely to be free to do what he wanted, decided sadly that he might well in his youth have behaved exactly as Alan had. He sought to formulate his next question, but she was ahead of him.

'I didn't do it on purpose, you know. And it was much more likely to be his than Nigel's.'

McLeish decided that, much though he would like to know what her plans were, they were not germane to the enquiry. What mattered was Fraser's potential paternity and the reactions this had inspired in other people.

'Were your parents much distressed?'

'Dad was furious.'

'What did your mum say?'

'How could I have been so careless?'

McLeish nodded. Dorothy Vernon was someone who took personal responsibility seriously, even when it came to her own beloved daughter.

'Does Nigel Makin know?'

'No.' She stopped. 'I didn't tell him. Unless Mum or Dad told him — they're both very fond of him. But I don't think they did.'

McLeish nodded, knowing he could depend on Davidson to flag the point.

'And your brother?'

'I didn't tell him. The parents may have, I suppose. He wouldn't have been much bothered — I mean, he wouldn't have felt it necessary to kill Alan for me.'

She started to cry again, and McLeish waited patiently for her to stop. He took her through the sequence of events at the tea table but it left him no better off. Plainly, anyone at that table could have dropped a fatal dose into Alan Fraser's thermos, including Sally herself — which, he reminded himself, he must not forget. This strong-willed creature might well have been angry enough to try and damage a man who was turning her down.

He left Sally in the study, having asked if they could have a few minutes before interviewing the senior Vernons.

'Would she have topped him, Bruce?'

'Just because he would'na marry her, having got her in the club? There's a few would be dead men if women behaved like that. Anyway, why would she have dropped a rock on him in Scotland? She didn't know she was pregnant, then.'

McLeish thought about it. 'He was probably playing her up in Scotland too,' he pointed out. 'You saw the way he went off, very pointedly, with Fran's brother to visit the Calendar girls. And made a hit there, Perry tells me. This was later, of course, but he probably always behaved like that.'

Bruce Davidson opined that he didn't see many violent girls in his circles; perhaps rich girls were different; what did McLeish think?

'I can't honestly see Frannie murdering someone in those circumstances — no.'

Nothing to do with money, it was that her judgement was too cool, he thought regretfully. It was just possible, but only just, to see her killing in defence of a brother, but not because a man didn't want to marry her. She would, no doubt, consider herself more than qualified to bring up any number of children on her own. He jerked himself smartly out of this line of thought and said to Davidson that they had to see the senior Vernons as a finish to a perfect day.

He put his head into the office and offered to interview the Vernons in whichever order they preferred, and found that Robert Vernon had volunteered. He took him patiently through his earlier acquaintance with Alan Fraser until the day of Alan's fall.

'Were you in the area that day?'

'You want to know whether I had an alibi?' Robert Vernon sounded grimly amused. 'I know where I was that day. I was fishing a loch on the same hill and I was by myself from lunch-time on. I came down at about six-thirty and picked up the Range Rover — there's a little carpark by the waterfall where the Carrbrae Road crosses the river. Then I drove back to the hotel — I was there about eight-thirty.'

McLeish nodded, remembering Duncan Mackintosh pulling over sharply to let the blue Range Rover through. The timing was about right, but it left Robert Vernon with no alibi; it had been five-thirty when Francesca had seen Alan fall, and Robert Vernon, by his own admission, had then not been far away.

McLeish took him equally carefully through the events of the day before, but he had apparently noticed nothing at tea, including the thermoses. If it was a sign of guilt to have noticed absolutely nothing, it was also a perfectly sound approach. McLeish considered his man carefully; the powerful compact body was tense in the leather chair and the bright brown eyes were very alert.

'Miss Vernon has told us that she told you the day before yesterday that she was pregnant, and that the most likely candidate for its father was Alan Fraser. How did you feel about this news?'

'Well, how would anyone? I was bloody furious, I can tell you.'

'Did you talk to Fraser about it?'

The brown eyes flickered. 'No, no, it was Sally's business and she didn't want anyone interfering. I think she was worried I'd clout him one.'

'And would you have?'

The man looked faintly disoriented and McLeish sat still.

'I might have.' He recovered rapidly. 'But I'd not have put poison in his tea, I'd have dealt with him straight.'

Now that, McLeish thought, rang true. He could not see Robert Vernon murdering anyone by that route — a swift blow with a shovel, perhaps, but not by poison. But he was lying about something — and Davidson thought so too, since he was scraping his chair. McLeish nagged away carefully but got nowhere, leaving Robert Vernon still tense.

He decided to change tack. 'Did you discuss the situation with Nigel Makin?'

'Of course not.' Robert Vernon sounded shocked, but relieved, as if he were on easier ground.

After a few more questions McLeish let him go. He swivelled his chair and looked enquiringly at Davidson.

'I think he did see Fraser, guv,' Davidson said quietly, an eye on the door.

'So do I. What did he say to him, do you think?'

'Never darken the doors of my building site again?'

'Fraser was still there twenty-four hours later — he'd have been out that day if Robert Vernon had wanted that,' McLeish sighed.

'He mebbe made a deal with him that he would marry the wee girl after all?'

'And left him working as a scaffolder while he thought about it? That's possible. OK, let's leave it for now and get Mrs Vernon in.'

McLeish rose as Davidson came back with Dorothy Vernon and thought again what a formidable creature she was. He looked at her carefully as she came quietly in and realized she was even more tense than her husband had been, and grimly determined to run the interview her way. He decided to calm her down by taking her very slowly through the preliminaries, so that after ten minutes she was glancing at the diamond watch which she wore, unusually, on her right hand, and was no longer tense but merely impatient.

She confirmed the details of the tea party, and left McLeish clear that the antihistamine could not have been in the milk or the tea but could have been in the sugar. She was roused to real eloquence as she described the general state of the canteen and, seeing her relaxed, McLeish slid in his enquiry about whether she had talked to Alan Fraser after Sally's disclosure of her pregnancy.

'No, I didn't, though I would have liked to. I did have a word with Nigel Makin, who has been badly treated.'

'Sally told him, then?' McLeish sounded as startled as he felt.

'No, and she hasn't yet. But she has broken off their engagement.'

'Before Fraser was killed.' McLeish kept his voice dead level but Dorothy Vernon looked at him sharply.

'Yes.' The confirmation was reluctant.

'I will, of course, be interviewing Mr Makin again — it was only a preliminary chat last night. Did Mr Vernon — William Vernon, I mean — know about this as well?'

'Yes, he did.'

'How did he react?'

Dorothy Vernon considered the point carefully. 'He was very distressed for her — I mean, she is his half-sister and they've been getting along quite well now they are on the same site. But they're not really very close — they were brought up apart. He was very angry for her, but not as violently so as some brothers would have been.'

She thought again, just perceptibly, chewing her lower lip: 'He behaved well and was nice to her, but I had the feeling he was not that unhappy that she was in trouble. He's got no cause to be fond of her; Robert's first wife brought him up to think of me and her as the enemy.' She looked him in the eye. 'He's not a bad lad, Chief Inspector, but he's no better than his rearing.'

McLeish observed neutrally that he had only had a brief preliminary interview with Bill but he intended to see him the next day.

Dorothy Vernon made to speak, then stopped, and McLeish enquired whether Nigel Makin was much distressed by recent events.

'Yes, of course he is,' she said, irritably. 'What man would not be? He wanted to go straightaway; he could walk into another managing director's job anywhere in the industry, but he said to me he'd not leave us with the Western Underpass contract barely started.'

She hesitated and McLeish sat silent, from long training. 'Robert's sixty-three, you see, and Nigel's the only one of the divisional MDs who can succeed him. He's not well known yet, but he is the only one who can take over from Robert.'

'I see.' McLeish saw the key fact, that Vernon Engineering might need Nigel Makin more than he needed the company. Rejected in quite such a public way by Sally Vernon, he might reasonably prefer to go elsewhere, leaving both Robert Vernon's treasured creations vulnerable to predators.

'Robert is fit to be tied,' Dorothy Vernon looked surprised at herself. 'He's very fond of Nigel, too, apart from seeing him as the natural successor.'

Any father might not unreasonably feel that Alan Fraser was a rotten bet as a son-in-law. Add to that the fact that Fraser was, by his very presence, threatening to weaken the managerial defences of Vernon Engineering, and you had a strong motive for Robert Vernon to get rid of Alan Fraser. The same, of course, might apply to Dorothy Vernon; he contemplated thoughtfully the firmly pressed lips and the strong, ugly, beringed hands. For his money, twinset and pearls notwithstanding, Dorothy Vernon was well capable of ruthless action to remove an obstacle. And poison was always said to be a woman's weapon. McLeish decided that he was not going to get a great more light on the subject from this interview, thanked her, and waited while her statement was typed.

CHAPTER 13

John McLeish dropped Bruce Davidson off at New Scotland Yard and decided he would call it a day himself. Francesca's telephone being engaged he took a chance on her being at home and drove over to her small house in Notting Hill. He paused at the gatepost and looked up towards the first floor; the big windows were open and he could hear singing. He listened for a moment, recognizing Peregrine's high tenor, and hoped fervently that it was a recording, not the man himself. The singer was embarked on 'Bridge over Troubled Waters', and, even longing as he was to have Francesca to himself, he stood still to listen to the matchless voice lift easily to the top notes. Presumably Perry would never need to murder anyone; like Alan Fraser, he had a secure talent and if he couldn't use it by one route, he would find another.

The singer stopped, was succeeded by a murmur of voices, and McLeish sighed, but pushed his way through the gate. He rang the bell twice; although he had a key to Francesca's house he didn't use it if he knew other people were there. His heart sank as the door swung open to reveal Tristram, one of the twenty-three-year-old twins, a taller version of Perry.

'John, come in. We're all here.' In common with the whole Wilson family, McLeish thought resignedly, that boy was confident that it could give nothing but pleasure to have all five of them together. They all had separate flats or small houses, but all treated each other's establishments as extensions of their own. Indeed, all their houses looked very much the same; all Victorian, all featuring a large living-room with a piano at one end and bookshelves all round. All five also owned enviable amounts of expensive electronic equipment, supplied by the phenomenally successful Peregrine.

He looked round resignedly at the familiar sight of the Wilson children gathered in one room. Three out of four of the boys had the same dark Norman looks as Francesca, dark-brown hair, long straight noses in long faces, with blue eyes and high, arched eyebrows. Charlie, the eldest boy and second child, by contrast was dark blond with brown eyes, but the same long nose. They were, as usual, all engaged in different and noisy activities simultaneously; his eye rested on Perry, immaculate as ever, who was fiddling with the video tape recorder at the same time as demonstrating vocally some point in an aria to Jeremy, Tristram's twin, who was reading a book. Charlie was sitting at the piano picking away at a piece of music, bending forward to squint at the notes and simultaneously telling his sister some history. She was listening while marking up a hefty-looking report. McLeish sighed inwardly; Francesca looked up and saw him and came to kiss him.

'I can tell them to go away,' she said in his ear, sounding amused. 'They're only messing about. I didn't know you were coming.'

'I didn't either,' he said, mollified. 'Seems a bit hard to throw them out.'

'John, telephone for you.' Peregrine had interrupted his activities long enough to deal with the phone and appeared at his side, trailing the lead.

'Sorry to get after you, John,' Bruce Davidson said wearily. 'I tried to fix to see Mr William Vernon first thing tomorrow but he's away to Edinburgh for a couple of days and wonders if we could see him tonight. We could get him to stop back from Edinburgh, of course?'

'No, no. Better not to mess people around unless we have to. Fix him for eight-thirty tonight at the Yard. Francesca's got her family here, anyway.'

He scowled round the assembled Wilsons and Peregrine grinned at him, unoffended and amused. 'It's just as well she's got us, John. Think what she'd otherwise get up to, with you working so hard.'

McLeish considered him thoughtfully. He was always caught out by the speed of reaction in the Wilson family; it was of course a direct result of having five siblings close in age who had to compete for very limited parental time and energy. Not for the first time he realized that his own background, as the eldest child of two schoolteachers, with his nearest brother a comfortable three years younger, might actually be less than an asset in a highly competitive world.

'I always think of that, Perry,' he assured him gravely. 'It is a comfort to me.'

'Come away to the kitchen, John, and I'll find you some supper — I can feed this lot later.' Francesca tugged at his sleeve.

'I'll come and get a drink,' Perry said, firmly. 'I know you don't want me, Frannie, but I've got some gossip for John which might be useful, and it won't take long.'

Perry got them all drinks, moving round his sister's kitchen as if it were his own, complaining about the quality of the tonic water and freeing the clogged ice trays with a running commentary on women who never defrosted their fridges.

'So, John.' He stopped to listen as a tenor voice from the room above started up. McLeish watched impatiently as both Wilsons listened, all their attention focused on the music, drinks unregarded in their hands.

'He's good, isn't he?' Francesca said.

'Oh, he always was. He's got a better range at the bottom than me. That's Tristram singing, John.'

Peregrine sounded totally untroubled, and McLeish remembered Alan Fraser telling Francesca, with just that same untroubled air, that Mickey Hamilton had more experience in Himalayan ice and snow conditions than he had. If your talent was secure in an area where it mattered, you could afford to be generous about other people who might be better than you at some things.

'Is it something else on Mickey Hamilton?' he asked, declining a second drink and looking hungrily at the steak Francesca was putting under the grill.

'Sort of. I'll tell you where it came from.'

'Always useful.'

'No need to be sardonic, John, I know you've had a long day. It's the steel-fixers on the new house who told me.'

'The place in Bertrand Terrace you were looking at?'

'I know you've been away, John, but you're well out of date. I bought it six weeks ago and the lads went straight on site — we're gutting it and putting RSJs in everywhere.'

'But you've only just finished the house you're in,' McLeish, sidetracked, objected.

'It's too small,' Perry said firmly. '*Much* too small.'

McLeish was relieved to see that Francesca was also unconvinced by the idea that a single man with an intermittently live-in girlfriend was inadequately housed in the terraced house with three double bedrooms and three large reception rooms in which he presently lived.

'Mind you,' Francesca said, turning the steak, 'we're all quite relieved that Perry is spending some of his ill-gotten gains on property, rather than on wine and women.'

Perry grinned at this sisterly observation. 'However,' he said firmly, wresting the conversation back, 'there are armies of steel-fixers working on Bertrand Terrace, and some of those guys are absentees from the Western Underpass site which isn't all that far away.'

'Perry! You are naughty. Do you mean they are still clocked on with Vernon?' Francesca sounded appalled.

'I haven't asked, Frannie, I really don't want to know. What she's saying, John, is that these chaps take jobs on the big sites and then go and moonlight for cash on little conversion jobs.'

'Does that matter?'

'Yes it does,' Francesca said, peering under the grill. 'The lads don't usually even try and do two jobs. At best they go sick for short periods from the big sites in order to work for private employers for cash. We were always losing gangs for the odd week when I was on a site. That means that an employer like Vernon is carrying all the National Insurance costs while the bloke is pocketing cash on a private job. I assume you're paying cash, Perry?'

Perry confirmed equably that, in common with every other homeowner in London, he was indeed paying cash to get anyone to do anything.

'At worst, these chaps clock on a big site in the morning then slide off when the site supervisor is not looking and do a day's work somewhere else, then get back on site just in time to punch a clock on their way out. That way they're drawing basic pay on the big site and earning a second wage in cash somewhere else.'

McLeish indicated that all this was dead interesting but he didn't see where it was going, and Perry said irritably that Frannie had introduced an irrelevancy.

'The point, John, if I may get back to it, is that some of the chaps who are fixing steel at Bertrand Terrace have worked on the Western Underpass site, and some of them also worked on a Vernon site in the Barbican. I know this because I tend to have tea with them all in the morning, *pour encourager*, you know.'

His sister observed that this simple human action must provide enormous inspiration to the men, and McLeish told her to shut up and let Perry get on.

'Anyway, they were telling the usual tall stories about the trade, and the lead steel-fixer said not only half the men but also much of the steel being used in London for a couple of weeks earlier this year had come off the Barbican site, *and* they'd all had another welcome load of cheap steel about three weeks ago off the Western Underpass. A lot of rebar — that's reinforcing bar, John — and some RSJs in standard sizes. All right, Fran, I know what you're thinking, but I'm paying the full price, I bet you, and no one told me at the time. Well, I thought it might be important, John, so I made everyone another cup of tea.'

Very possible to imagine the scene, McLeish thought — the gang flattered by having a celebrity waiting on them and eager to hold his interest.

'It all took rather a long time to come out, but it appears that the steel walked off the site on the back of several lorries in the middle of the night on to little sites where it was received gratefully by assorted steel-fixers and scaffolders. And all this was done with the full authority of a bent gaffer.'

'Well, it would have to be, wouldn't it?' his sister said scornfully. 'I mean, that's a major operation, it's not just a few bags of cement in the back of a van.'

John McLeish had stopped eating, remembering what Robert Vernon had said about theft from the Western Underpass site. 'The steel vanished on to a dozen little sites, then?' he enquired, seeing in his mind's eye the heavily laden flatbed lorries pulling out of the main gate.

'So my conversation about people taking a few days off big sites may not have been at all irrelevant,' Francesca said, triumphantly. 'The scaffolders, steel-fixers, whatever, were involved in the scam. They organized their material off a big site, and then took a few days off to fix the steel on whatever site it went to. John, darling, do eat — you'll have to go in ten minutes.'

'That's theft,' McLeish said, soberly. 'And on a large scale. What was all that worth, Perry, did they say?'

'No. But I pay bills so I know what steel costs — you're talking in the hundred thousands rather than the tens.'

'The site accounting system should tell you,' Francesca pointed out.

'Hang on, Perry, how does the steel get off the site? I mean, who loads it up, and doesn't anyone notice?'

'I don't know, actually.'

'*I* do.' Francesca was sounding smug. 'It never got on site.'

Her brother and her lover looked at her blankly.

'It's the classic lorry fiddle. It's terribly simple — eight lorries leave the depot, only seven arrive on site. Deliveries to central London sites tend to be made at night or very early in the morning because of the traffic, so there aren't that many people there, anyway. All you need is someone to sign for eight lorries. By the time it's all unloaded it's pretty difficult to sort out how many brought it.'

'And lorry number eight is offloading somewhere else?'

'That's right. But a staff man has to sign the lorries in, so someone reasonably senior has to be in on the fiddle. I helped check lorries one night with a boyfriend on the site, that's how I know.'

'I'd like to talk to these lads of yours, Perry,' McLeish said longingly, 'but I guess all that would happen is that you'd turn out to have misunderstood every word said to you, and half an hour later you wouldn't have a labour force.'

'For you, John, I'll risk that. I do understand that having a sister take up with a senior copper involves certain responsibilities.'

'I'm honoured. No, I don't need to do that yet. I'll get the site records checked, see if anyone on the steel-fixing or scaffolding side was working late any time in that month and who left the site around then.'

'You may not find them again, John; it's that kind of trade. The Irish will be off at the first hint of trouble, for a start,' Perry observed.

'I'll find the staff bloke who covered for them, if no one else. No?' He looked enquiringly at Francesca who was frowning doubtfully.

'Well, darling, *staff* don't clock on or off. No nonsense about democracy on a building site, it's them and us. Also, of course, staff don't get overtime. I mean, whoever was on duty checking lorries then might well not have been recorded as being there.'

'I'll have to start with the clock records, anyway. It was a scaffolder, after all, who was murdered.'

He looked across at Francesca who was drinking tea. She nodded. 'The trades are to some extent interchangeable. I mean a scaffolder can certainly fix RSJs. I was just wondering who you were going to turn up.'

'Yes, I was too.' He finished his coffee and hesitated, watching Perry who was getting himself another drink.

'I've gone, sorry John. Ruined your evening, but I thought you'd better know. Nice to have seen you.' He vanished upstairs with his glass.

'I hope Alan wasn't in on it.' Francesca was looking anxious.

'So do I. I don't like the timing — he was killed just before he could have a drink with me, and I'd had to tell the site management I was police in order to get a message to him. This one's a bit close to home for us, isn't it?'

'Worse for you. I wasn't as fond of him as you were.'

'You think he'd have been in a major theft?'

'Well, he only wanted to climb, didn't he? I mean nothing else quite mattered enough to him. So, if he saw a reasonably risk-free way of making some cash, then yes, it wouldn't amaze me.' She rubbed her forehead. 'I don't quite know what would have happened with Perry, if he hadn't always been able to do exactly what he wanted. He only wants to be a successful singer, nothing else matters when push comes to shove. Tristram's the same — we'll just have to hope he can get there easily, like Perry.'

McLeish moved to sit next to her and put an arm round her. 'Why aren't you like that?'

'Maybe because I'm not talented enough in any one thing. I don't feel like that about anything — you know, that I *must* have it, at all costs.'

No, McLeish thought, you don't, do you? You don't feel like that about any one person either, more's the pity. He got heavily to his feet, trying to concentrate his mind on the coming interview with Bill Vernon.

'Can you come back afterwards?' Francesca was putting a packet in the pocket of his jacket. 'It's just an apple and a biscuit.'

'Please not one of the biscuits you gave me yesterday. I felt like the prodigal son.'

He laughed at her as she frowned in concentration.

'Ah, the husks that the swine would not eat. They aren't that bad, you ungrateful monster.'

'No, just a *bit* husky. Thanks for supper — I'll try and come back, not too late.' He kissed her and got into his car, and waved as he went, but she had already gone back into the house. Perhaps no one who wanted things or people passionately and exclusively could be married to a policeman; the job would be too much of a rival. In that sense he was lucky: he did not have to worry, as so many of his colleagues did, about a wife sitting at home waiting longingly for him to arrive. Fran would be with her brothers, or working at the Department, or organizing the College Appeal, or something of that order. It ought to be a thoroughly satisfactory arrangement, but he sometimes felt a few tears and reproaches when he was late or absent would not come amiss.

He drove into the New Scotland Yard car park and checked his office, finding Bruce Davidson waiting for him.

'Got some dinner in, or was she too cross with you?'

'Yes. She wasn't all that bothered, the brothers were there. Peregrine had some useful information too.' McLeish brought Bruce Davidson swiftly up to date.

'Well, if Fraser was in it, so was Hamilton, wasn't he? Or could Hamilton have been running a wee bit of private enterprise, and then killed Fraser to prevent him telling the sponsors?'

Both of them considered this.

'I don't think so, Bruce. They're partners. The records ought to give us a lead, but I think they were either both in it or neither was. Hamilton could have killed him for a bigger share, though.'

'What about the gaffer, whoever he was?'

'I'll pick that up tomorrow with Mr Makin. Oh, thank you, Sergeant — Bill Vernon's here, Bruce.'

McLeish went ahead of Davidson into one of the small interview rooms and greeted Bill Vernon, who was looking vaguer and more gangling than ever. McLeish went through the usual preamble, explaining that the case was now beyond doubt one of murder and linked to an earlier attempt in Scotland.

Vernon nodded. 'I can't quite remember where I was the day that Fraser had that fall in Scotland,' he said, anxiously. 'I know I was in the bar about seven-thirty because I can remember hearing about it then. I was fishing in the afternoon, but I packed that up early and just mooched about, had some tea on the hill . . . I really couldn't be exact about any of the times.'

'It was about five-thirty that Fraser fell.'

'I'm sorry, I really couldn't be sure where I was, but I was a good couple of miles from the Wall.'

Another missing alibi, McLeish thought; but it wasn't unreasonable, given the nature of people's occupations on a holiday in the Highlands. Mooching about was one of the great pleasures of the place for a good walker — and all the Vernons were that, including Dorothy, who would walk miles to fish the hill lochs. He turned his attention to the events at the Western Underpass site.

'The estimators didn't put in nearly enough for the Section I groundworks, and there's obviously been some misunderstanding. I'm a quantity surveyor and responsible for measuring what actually does get in, and it's not our fault. But Nigel Makin, who is running very fast to the top, behaves as if we had personally got the figures wrong. We're working together to see if we can claw any of it back from the client,' he finished importantly.

'How is all that going?'

'Not too bad. I don't mind old Nigel, he's alright when you know him, and we've found quite a lot of room to manoeuvre.'

McLeish, who had perceived Nigel Makin as a hard man, decided he must also be a good manager of people; he was obviously getting the best of what there was out of this not very competent employee.

'You've been on the Western Underpass site from the beginning, then?'

'Yes, since April. I was on our other major London civil engineering site at the Barbican before that, but not for very long.'

'I understand from your father that there is some concern on this site about possible theft?'

'That's always a problem on a major site, particularly in London.'

'I'm asking, because it might in this case have some bearing on Alan Fraser's murder. Anything you can tell me may be useful. I'll take it up, of course, with Mr Makin but I've not had a full discussion with him yet.'

The tall man opposite looked back at him blankly. 'I'm sorry, I can't think of anything useful. I know Nigel has been very worried about theft from the site. I don't quite know what his specific worry is. I don't even know if he thinks Fraser was involved.'

McLeish decided this avenue of enquiry was proving unremunerative and proceeded to ask about the Vernon family relationships. 'I believe that you are the son of Robert Vernon and his first wife?'

'Yes, I am. My mother has not remarried so she is Mrs Vernon, too. Very confusing. What has that to do with Alan Fraser's death?'

Not as green as he's cabbage-looking, McLeish thought sourly in the argot of his childhood.

'Alan Fraser seems to have been fairly involved with the Vernon family; I was trying to establish how they all fitted together.'

'You've talked to Sally, and you therefore know she's pregnant — possibly by Fraser?'

'Yes. When did she tell you?'

'Two or three days ago, I suppose. I was very sorry for her. She'd obviously got herself into a real mess.'

And her half-brother was not at all displeased, McLeish noted; the undercurrent of satisfaction was unmistakable.

'Did you offer her any advice?' he asked, with interest.

'No, no, it was obviously a situation beyond advice. She'd told Alan, and he'd said he really didn't want to marry her, he wanted to go to K6. He's always only wanted to go to K6; he'd do anything to get there and I would have thought she knew that. She'd have been much better to stick to Nigel Makin — he's going to take over from Robert in the fulness of time and she'll have it all that way. Not that she needs it: Robert's settled money on both of us already.'

'Is it a substantial amount?'

'I'd call two million-odd substantial, yes. It's going to buy me a decent-sized farm. Sally got the same — in fact she's got it already; my settlement's still going through. I had a small sum before, but Robert has decided to give me the same as Sally.'

'Was this recently?'

'I don't know when he decided. He told me when we were all in Scotland, and the lawyers are still messing around with the detail.'

'That must have been a very pleasant piece of news.'

'It was indeed. I'd been hoping to get out of construction and into running a farm, but I thought it was going to take a very long time. I'm going to buy in the Borders when the lawyers get through — it's hill land, of course, but the people there make a very decent living, and it's a very pleasant way of life. Lots of hunting. My mother's people came from there.'

McLeish considered him with interest; he had relaxed and was obviously happy. He wondered idly whether Bill was going to be a good farmer where he had not been particularly successful as a quantity surveyor. Disconcertingly, Bill read his mind.

'I'm good with animals,' he said. 'And I love the country. My mother pushed me into being a quantity surveyor because she thought it would please Robert. He has enough sense, does Robert, not to care whether he has a son to follow him; he's got Nigel — or he had Nigel — and that's all he needs.'

'You think that Nigel — Mr Makin — will want to do something else now?'

'Well, I would, wouldn't you? I don't think I'd want to stay in the same company as my fiancée who'd got herself pregnant by someone else, ambitious bugger though he is. No, I'd expect him to be off.'

'Even in the middle of an investigation of theft on site?'

'Well, I don't think he'll get very far with that. One usually doesn't, you know; everyone involved tends to drift away.'

'Or to fall from a scaffolding tower.' McLeish spoke more sharply than he had meant to, and the man opposite blinked.

'I'm sorry? Are you saying Alan Fraser was involved?'

'What do you think?'

'I'm afraid it's possible.' Bill Vernon sounded uncomfortable, bending his head so the dark cowlick fell into his eyes. 'He only wanted to climb, you see, and he desperately needed money. If it was easy for him, he might have been involved. But I don't *know*, and I oughtn't to be speculating like this — poor Alan is dead, after all.' He gazed at them both reproachfully, obviously distressed by the line the questioning had taken, and McLeish looked back at him thoughtfully.

'It's been suggested to me that there was a lorry fiddle.'

Bill Vernon looked at him, blankly. 'Oh, sorry, yes, see what you mean. Where not all the lorries unload. That is the easy way of stealing materials, yes.'

'Who would have been responsible for checking the lorries?'

'Oh, you'll have to ask Nigel Makin that, or Jimmy Stewart. That's a matter of site management, if Nigel's still interested enough.' He bit his thumbnail thoughtfully. 'I can't believe that he will be, though.'

McLeish persevered for a few minutes more, then thanked Vernon and left him with Davidson to get the statement typed up and signed. The Western Underpass site was on his way home, and he decided to stop there. The site was not working but the fence was brightly lit and there were lights in the Section I offices. The tower from which Alan Fraser had fallen had grown to an unrecognizable shape but it was still possible to see on the ground the remnants of the chalk outline he had drawn round Fraser's body, even though the pile of steel over which Fraser had broken his back had been moved. As he watched, the big gates of Section I opened to admit two lorries, loaded with some sort of steel. He moved closer to look and found himself a few yards from Jimmy Stewart, clipboard in hand, conferring with the first driver.

McLeish nodded to him and waited patiently till the lorries were through.

'Good evening Chief Inspector.' Stewart was looking wary.

McLeish greeted him and chatted idly about the site until the man had relaxed.

'Do you always check the lorries in yourself, then?' he asked, following a general question about progress.

'No. Some of our steel went walkies before it ever got here, so I'm checking. I'm not having theft on my site, so I'm here to make sure everyone gets the message. The sub-agents can do it from next week, though, I hope. I don't want to have to do this right to the end of the job.'

McLeish expressed polite pleasure that Stewart's burden would be eased in the near future. The system of checking loads had plainly been inadequate and Stewart had done exactly as McLeish or a senior policeman would have in the circumstances — made certain that for the future responsibility rested unequivocally in senior hands.

'Is Hamilton back with you on the scaffolding or is he still away?' he asked, out of curiosity.

'Came back this afternoon, but only to ask about his pay. He's got an interview tomorrow, hasn't he? But he'll not be back, he said. The Doolans, well, they're Paddies, aren't they? They've gone, they're too superstitious to carry on, now.'

McLeish felt that anyone might reasonably have taken a scunner to a site where their foreman had fallen to a sickening death in suspicious circumstances before their eyes, and said so, mildly. Jimmy Stewart visibly thought about the whole question again, and agreed that it might have been a discouraging experience.

'They're away to Ireland, anyway,' he observed, 'so they really did take a scunner. They could have been down the road on another site the day after they left here, we're all short of steel-fixers and scaffolders.'

'They've gone back to Ireland?' McLeish enquired.

'I'm sorry. Perhaps I should have told your people?'

'No, it's all right, we can get them back if we need. Lost their bottle, though, didn't they? I suppose they did actually go?'

Jimmy Stewart said drily that his information came from the core of the farewell party that had paraded to put the Doolan brothers on the boat train. McLeish leant against the gate, wondering about the Doolans. Neither had been in Scotland but on the other hand both had excellent access both to Fraser and to his thermos. It was, he decided five minutes of rumination later, simply flying in the face of instinct and experience to see the Doolan brothers as sufficiently well organized and knowledgeable to have sought to murder Fraser by that particular method. So why had they made a run for it as soon as they could? Once you discounted superstition or grief — although you could easily be wrong to leave either out of consideration — you were left with the likelihood that they were avoiding trouble of some sort. And trouble there was in plenty, with a major theft of materials still unresolved. If Alan Fraser's gang had all been involved in that, then the Doolan brothers' run for home made a lot of sense. They could go to ground over in Ireland for a very long time if they felt like it. It was becoming increasingly important to find out how Nigel Makin's researches were coming on.

CHAPTER 14

'Yes, of course, Chief Inspector, I'm coming up to the Western Underpass site later in the morning, and I'll stop off at Edgware Road if that's convenient. About noon?'

John McLeish put the phone down on Nigel Makin's flat London accent and logged the arrangement in his diary. He had spent the night with Francesca after he had seen Bill Vernon's statement signed off, and was feeling restored by having had time away from the case. He glanced at his notes, remembering that Mickey Hamilton was seeing the sponsors' committee for K6 this morning, being presumably sure of a place if there was one. He thought about Mickey, grimly. The old rule about considering who benefited from a death was ignored at your peril: Mickey had now got an undisputed run at a place on an expedition which he had passionately wanted. He had loved Fraser, no doubt about that; but perhaps that had not been strong enough to overcome the jealous rivalry he felt, combined with the realization that Fraser was never going to return his love in the same way.

Mickey was highly credible as a suspect, not only on grounds of motive, but of means — he had done two years in medical school and would have known how much antihistamine was needed to render Alan Fraser helplessly dizzy — and of opportunity. That was not quite enough for an arrest, yet, unless some supporting evidence could be found. Two detectives were even now touring major chemists with pictures of all six suspects, and you never knew what that might turn up. Forensic had opined that the thermos which held three cups of tea had probably also contained thirty antihistamine tablets, their taste masked by the four tablespoons of sugar with which Fraser habitually laced the tea in his thermos. Two of the largest packets sold over the counter would have been more than enough and, as McLeish knew, Francesca, who had to take three or four a day in the main hay-fever season, regularly bought that many. Indeed, he remembered that when she had cleaned out the bathroom cupboard she had produced thirty-odd pills from the various shelves and a further twenty from the recesses of two handbags. He could still see the packets neatly rearranged on a top shelf.

Still, there was nothing to do at this stage but let Mickey run free, although, as McLeish admitted to himself while he gulped his coffee, if he *were* offered the place on K6 it would be a very difficult piece of judgement as to whether or not to arrest him. Once out of England, Mickey could easily disappear, leaving CI looking like Slipper of the Yard, a fate which any senior policeman would go a very long way to avoid.

His secretary put her head round the door. 'It's Francesca for you. She says, please, it's urgent.'

'Put her through.' Francesca, a fellow public servant, never interrupted him unnecessarily.

'Darling, I've got a difficult question. We were discussing offering Robert Vernon a government job, and all was going fine when Bill Westland said what about this murder investigation? He'd picked up somewhere — not from me, but you know what he's like — that Robert Vernon might be involved, and he didn't want to offer anything until he knew it was alright. I mean, it *is* alright, isn't it? No need to hang around?'

McLeish sighed. 'It's too soon, darling, to say that anyone's in the clear.'

'But *Robert*?' Francesca was incredulous. 'Why would he want to kill Alan?'

'I shouldn't be discussing it, Frannie, but maybe he didn't want Alan as a son-in-law.'

There was an appalled silence at the other end of the line, and McLeish followed up promptly: 'It may be nonsense, but you know that the list of suspects has to be limited to the six people who were in Scotland *and* on the site, and Robert Vernon is one of them. No one can say yet he's in the clear.' No, indeed, they can't, he thought, not after that disconcerting hesitation under questioning.

'He wouldn't have killed Alan himself, no matter what.' The clear voice was confident and McLeish grinned to himself.

'Might have got someone to do it?' he suggested, more out of curiosity than out of conviction. There was a pause.

'Just possibly.' Francesca sounded shaken but thoughtful. 'He'd be more likely to have used money than personal violence, I would think. My dad always said he was a hard man, but then you'd have to be in that trade, starting from nowhere. All right, Detective Chief Inspector, I hear what you're saying. Just remember HMG needs him, always supposing that he isn't a killer. Are we having supper tomorrow?'

They made one of their necessarily elastic plans and McLeish left for Edgware Road.

Nigel Makin arrived exactly on time, dropped by a Vernon Construction driver, and could be seen finishing off a telephone call from the car before sending the driver on with a pile of papers. McLeish and Davidson waited in an interview room for him to be brought in by a uniformed policeman.

'Since we spoke briefly at Western Underpass, I have talked at more length to Mr and Mrs Vernon, Mr Bill Vernon and to Miss Vernon and Michael Hamilton,' McLeish began, formally, the introductions completed. 'I have said to all of them that we are treating Alan Fraser's death as murder, and linking it with an attempt on his life in Scotland last month.'

'So, all of us who were in Scotland as well as on site when it happened are on your list of suspects.'

'That's right.'

'Do you also know that Sally — Miss Vernon — terminated our engagement earlier this week?'

'She told us, yes.'

Nigel Makin gazed at the blank and unpromising side wall of the interview room, and unexpectedly fished for a handkerchief and blew his nose. McLeish let the pause stretch, both he and Davidson sitting absolutely still.

'He'd never have married her,' Makin observed, to his hands. 'But he's messed us up completely by getting himself killed. *I* didn't kill him — I knew he'd go off to K6 if he got the place.' He looked at McLeish directly. 'I'll tell you what I was doing, and I'm not proud of it. Fraser was there or thereabouts on a couple of fiddles, one at the Barbican in February, one here in the last four weeks. I've been trying to nail him, but I couldn't quite do it.' He inspected the side wall again. 'And then I thought, bloody hell, why don't I just leave it alone, let him take whatever cash he got as his share and get off to K6 or wherever it is, out of Sally's way? So I'd decided to stop trying to find the fiddle, just to make bloody sure it didn't happen again and let anyone I thought might have been involved know I had my eye on them — get Stewart to move one or two people. Anything, just so Fraser would disappear to the Himalayas.'

He scowled at McLeish. 'Now the whole thing's buggered. Fraser's dead, and Sally's pregnant — yes, she told me this morning but I understand everyone else but me knew two days ago. I wanted to leave the company but Robert Vernon's asked me not to do that. Well, I owe him that, so I'm staying, at least for a bit. But I'd rather have Fraser alive and on his way to the Himalayas than dead.'

McLeish let that verdict stand in his head, and wondered whether Makin had really not known that Sally was pregnant until that morning. Makin's thesis — that Fraser was more of a barrier to him dead than alive — made sense, and this was a logical, well-trained successful man, on the edge of a major managerial breakthrough. There was, however, no predicting the effect of having a much-loved fiancée break off an engagement; the additional misery of knowing that she was possibly pregnant by a rival — if he *had* known — might have been the final straw.

'I expect you want to know where I was and what I was doing both times, though?' Makin offered and McLeish agreed, taking him patiently through his movements.

'I can remember exactly what I was doing at the time when Fraser came off that cliff,' he said, surprisingly. 'I'd had a miserable afternoon. I'd had lunch with Sal, and she just wasn't with me, I knew. I went off and walked and fished after lunch — I didn't want to be with anyone, I'll be honest with you — so I didn't go with Robert. I didn't catch any fish either, and I came back, walking, oh, at about seven o'clock. The first thing I heard was that Fraser was in Oban, injured, and I was dead pleased, I can tell you. Then we heard he'd been picked up by a tourist and was hardly hurt at all. And he was back two days later, good as new.' His eyes focused on McLeish who was trying to look as much like a chair as possible. 'It was you of course, I'd forgotten. You liked him, didn't you?'

'Yes.' The monosyllable echoed in the room, and Makin waited to see if he was going to go on.

'No one saw me — I suppose I could have pushed him off a cliff or whatever it was happened to him.'

McLeish left it after a few further questions. The Scots might pick up some corroborative evidence or they might not. If Makin had tried to kill or injure Alan Fraser that day, it was sensible and realistic not to try and establish an alibi. Neither Robert nor Bill Vernon had an alibi, come to that, and Dorothy Vernon's statement that she had been having a rest before supper could not, in the nature of things, be proved either. Sally Vernon had at best a partial alibi, and Mickey none at all.

About the events on the Western Underpass, Makin's memory was even sharper. 'I'd had a lousy couple of days then as well,' he said sourly. 'Sally had broken off our engagement the day before, and I'd rather not have been on that site at all — but the costing system still isn't right and you have to get it right early, you lose a fortune on groundworks if you don't. Anyway, I'd decided to stay and work on late; the sooner I could get off that site the better. So I got Bill Vernon to agree to stay as well — he's not one to put himself out, particularly now he's going to be a rich man, but he did agree. I decided to get a meal in the canteen. It isn't much good, but I don't care what I eat when I'm working.'

'Did you know the senior Vernons would be there?'

'No. Everyone knew Robert was coming to see the site but he isn't interested in canteens. I wouldn't have expected to see him there. I don't think anyone knew Dorothy — Mrs Vernon — was coming. Bill didn't know, he was with me. I don't know if Sally knew, I hadn't spoken to her.' He thought for a minute. 'Even if I had known Mrs Vernon was coming, I wouldn't necessarily have expected to find her there. No, I'll tell you, the other one I didn't expect to see there was Fraser. I knew he was meeting you at six, you see, and I thought he'd not bother with tea.'

'How did you know that?'

'Stewart rang me and asked me to deliver the message — well, he didn't know, did he? I didn't want to say no, so I took it and of course I recognized the name. I didn't give the message to Fraser myself — I might have hit him if I'd had to talk to him — so I passed it on to Bill Vernon. He passed it to Hamilton. Gives me the creeps,' he added, *obiter dictum*.

'What time was this?' McLeish asked grimly.

'Just before dinner. Eleven-thirty or so?'

'You didn't talk to Sally that day?'

'No I didn't. I stayed out of her way.'

But Bill Vernon might easily have told his sister about the meeting, though, McLeish thought. He had faced the realization the day before that his meeting with Alan Fraser might have precipitated a tragedy, and at least three of the main suspects had known of that meeting. He took Nigel Makin patiently through the events of tea-time, but, not surprisingly, his attention had been on his own problems at the time and he had not registered much detail. Or if he had, he wasn't letting on. No, he had not known Fraser was a regular user of antihistamine; why should he? And no, he himself did not suffer from hay-fever and had not had occasion to use antihistamines of any sort.

'I didn't kill him, and I'm worse off with him dead,' Nigel Makin repeated uncompromisingly at the end. 'I thought he was probably bent — and now he's gone I'll find and sort out anyone else who was in that particular fiddle. But I've had fifteen years in this trade without killing anyone, and I didn't start with a pretty boy like Fraser.'

McLeish found himself resenting that crack on behalf of the dead man; Fraser had been a good deal more than a pretty boy, as indeed the short obituary in *The Times* had made clear.

'Well, he wasn't after your girl,' Nigel Makin said bitterly, and McLeish realized that his face must be giving away more than he intended.

'I do see that,' he said, formally. 'He was a good climber, though.'

'I understand that.'

It was a handsome concession and McLeish took it as such, and found himself liking the man better than he had before.

'This fraud, on the site — are you looking for a lorry fiddle?'

Nigel Makin's head came up and he inspected McLeish with interest. 'Yes, I'm sure that's how it was done, on both sites. Fraser, Hamilton and their gang were on the sites, though actually they weren't there on the night the stuff was delivered — or not delivered.'

'Were they somewhere else waiting for it, maybe?' McLeish decided to test Perry and Francesca's hypothesis, and Nigel Makin's eyes widened.

'Of course they bloody were, weren't they?' he said, softly. 'Clocked off my site for a few days, or maybe they were even still on the clock for some of it, but were actually somewhere else. I'll look for that.' He considered, eyes slightly crossed, looking through McLeish. 'But the bugger who did a false count on the lorries had to be on site, and it's him I'm after now; Fraser's dead and his gang will be away. Still that's useful.' He nodded briefly to McLeish, and had to be restrained from leaving without waiting for his statement to be typed up.

McLeish stood by Davidson, who was threading paper into an ancient Edgware Road typewriter. 'Ye'll remember that Sally Vernon is a rich young woman, as well as his ex-fiancée?'

'I'd not forgotten. I'm not sure he minds all that much about the money — he's on near enough £60,000 a year and share options, according to his guv'nor.'

'I'd still mind on a couple of millions if they came with the girl I wanted to marry.'

'Yes, all right, Bruce, but killing Alan Fraser doesn't seem to have left Mr Makin in pole position.'

'Mebbe not just yet awhile. But the wee girl's pregnant and she's no father for the bairn.'

One had, McLeish thought, to make substantial allowances for Bruce Davidson's admirable, Scots working-class upbringing. Nonetheless he had a point; with Alan Fraser dead, Nigel Makin might well find himself back in the field.

'If there was a fiddle on site,' he said, 'who else of this lot'd have been in it?'

'If Fraser was, then Hamilton, I'd guess. They're partners.'

'And rivals. But you're right, Bruce, partners on site, whatever was going on. The Doolans were in it, too; that's why they've scarpered. Hamilton's already got one strike against him, with a dodgy bit in his youth and being gay as well.'

'It keeps coming back to him, doesn't it?' Bruce Davidson observed, neutrally.

'What are you betting, Bruce?' McLeish was wont to apply this test at some stage during an enquiry; he found it sharpened his thinking as well. Davidson considered, and wrote in the cover of his notebook, crossed out a couple of numbers and substituted others.

'I'd say 7 to 4 on Hamilton; Makin 5 to 2; the wee girl and her father both 3 to 1; 5 to 1 Bill Vernon; 10 to 1 Mrs Vernon.'

Yes, so do I, McLeish thought, grimly. Not only was Alan Fraser in direct competition for the coveted K6 place but he knew an uncomfortable amount about Mickey and could have found a way to use it — an anonymous note to the committee would have been all it would have taken. On this thought, there entered a sergeant bearing a message.

'I hope it makes sense, sir.'

'Yes. Yes it does.' He showed the note to Davidson.

'So Hamilton got the place, after all. What are you going to do, John? They'll need to be away in a couple of weeks.'

'As things stand, he can't go and that's all there is to it. He must know that; that's why he's telling me.'

'Daring you to stand in his way? It'll cause a row.'

'It will, won't it? Well, we'll just have to find the killer, be it him or someone else.'

'I've been thinking.'

McLeish waited for the fruits of this process to emerge.

'Does it have to have been the same person had a go at Fraser in Scotland as killed him down here?'

It was a sound question and McLeish sat down to brood about it. 'Why would they be different, Bruce?'

'Well, mebbe someone wanted different things — I mean, mebbe it was worth Mr Makin's while to put young Fraser into hospital for a bit so he could get his girl away — there's not much glamour in a bloke who is flat on his back with a leg up in plaster. So maybe Makin did the business in Scotland, and someone different actually killed him in London. We've been looking for a murderer who could have done both. Perhaps we should take these two separately?'

McLeish nodded. 'I have been looking at them separately to some extent — I just couldn't get enough on the Scottish attack, even though I was there, so I have been thinking about London separately. But you're right, I must watch that. It needn't be the same person. Hamilton could have wanted to put Fraser out of action without killing him.'

Both men considered this hypothesis, but it was McLeish who decided it was flawed. 'Our man couldn't have been sure he was just putting Fraser in hospital: he could just as easily have been killed falling off the Wall. Equally, he needn't have been sixty feet up in London when he turned giddy.'

'A bittie opportunistic, both times?'

'Yes,' McLeish agreed soberly. 'Yes. The murderer couldn't have been absolutely confident he'd kill him, but could reasonably have expected to do serious damage.'

'Which points to Hamilton again, or Makin in Scotland?'

'But not Makin in London. By then it would have been worth his while waiting to see if the K6 expedition was going to take Fraser.'

'That's right,' Davidson agreed.

'I can't get away from the timing,' McLeish said, after a period of contemplation. 'Fraser gets knocked off just before he sees me. Someone thought he was going to tell me something.'

'If you'd been able to talk to him, John, what would you have said to him?'

'Oh Christ,' John McLeish suddenly felt the full painful weight of grief and anxiety. 'I'd have told him someone was laying for him, and have got him to think who it might be. He'd have been warned. We know he felt peculiar on that scaffold, and he would have known to be more careful, to come down immediately instead of just assuming the dizziness would go away.'

'What would he have said to you?'

'You mean would he have told me about Sally? Or about the fiddle he was in — if he was in it? I can't see it, can you? But someone thought he would.'

Bruce Davidson sighed, evidently feeling he had shot his bolt, but McLeish's mind was working again. 'He may have known who was involved in the lorry fiddle, even if he wasn't himself. And that would have made it worth someone's while to top him rather than have him talk to the police. The sooner we get to the bottom of that fiddle, the better.'

'Well, Mr Makin's doing that, isn't he? And he won't have been in the fiddle.'

McLeish shook his head. 'I'm not going to assume anything, Bruce. Makin's an intelligent bloke, he could be covering his traces. We'd better put one of our blokes on, assuming you can find anyone left who can read and write. You may have to do it. Yes, Woolner?'

'Sorry, sir, it's your secretary.'

Jenny had a message from Francesca; could he please ring her urgently. 'She was very apologetic, John; says to tell you she must speak before lunch.' Jenny was sounding disapproving but McLeish knew his girl and rang straight back.

'Darling, Robert Vernon has just rung and said was I free for lunch tomorrow. My mind wasn't on him because I was adding up numbers, so I said yes. I'm sorry; perhaps I shouldn't be doing that?'

'No, that's all right. He knows about us,' McLeish said, reluctantly. 'Just try not to talk about the case, all right? I don't want the evidence to come unstuck when we get whoever it was.'

'Are you getting anywhere?'

'Not really, but I don't feel any worse about Robert Vernon than anyone else.'

'You haven't got *anywhere*, in short.'

'Go away, Frannie.'

'Sorry, sorry, just an observation. I'm sure it's all going better than that.'

He put the phone down, grinning to himself reluctantly, and told Bruce Davidson the latest.

'Is he going to tell Francesca something he'd rather not tell us?'

'Possibly, blast him.'

* * *

Back in the Georgian house in the West End, Robert Vernon was sitting beside his daughter's bed, visibly fussing. 'What are you going to do now, Sal?'

'Do you mean am I still going to have the baby?'

'I suppose I do,' her father conceded reluctantly, looking so utterly dispirited and suddenly so old that she was appalled.

'Dad, I don't know what I want to do. I've been thinking, though. Alan wouldn't ever have married me, would he? I mean, even if he hadn't died.' Tears spilled out of her eyes and she wiped her face unceremoniously on the bedspread. Her father reached out awkwardly and gathered her into his arms.

'I don't think so, no Sal.'

She looked at him sharply, puzzled by his uncharacteristic hesitancy, but he avoided her eyes. She was about to question him further when her mother came in, holding herself very erect with her head up, and father and daughter wordlessly braced themselves, recognizing the symptoms.

'That was Nigel on the telephone. He'd like to see you for a few minutes, Sal. You ought to see him.'

'I know I ought to,' Sally agreed, 'but I'm not going to yet, Mum, I'll see him tomorrow.'

The two women looked at each other across Robert Vernon, who found himself feeling uncomfortable in a way he hadn't for years.

'I want to think it out, Mum, and I don't want to see Nigel until then.'

Dorothy Vernon considered her daughter. 'But you will see him tomorrow?'

'Yes, I promise, and you can tell him so.'

Robert Vernon, with a strong feeling that he had put his foot on a step that wasn't there, opened his mouth to speak and closed it again.

'Bill rang too, by the way, asking how you were.'

'That was nice of him,' Sally sounded surprised. 'He warned me about Alan, told me he had another girl.'

Robert Vernon blinked. 'That's more than he told me.'

'He may not have thought it was your business, Robert.' Dorothy Vernon sounded uncharacteristically snappy. 'He's on the Underpass site for another couple of days, he tells me?'

'That's right. He's being very good about finishing up — he's told me he wants to go up and look at a farm at the end of next week, and I don't think we'll get much useful work out of him after that. But he's doing well.'

Robert Vernon was obviously pleased and Dorothy relaxed a little. 'Anyway, Sally, he said to tell you he was there if he was wanted. You rest now for a bit and maybe you'll get up for supper?'

* * *

On the Western Underpass site, Bill Vernon was struggling with last week's paperwork. He lifted his head and looked out of the window, scowling at the back of a dumper truck which filled the immediate horizon. He blinked a moment later as Mickey Hamilton appeared at the window.

'Hello, Bill, I've come to get my pay. I've got the place, I'm going to K6.'

'Oh, well done, Mick. You want a drink on it? I'm not making any progress.'

'Thanks Bill. I'll just get my envelope.'

He appeared a few minutes later and the two men left the site together, turning automatically into the Duke of York.

'Champagne, Mick?'

'They'll not have it here, will you, Deirdre?'

The black-haired girl smiled at them demurely and asked whether non-vintage Dom Perignon would do because that was what they had cold, and both men laughed, appreciating her moment of triumph.

'So that's it then, Mick?' Bill Vernon said, watching appreciatively as Deirdre expertly flipped off the cork and caught the first drops in a glass. He waited till she had filled both glasses and raised one to Mickey. 'To K6.'

'To K6,' Mickey repeated and drank a large mouthful. 'Christ, it feels good.'

He looked a size larger and five years younger than usual, Bill observed, the tense lines in his face relaxed.

'Damn.' He put the glass down and winced, then laughed. 'My shoulder still twinges but it doesn't matter; it'll get right by the time we do any serious climbing.'

'When do you go?'

'With the rest, in two weeks.' He took a swig of the champagne, and poured himself another glass without asking, then blinked as he realized what he had done. 'Sorry, Bill, could have waited. I suppose I'm just a little worried about whether I'll be let go on time, with this investigation going on. Christ, I'd forgotten about Alan for a minute.' The lines in the face were suddenly back in place, Bill observed, fascinated. 'He'd not have grudged me, though.'

'Why don't you just go now?' Bill Vernon refilled both glasses. 'I mean, no one's going to bother to bring you back.'

Mickey Hamilton looked at him over the top of his glass. 'That's a thought, isn't it? No point hanging round here — I couldn't bear to go back on the tools after what happened. I could be away, get some training in.' He looked past Bill, out of the window, seeing a vision. 'Save a lot of trouble too, that could,' he said, and looked sharply down at his glass. 'I'll think about that, I'd like to be out of all this — I mean, what with Alan gone,' he ended, bleakly.

'That must have been awful for you,' Bill said, quietly.

'He was a good mate.' Mickey sounded desolate, and gulped down the rest of his glass. 'He was a better climber than I am, too,' he said, to his empty glass, 'and if he'd been here he'd have got the place, God rest him.' His voice roughened on this epitaph and Bill waited, not wanting to speak into that silence.

Mickey drew a breath from his boots and looked up. 'Thanks for the drink, Bill. I appreciated that, and I'll think about going now. You off now?'

'No, I'm going back on site for a bit. I've got nothing done all day. I've had Nigel Makin buzzing round me like a wasp all day, looking at the books for the last two months.'

Mickey's hand tightened on his glass. 'Oops, sorry Deirdre, clumsy. I'll pay for it.'

'Away with you — what's the odd broken glass between friends?' Deirdre had materialized from down the bar and was dealing competently with the damage.

'What's he looking for?' Mickey asked.

'Oh, he's decided after all to try and find out why the steel deliveries were short. He thinks they went adrift to somewhere else, probably with people off the site here. Same as at the Barbican, he thinks.'

'Can he prove it?'

'I shouldn't think so. But you know our Nigel — he'll keep on, won't he?'

'Yes,' Hamilton agreed, on a long indrawn breath. 'Yes, he will.' He looked past Bill, seeing his vision again. 'Thanks for the drink, Bill.'

He shook hands and went, finding his way easily through the crowded bar, going fast without seeming to hurry.

* * *

Across London, John McLeish was sorting papers and rereading the statements in the case. His secretary, coat on and shopping bag in hand in a definite statement that she was going home and would not be willing to engage in any further duties whatsoever that night, placed in front of him a copy of the statement which Nigel Makin had made that morning. McLeish methodically read it through, noting the neat signature at the bottom of every page. You could depend on Davidson to get his paperwork right. He read it twice, and sat back, allowing himself the luxury of trusting his instinct. Somewhere in that statement lay the possibility of progress, but it wasn't obvious where.

He sat quietly in the silence of his room, letting himself drift, then pulled himself awake with a start and decided he needed a meal. Francesca, he remembered, was out, so he decided he would go down, eat near the site, and see if inspiration would visit him. He thought about Nigel Makin again, and on impulse rang the site number.

'Yes, I'm glad you rang. I'm here for a bit if you want to come down,' Makin said. He raised his voice: 'No, I'll lock up, Fred. Sorry, just telling the nightwatchman. I'll tell you something very odd: I'm working here on copies of the wages print-out for the Barbican for February and this site for the last six weeks and . . . I spilt my coffee — I'm tired, I suppose. So I tapped into the computer for another copy. They aren't there — I mean they've gone, kaput, destroyed. Head Office is going spare, wants to take my copies away from me, coffee and all.'

'Are you sure?'

'Yes.' The monosyllable admitted of no doubt.

'That's odd, isn't it?'

'It is.'

'Mr Makin, are there other people around where you are?'

There was a long pause.

'Fucking hell,' Nigel Makin said, with something like reverence. 'I'd never have believed this. I'm going to get off site and make a couple of copies — I'll go up to Criterion Place; they've always got a secretary on.'

'Why don't you meet me at Edgware Road police station — they've got photo-copiers.'

'I still don't know what I've found,' Makin objected.

'Maybe we can both look for it?'

'Two heads probably are going to be better than one,' Makin agreed, still sounding incredulous. 'I'll do that. Give me ten minutes.'

'It'll take me twenty to get there myself, but you go there now. I'll telephone them to expect you.'

CHAPTER 15

In the event it took McLeish thirty-five minutes to get to Edgware Road, the traffic being heavy in the pouring rain.

'You got my customer? Mr Makin?' McLeish asked the desk sergeant, showing his warrant card and peremptorily ignoring the demands of a large West Indian lady who was working herself up to have a shouting match.

'No, sir, no one's came,' the sergeant replied ungrammatically, grateful for the diversion.

'You're sure?' McLeish demanded, so urgently that the fuming West Indian lady shut her mouth on whatever protest had been about to emerge.

'Yes, sir.'

McLeish looked at him carefully. The man was unfamiliar but was a type he had worked with before — a careful deliberate bloke not given to mistakes.

'Then where is he?' he asked rhetorically, realizing he was rattled.

'Where was he coming from, sir?'

'The Western Underpass site. He left half an hour ago.'

'Should be here, then.'

The two policemen looked at each other.

'I'll go and look. If he turns up here, you hold on to him, sergeant!' McLeish nodded to the West Indian lady and, mindful of relations with the public, apologized for interrupting; he was taken distinctly aback when she beamed back at him, a huge smile revealing far too many, far too white teeth for her substantial jaw. He ran for his car, the rain so heavy that he was perceptibly wet by the time he had covered the fifty yards separating it from the steps.

He switched on the engine and sat for a few seconds, thinking about his route. He had, of course, no idea what car Nigel Makin was driving; he'd just have to come back again if he couldn't find him. The traffic was still heavy and it took him a good ten minutes to get to the caravan site which bordered the underpass site; as he moved slowly forwards in a queue of cars he glanced sideways to see Mickey Hamilton, carrying a huge rucksack and moving purposefully into the caravan site. Not unreasonable, McLeish thought a minute later; chap had to live somewhere, and the caravan was still there and doubtless now stripped of all traces of Fraser's occupancy.

He swung his car as close to the wire fence as he could get it, crawled out over the passenger seat and spent a damp five minutes attracting the attention of the nightwatchman. He stood, itching with impatience, as the figure moved slowly towards him, noticing that this one was well within the proud tradition of nightwatchmen everywhere, being oldish, bowed by a serious chest complaint and limping heavily on a gammy leg. Not for the first time he wondered why major industrial concerns habitually entrusted the security of their undertakings during the hours of darkness to men who would be handicapped in a fight with a ten-year-old girl.

He shared something of this thought with the bundled-up wheezing figure who admitted him to the site as they trekked unhopefully towards the darkened Section I offices.

'When I'm on me own, I only have to press the button, guv.'

McLeish considered the top of the venerable grey head with exasperation.

'Where's the button then, uncle?'

'Well, in the offices, isn't it?' The man sounded world-weary, but the thought penetrated, and he stopped to consider it.

'Never mind, uncle,' McLeish urged him on; 'just you stay close to that button. Now, when did you last see Mr Makin?'

''Bout twenty minutes ago. 'E said for me to go on with my rounds, 'e'd be finished soon, then 'e'd be off.'

'Did you see him go? Did you close the gate?'

'No, 'e told me not to bother, it was a lovely night, and he had a key. 'E forgot though.'

'What do you mean?'

'When I let you in, the gate wasn't locked, it was just closed.'

McLeish, who had not even tried the gate, assuming that it was locked, swore inwardly.

'I'll come into the offices anyway, and use the phone.'

He stood aside while the older man wheezed his way up the three wooden steps into the Portakabin. He followed him and stopped, the hair at the back of his head prickling. 'Come back, uncle. Come behind me!' He reached for the light switch, illuminating a bare corridor and six closed doors. The seventh stood open, and McLeish was by it before his companion had adapted his eyes to the light. He pushed the door inwards with his right shoulder, reaching for the light switch with his left hand. 'Jee-sus!' He jerked his left foot back from something and stared down at the still body of a man, lying face down, one arm crumpled under him and the other flung out at his side, almost underneath McLeish's foot.

'Press the button, uncle. Do it now!'

He knelt by Nigel Makin's side while the electronic alarms started to whoop above his head. Makin had been coshed, the dent at the back of the skull would have told anyone that, but he was breathing. McLeish picked up the phone beside him and found himself talking to the Edgware Road desk sergeant, who confirmed McLeish's good opinion of him by having followed meticulously the agreed procedure when the site alarms went off.

'I'll send the poor old tortoise on the nightshift here to open the gate. If he starts now he'll just about meet the ambulance arriving.'

McLeish slammed the phone down, dived down the passage and took a careful minute to ensure that the night-watchman understood his instructions exactly and was not too shaken to carry them out, before returning to Makin, who was breathing steadily. The office looked as if it had been hit by a typhoon — papers were everywhere and every drawer of the big filing cabinet was open. So, McLeish realized grimly, was the safe: wide open and innocent of everything but the petty-cash box and some keys. No sheaf of computer print-out, coffee-stained, was anywhere to be seen. And all this had happened in the forty minutes or so it had taken him to arrive.

He sat back on his heels, one part of his brain registering the distant noise of an ambulance in a hurry, and thought about that forty minutes, then reached for the phone urgently to put out an order to pull in Mickey Hamilton and to organize a warrant.

'He was not a hundred yards away. I saw him myself,' he said grimly to the detective sergeant who was the most senior officer Edgware Road could muster at that point. 'I'd go myself, but I daren't leave Makin in case he says something. But hurry, will you?'

He was shouting by now to get above the impressive amount of noise being made by the arriving ambulance, but he heard his colleague confirm that he was off now.

He knelt again by Makin, who appeared to be in much the same state as before, and indicated as much to the senior casualty officer who had come with the ambulance.

'Nasty,' the man observed dispassionately, checking for other, less obvious, injuries. 'We'll take him in — are you coming, Chief Inspector?'

'Not if I can find a sensible constable to go with him,' McLeish said, peering out of the window at the arriving might of Edgware Road. 'Woolner!' He pushed open the stiff window and shouted, and young Woolner, pale but evidently still keen, looked up hopefully. 'Job for you. Stay right with this chap — Mr Makin — whatever they want to do at the hospital. I want every golden word noted down, and I'll come by later and collect them. Don't even leave him long enough to phone me, all right?' He looked carefully at the young constable to see that he had understood.

'I've got it, sir. I'll just tell Sergeant Williams where I've gone.'

'Right.' McLeish mentally gave him points for keeping his head and remembering where the chain of command lay. 'Got your notebook?'

'Sir.' The young man grinned, the blond hair, pale skin and bright blue eyes suddenly very much in contrast, and revealing a rather older and more sophisticated personality than McLeish had seen hitherto. 'I used occasionally to forget it, but I've been in three years now!'

'Have you now? Graduate entry?'

'Yes, sir.'

'So was I.' McLeish nodded to him to follow the stretcher, and watched him walk away, noting him for future use.

He hesitated, torn between getting back to a police station and the attendant facilities and the need not to waste precious minutes in checking up on the whereabouts of anyone else who might have wanted to halt Nigel Makin's investigations. He decided on the telephone in the next-door office, which meant also that he could be on site to meet the Forensic team when it arrived.

He got hold of Ian Michaels and sent him round to what he now thought of as Fort Vernon, ostensibly to break the news and enquire where Nigel Makin's next of kin could most easily be found, but actually to establish who was there and what they had been doing. Neither Bill Vernon nor Sally lived there, but he knew Sally was staying there and he dispatched a spare sergeant to Bill's Chelsea flat.

These works accomplished, he sat down and looked hopefully at the telephone. By now the party sent to arrest Hamilton should have found him and be reporting in. He sat, twitching with impatience, watched uneasily by a young policeman, posted on the doors to await the arrival of Forensic.

'Francesca,' McLeish said aloud, seriously rattling the young policeman whose given name was Francis.

'Sir?' he said, cautiously.

'Constable, would you listen for the phone? I'll find another one. I'm just along here. Call me if I'm needed.'

McLeish plunged into another office, then checked as he remembered Francesca would be out that evening. The recollection gave him time to reflect. Robert Vernon would either cancel the lunch they were having tomorrow, or he would keep the date; in the first case no harm could come, and in the second they might all learn something. He considered this line of reasoning and decided definitely that he was not prepared to see Francesca exposed even to the smallest danger. Whoever had coshed Makin was presumably close enough to the Vernon computer system to have removed data from it, and that put Robert Vernon along with his wife, his son and daughter, right in the frame. So he would let Francesca keep that date, but she would be accompanied every step of the way, even if it meant several budding detectives doing themselves a bit of good at the Savoy. For her protection he would tell her that Makin had been attacked and that Vernon — all the Vernons, indeed — were suspect unless and until Hamilton turned out to have done it. But he would not tell her she was being minded.

The phone in the next-door office rang sharply and he was there almost before the young constable had time to answer it. 'You got him? Good. He say anything? All right, take him over to Edgware Road, will you? I'll meet you there.'

McLeish didn't try to hurry: there was no point. Hamilton had said nothing useful when arrested and all experience suggested that people either said something revealing at the moment they saw the arresting officer or else sweated out hours of questioning before anything emerged. Before taking off for Edgware Road, he made two more calls, explained to the incoming Forensic team what he wanted, and rang Edgware Road again to make sure they got a set of Mickey Hamilton's fingerprints.

* * *

'Why am I here?' Mickey Hamilton was even paler than usual, either from fear or temper. 'I'm free to leave the country, aren't I? You can't just arrest me. Do you have a warrant?'

McLeish considered him and indicated to the arresting officer that he would be glad of a word outside the interview room.

'You just pulled him in? Didn't tell him Makin was attacked?'

'No, sir. He had his passport on him and he was packed to go.'

McLeish nodded. Mickey Hamilton had something on his mind, that much was obvious.

'OK, let's go back in. I'll play it by ear. There's a warrant on its way.'

He banged his way into the interview room and sat down opposite Mickey Hamilton.

'Why am I here?' Mickey demanded again.

'You are here because Nigel Makin was violently attacked in the Underpass site offices in the last couple of hours. I was on my way to meet him and saw you turning into the caravan site.'

Mickey turned even paler if possible and gaped at McLeish. 'Why would I want to attack Nigel Makin?' he asked breathlessly, several seconds later.

'I don't know yet, but I will as soon as Makin comes round. You could save us all some time by telling me now. Was he on to the fiddle you were in?' McLeish was watching the young man's mouth as he spoke for the small twitch at the corner which indicated shock with the most controlled people, but he needn't have bothered. Hamilton all but jumped out of his chair.

'I don't know what you are talking about,' he said flatly, pushing himself back in his chair and folding his arms, and the two policemen took in this unequivocal piece of body language with real exasperation.

'Oh, come on, Mickey,' McLeish snapped, 'the lorry fiddle on the Barbican site and the second one here! I don't yet know whether you were on site or off site somewhere, waiting for the steel, but the Vernon computer will help there. And Nigel Makin's notes.'

'You'll have to prove anything you say,' Mickey said doggedly, arms still tightly folded. 'I didn't know Nigel Makin had been hurt, but if he isn't talking he's badly hurt, and I'm not answering any questions without a solicitor here. I'd like to telephone. My uncle's a Writer to the Signet in Edinburgh and I expect he'll know someone here.'

McLeish opened his mouth to say he didn't care if Mickey's uncle was the Attorney General and closed it again, on reflection. If Mickey was a murderer, then how he was treated and how any statements were taken from him mattered very much, particularly with a family alert to all the niceties. He was under lock and key on McLeish's own evidence, and that was where he was staying, be he nephew to all the Lords of Appeal in Ordinary.

'Suit yourself,' he said, pushing his chair back. 'Ring your uncle by all means — the constable will bring you a telephone. Get yourself a brief. But none of it, so help me, will be any good to you if you're involved in this.'

He collected Davidson and left, his mind going to the next stage.

'Likely if his uncle practises in Edinburgh he'll not know any lawyers in London,' Davidson offered, with the West Coast contempt for Edinburgh.

McLeish grunted. 'I've got other things to worry about. I sent what's-his-name, Michaels, up to the Vernon place to find out where everyone was — he should be reporting in. Christ, it's ten-thirty.'

'Sir?' Sergeant Michaels was at the door of his own office. 'Mr Vernon and Miss Vernon were very distressed, and Mr Vernon was going to go to the hospital as soon as Mrs Vernon got back — she was out seeing a friend.'

'You saw them both? What time did you get there — eight-thirty-five? Makin was attacked between seven and seven-forty. One of them could have got there and back in that time.'

'The man-servant, Luigi, was there and says neither Mr Vernon nor Miss Vernon went out. Been there five years, saving up for his own restaurant,' he added in parenthesis, consulting his notes. 'And the house car was out of action, too — the driver had gone home early with it because he was putting it into a garage for some minor thing. Mr Vernon plans to go to the hospital later in a taxi — they're CabCall subscribers. Mrs Vernon had been dropped off by the driver on his way home to do some shopping. At Harrods.'

'Harrods isn't still open at ten-thirty, is it? Where is she?'

'I haven't managed to have a word with her yet, sir, but Mr Vernon has spoken to her. She was having dinner with a friend apparently, and arrived there about eight-thirty.'

'Well done, sergeant. Where was the dinner?'

'Clarendon Road, sir, W11 — do you know it?'

'I do indeed. What is it, ten minutes from the Underpass site? How did she get there from Harrods?'

'I assume she used CabCall, sir. They're all black taxis, but a lot of them work full-time on account business. Mrs Vernon doesn't run a car, and the business doesn't run one for her, so most places she wants to go to she goes by taxi, unless Mr Vernon's driver is free.'

McLeish considered him. 'You've been busy, sergeant.'

'It's a bit easier than it looks, sir. My brother-in-law drives for CabCall.'

'Saves a lot of work. So, what do you reckon, Michaels?'

'Was Mr Makin sitting down when he was attacked, sir?'

'Probably.'

'A lady could have done it, couldn't she? Particularly one he knew and wasn't frightened by.'

McLeish reluctantly examined the picture in his mind of Dorothy Vernon, dropping in on the offices to talk to Nigel Makin, leaning over his shoulder while he explained some of his findings, then felling him with a cosh.

'The site gate wasn't locked,' he observed, aloud. 'She could have got in.'

'Taking a bit of a risk, sir?'

'No, why? It's her site. Short of being caught actually in the act, she'd hardly need to explain what she was doing there.'

'I suppose that's true. You'll be wanting to talk to her yourself, then?'

'I'll have to. But thank you for your help. You doing the exams?'

'Yes. I reckon I'm about ready, but it's difficult to get the course work done.'

McLeish sympathized. Michaels was not a graduate and, though a good policeman, was one of the people who had difficulty absorbing the endless detail required to pass the exams for Inspector. Bruce Davidson, looking a trifle narrowly at Michaels, came in with the news that Nigel Makin had a fractured skull, was currently on the operating table, and young Woolner, got up in all the gear, was in attendance in the theatre itself.

'Makin's not going to say anything under anaesthetic, is he?' McLeish asked, startled, and Davidson grinning said that DC Woolner had taken the line that he had been instructed to remain at his charge's side and there he was going to stay, even if it involved standing through a major operation.

'I suppose I was once twenty-three and that keen, but I've forgotten it all,' McLeish said, holding his head. 'No, never mind, I'll go down there. Look, I want someone to babysit Francesca tomorrow — she's having lunch with Robert Vernon. You won't do, Bruce; she knows you. What about you, Michaels? I expect you'd like lunch at the Savoy, wouldn't you? Take another officer with you — I'll sign for it.'

Michaels opined, grinning, that there was going to be no shortage of volunteers for this particular task. What did Mr Vernon, or indeed Miss Wilson, look like? McLeish scrabbled in his file for a photograph of Robert Vernon, producing finally a file photo culled from a newspaper. He considered it critically. 'Taken a few years ago, I'd say, but it's good enough.' He hesitated, then took out his wallet and carefully extracted the picture he had taken on their last day in Scotland: Francesca, grinning confidently into the camera, her hair blowing into her eyes. 'And that's Miss Wilson — I'd like the picture back.'

Michaels nodded, taking both pictures carefully and putting them in an envelope. 'I'll look forward to this,' he said, not looking at McLeish. 'Thank you, sir.'

* * *

At lunchtime the next day, Michaels felt less confident. The floor manager looked carefully at himself and his fellow sergeant and allocated them a small corner table near the kitchen. Michaels, looking past him, saw Robert Vernon being shown to a table in the window, a flurry of waiters in attendance, the head waiter pulling out a chair for Francesca and pressing a napkin upon her. 'No,' he said stolidly, 'we'd like to be a bit closer to the window.'

The floor manager hesitated, and for a minute Michaels wondered if he was going to have to use his warrant card, but he gave way, ungracefully, and Michaels found himself with an excellent view of his charge. Good-looking girl he thought, now much tidier than in the photograph.

He watched her from behind his menu, noticing the way she was looking round the big room, openly considering the details of the décor. The photograph had got her right, though; this was a confident young woman who saw no necessity to pretend she ate at the Savoy all the time. She turned her head suddenly and looked at him like an animal suddenly sensing it was being watched, and he froze. He managed to get his mouth open to speak to his fellow sergeant, who was staring incredulously at the Savoy's prices, and by the time he had managed to reassure him, Francesca's attention was back with her host.

'You heard about Nigel Makin?' Vernon was saying. 'They had to operate, you know, but they reckon he's not in immediate danger. What does that mean, Francesca — did your boyfriend say?'

Relieved at having got the subject of John McLeish's involvement with the case so quickly on the table, Francesca replied that it was apparently unlikely that Nigel Makin would die but no one knew quite when he would be fully conscious.

'They lifted the piece of bone that was pressing on the brain, John says, but he still hasn't come round,' she said, looking appreciatively at the huge plate covered with beautiful thin slices of smoked salmon. 'I'm sorry, it must be another worry for you.'

'I'd not want to lose Nigel, that's for sure,' Robert Vernon agreed. 'But even if he's going to be all right — and he's got the best care where he is, I made sure of that — I may have to manage without him. It's a bit much to expect him to stay after what that girl of mine's done to him.' He shook his head, sadly, squeezing lemon over his smoked salmon, and Francesca watched the stubby fingers compressing the wedge of fruit.

'Sally almost told me in Scotland that she and Alan were having an affair,' she said and stopped, realizing that her next projected sentence was going to land her in difficulties.

The burly man on the other side of the table glanced up at her. 'What were you going to say?'

'Well, I was going to ask if you would have minded all that much if she'd married him instead of Nigel, and then I realized I would sound like a policewoman. And a nosey one at that.'

'You're very like your dad.' Robert Vernon was only mildly disconcerted. 'He always told you the truth when you asked him.' He attacked his smoked salmon with relish, while Francesca, embarrassed, fiddled with her lemon.

'Give it here, girl, you'll never get any out that way, these little squeezer things are no use — yes, Alberto, you know I need fingerbowls, just bring them, will you? Fraser wasn't going to marry her, Francesca, it just wasn't an option. Not the marrying sort, that one; didn't want the responsibility.'

He dunked his fingers decisively in the fingerbowls that had materialized instantly, even in that busy dining-room. Francesca, riled by his certainty, reflected fair-mindedly that this was a man who had always carried massive responsibilities: his own business when he was nineteen, and a wife and baby by the time he was twenty-two. She drank half a glass of wine rather too fast to give herself time to reflect and felt it going straight to her head.

'I didn't ask you to lunch to talk about Sal,' Robert Vernon was saying. 'I want you to come and work for us — I don't know why I didn't think of it before, but I need someone like you as a personal assistant to help me with our public relations, our shareholders, government, all those things.'

'Dorothy — Mrs Vernon — does all that, surely?'

'We're getting too big for her to do everything. You're your father's daughter, you can do all that. What are you being paid where you are?'

'£20,000, give or take. And an index-linked pension.'

'You get a car? No? Expenses? No. Why are you doing it, Francesca? You could have twice that with us, no trouble at all. You could be my personal assistant.'

Francesca, even flushed with a glass of wine, felt imagination boggle at the idea of being this one's right-hand girl, never mind the hazards of skirting around Dorothy Vernon.

'You are kind, Robert, but it's not my thing. My personality is all wrong to be anyone's personal assistant. I need to have my own command. I could maybe run a site if I'd started younger or was an engineer, but I couldn't look after public or government relations.' She struggled to express her objection. 'It's not that it's not interesting — I'd only be interested for about ten minutes a day and that just isn't enough. I'm sorry, Robert, I'm not making myself clear.'

'Yes, you are.' Mercifully he seemed to be amused. '*I'm* only interested for ten minutes a day, so's Dorothy. No point having three of us. God, you are like your dad. Not that interested in money either, are you?'

'More interested than he was.' The response was sharp enough to cause Robert Vernon to stop in mid-attack on his steak. 'I'm very keen on having my own good job and my own good pension. There's no way I'm ever going to be financially dependent on anyone.'

'You'll have to be when you have children. You are going to marry your policeman, aren't you?'

'I'm not going to marry anyone if it means being dependent on them.'

'But Francesca.' Robert Vernon was so distressed that he put his knife and fork down. 'What's up with all you girls?'

She looked back at him, pink with anxiety.

'I suppose I understand,' he said, slowly, pouring her some more wine. 'My father died young, too, and I saw what happened when there wasn't a wage-earner in the family. It's different now, though.'

'You cannot have looked at the rates of pension payable to the widow of a Detective Chief Inspector.'

'Good heavens, girl, is that the first thing you enquired about when the poor bugger asked you to marry him: how was the pension scheme?'

Francesca started to laugh, and choked on her steak, accepting gratefully the glass of water pressed on her within seconds by a hovering waiter. 'No, Robert, not quite like that. John couldn't understand the bumph about the ways of opting in, out, or sideways to the main Metropolitan Police Pension Scheme. I can read anything financial rather quickly, so he showed it to me. Disheartening reading, I'd have to say.'

She looked round for the waiter to get another glass of water, and found her eye drawn to the two sober citizens, sharing a half bottle of wine at a table three away from them, whom she had noticed before. They both looked away from her quickly, and she wondered idly what they were doing here. Not tourists; her eye, trained by months of bankrupt textile companies, told her that — their suits were English and mass-produced, probably for Austin Reed or Marks and Spencer. Unlikely for the Savoy, somehow.

'How *is* Sally?' she asked giving up the small puzzle.

'Better in herself today. She was very upset about Nigel, of course. I still think she'd have come back to Nigel — they get on all right — but of course with Fraser dead, it's made things pretty difficult.'

'You think that if Alan had actually got that place on K6 he'd have gone and the whole affair would have collapsed?'

'I'm sure of it.'

Francesca blinked at the confidence of the response, and stared across at Vernon who looked away.

'You talked to him,' she said, suddenly and unreasonably certain. 'You offered to pay him to go away.' She sat looking at his bent head as he went slowly scarlet across the cheekbones. 'And he took it — I mean he agreed,' she said, speaking out of the same certainty. 'Oh, Robert! What a thing to do.'

'He wasn't going to marry her, whatever I did.' Robert Vernon was searching the table for his glass in an agony of embarrassment. 'I wanted him *out of the way*.' He looked up, startled, and Francesca and he stared at each other across the table, the words echoing between them.

Michaels, three tables away, kicked his companion sharply and unobtrusively organized himself to move fast if he had to.

'But did you succeed — I mean, did he agree to go, for money?' Francesca was after the point like a terrier.

'Yes. We'd made a deal and he was taking twenty-four hours to sort out the price. He wanted me — the firm — to provide enough sponsorship for a place for that oppo of his, too — Hamilton. Didn't think it right, he said, just to take it for himself.'

'How did you feel about that?'

'I thought he had a nerve, asking for two places, but I did agree. I didn't want him as a husband for my Sally. He said himself that climbers shouldn't marry. Don't look like that, Francesca — even if they'd married, where would my Sally be with a husband dead on some mountain and young children left? He was right about that.'

'I'm sorry. I was remembering Alan. Very like him, wasn't it? And someone killed him.'

'Well, not me, girl, not for the price of two tickets to K6. He thought it would have cost about £200,000. It's deductible from tax and we'd have got some good from the advertising.'

'What would you have told Sally?'

'That was Fraser's job. He said he'd already told her he wasn't prepared to marry her.'

'But Robert, he'd have gone, anyway — I mean, you didn't need to bribe him?'

'We had to teach your dad not to use words like that. Yes, he'd have gone *if* he was offered a place — I was just making sure he *was* offered.'

He scowled across the table, but Francesca kept her head. 'You must tell the police this, Robert; it's material. It lets you out anyway.'

'They surely don't suspect me?' Robert Vernon said incredulously.

'Of course they do,' Francesca said implacably. 'Though, come to think of it, John said no more than anyone else involved. Yes, I should like some pudding, if that's all right?'

Robert Vernon assured her impatiently that she might work her way from one end of the trolley to the other with his blessing.

'Why didn't you tell the police anyway?' she asked, accepting a mixed bowl of raspberries, strawberries and trifle.

She considered him, frowning. 'You weren't concerned for yourself, although you should have been. You were worried about someone else, and now you're not or I'd never have got this out of you.'

'I'm glad you don't want to work for me,' Robert Vernon said, after a pause. 'I'm not going to tell you what I was worried about, clever clogs, but you're right — I'm not now. Do you want a second go at the trolley, since the first lot's gone down in one swallow?'

'How kind. Yes, please, it's not every day I see a trolley like that. Look, Robert, I'm sorry, I know you've gone off me, but you *must* tell John all this.'

'I've not gone off you exactly,' he said thoughtfully, watching her. 'I'd just forgotten what your dad was like, awkward bloody genius that he was. I'm sorry I offered you a job in public relations though; you'd be terrible. I probably should have offered you managing director.' He reached over and patted her hand. 'I'll talk to your John this afternoon. Will he be very annoyed?'

'Yes and no.' Francesca noticed that the two men at the nearby table had paid their bill but were still sitting drinking coffee, and suddenly understood who they were and why they were there. 'Yes, for the waste of his time; no, because if he had a daughter he too would protect her from the winds that blow, to the point of gross interference. He'll understand.'

'You don't let him protect you,' Robert Vernon observed. 'You should. It's what men want — someone to look after.' He indicated to the head waiter that he would welcome a bill, and checked every item before signing it. She watched him, observing each detail. 'Your dad tried, you know. He couldn't help dying at thirty-seven.'

'I know. Thank you for lunch, Robert.'

They caught each other's eye and both started to laugh.

'Ah, Francesca, any time I want my character back in my face I'll buy you lunch.' He rested a heavy hand on her shoulder as he steered her out of the restaurant and up the stairs to the main lobby. 'You'll be all right with a man and kids of your own. Don't you pass up a good man like my Sally's just done, there aren't enough to go round. Can we take you to your office? I'll ring your John as soon as I get back.'

Francesca hesitated, mindful of the watchers who were now standing just outside the main door studying the programmes at the Savoy Theatre. 'My office is in the opposite direction to yours,' she said, pitching her voice so they could hear. 'Would it not be better to get me a taxi? The traffic looks awful.'

Robert Vernon glanced at his driver who observed neutrally that there was a demonstration which was causing difficulty.

She kissed Vernon goodbye, nodded to his driver, and hesitated by the door of the taxi which the commissionaire was holding deferentially open, wondering irritably whether to tell her watchdogs they could go home. But she suddenly heard Robert Vernon's voice in her head and in a blessed moment of clarity understood that she was being ungracious. John McLeish had provided secure protection for her, and that protection should be accepted in the spirit in which it had been offered. It was for John to tell her afterwards, if he chose, that she had been well looked after.

She smiled at the commissionaire, told the taxi-driver where to go in tones that the watchers could not fail to hear, and sat back in the cab without looking in their direction.

CHAPTER 16

Three miles away, John McLeish was spending his nominal lunch-hour reading irritably through the statement he had collected that morning from Bill Vernon. A sergeant from the uniformed branch in Chelsea had waited for five hours from nine p.m. to two a.m. at the door of Bill's flat and had been just about to give up and get some sleep when its owner had arrived home with a girl both of them flushed with drink, having spent the evening blamelessly at Tramps. They were vouched for by several well-known names, including the owner who had been roused from sleep at his house in St John's Wood to confirm the story and had observed with no discernible trace of sarcasm that he never slept that much anyway.

It was, of course, interesting that Bill had a drink with Mickey Hamilton around six-thirty that evening, which meant he had been in the right place at near enough the right time to attack Nigel Makin at about seven-thirty. He had left the pub with Hamilton, at about seven, certainly not later, and had not gone back on site. 'I mean, I wish I had, but I had no reason to, and I knew I'd left none too much time to get back and change before picking up Susy. He had picked up the said Susy, having changed and bathed, at eight-thirty on the other side of London, which made it just barely possible, but unlikely.'

McLeish rose heavily to his feet to return to the interview room where Bill Vernon was waiting to sign his statement, and paused at the door to consider him. He was reading a paper peacefully in the small unwelcoming room, looking uncomfortable but not unduly so.

'If there is any more coffee, I'd be very grateful,' he said, mildly. 'My head's still a bit sore.'

McLeish called down the corridor, feeling that he had been guilty of a breach of hospitality. 'Did we offer you any lunch?'

'I turned it down. It seemed a bit early.'

McLeish decided Bill Vernon must really have been over-indulging. 'It is two o'clock,' he observed.

'I hadn't realized.' Bill Vernon glanced at his watch and McLeish followed his gaze. 'It's stopped, that's why. Never mind, coffee is what I need, thank you so much.' He bent his head to adjust his watch.

McLeish saw the uniformed constable put the coffee down, and observed that Bill Vernon's hand was unsteady as he picked it up. A monumental hangover, evidently.

'I'll leave your statement with you to check. I'm afraid you have to sign every page, in the presence of an officer.'

'Fine. No worry.'

He might not have any worries, McLeish thought sourly, but he was the only one here who hadn't. He thought he knew who had attacked Nigel Makin but he had an uneasy, edgy feeling that there was more to come and he didn't know where it was coming from. He thought of Francesca lunching at the Savoy, nursemaided by Michaels. Not a lot could go wrong there, but he would be more comfortable when she was back in her office. He walked back to the interview room where Bill Vernon indicated that he was nearly ready.

'So you're off to Scotland?' McLeish said pleasantly, when Bill had signed all five pages of his statement.

'Day after tomorrow. I am just finishing some work on site. I can't wait.' The rather heavy face under the floppy dark cowlick was suddenly animated. 'There's a couple of farms coming up at auction — I thought I might make an offer ahead of the auction, see if the old chap would bite. The settlement is all ready for signature, so the money's there.'

'Well, good luck with it. We'll need to have an address where we can find you — this business here isn't over yet.'

Bill Vernon looked surprised. 'I thought you'd arrested Hamilton? I mean I was very surprised, but I thought you were confident. I'm sorry, perhaps I shouldn't ask.'

Mickey Hamilton had appeared in front of the magistrates that morning, as required by law, and had been remanded for seven days for further enquiries. McLeish was not, however, inclined to discuss police business with Bill Vernon, who had been close to the site the previous night and had also been present when Alan Fraser fell to his death. He declined, stuffily, to comment and said goodbye.

Back in his office, he threw Bill's statement into the out-tray for photocopying and filing, sat down and looked anxiously at his watch. Quarter to three: Francesca should at least be on her way back from lunch. His telephone rang and he snatched it up.

'Chief Inspector? Robert Vernon here.'

'What can I do for you, Mr Vernon?' McLeish asked, when the pause had stretched itself.

'I've just had lunch with Francesca. At the Savoy.'

McLeish attempted a sentence expressive of both pleasure and surprise, but realized that the man at the other end wasn't listening.

'I should have told you before about a conversation I had with Alan Fraser. Look, I'm in the car and we're on your doorstep. Shall I come up?'

McLeish, galvanized, said he would come down, now, to meet him. 'Is Francesca with you?'

'No, no, she's back at her office, or should be by now.'

'See you in five minutes.'

'Sergeant Michaels on my line, John,' his secretary called from the outer office and handed him the telephone while she took her coat off.

'She's back safely, sir,' Michaels reported. 'I've just seen her into her own office. Vernon went off in a different direction, and we didn't try to follow.'

'Quite right. He's come here. Get back, will you, quick as you can? And thank you.'

McLeish collected Davidson and rushed downstairs, realizing that Bill Vernon had probably missed his father by only a few minutes. Robert Vernon, looking uncomfortable but resolute, recounted the critical interview with Alan Fraser, Davidson's pen flying.

'Let me get this straight then,' McLeish said, furious and formidable. 'Fraser said he would go willingly to K6, provided a place could also be found for Mickey Hamilton. You, or rather Vernon Engineering, were going to negotiate an amount of sponsorship in exchange for those two places. Fraser was to explain his departure to your daughter.' He considered this substantial piece of projected interference and thought about the stubborn, wily, determined man sitting across the desk.

'He wasn't going to marry her anyway, Chief Inspector, whatever I did, so I wanted him gone. It was what he wanted, too.'

'The only explanation you owe *us*, Mr Vernon, is why you didn't tell us this before. You must see that this is important evidence.'

'Well, I'll answer that. I didn't know who he had told, did I? I didn't know whether he'd talked to Sally and I didn't know whether she'd been angry enough to do him harm.'

'And now you do know?'

'What I know, Chief Inspector, is that Sally was home with me last night, watching the telly, and not at the Underpass hitting Nigel Makin over the head. It has to be the same person doing all this, doesn't it, or it doesn't make sense?'

'No.'

'What?'

'No, it doesn't have to be the same person. As you know, Nigel Makin had found a lorry fiddle on two of your sites. When he talked to me yesterday he had also found that relevant material had been extracted from your computer system, and that he probably had the only copy left. It is now missing. The lorry fiddle and the murder of Fraser may be separate crimes, committed by different people.'

'Jesus Christ!' Robert Vernon had turned white and for a moment you could see that he was over sixty.

'You thought your daughter might have tried to do Alan Fraser harm? She knew if she laced his tea with antihistamine it would make him dizzy, didn't she? She'd been with Francesca when she'd turned dizzy on only a couple of the same pills.'

Robert Vernon sat back in his chair and glared at him, the colour returning to his face. 'I'll have you off this case.'

'It's too late for that, Mr Vernon. You can probably get me taken off this case if you complain loud and long enough to enough people, but the information is all on file. There are other Chief Inspectors who'll take up exactly where I left off, and who'll feel just the same as I do about people who hide vital evidence.' In the background he could hear Davidson shifting his chair in warning but he decided he didn't care. 'You may even have precipitated a murder by interfering as you did. If I thought that was why you hadn't been willing to speak up, I'd feel a bit better about you. But as it is I don't even know why you decided to give us your confidence, and I've no idea whether you're telling the truth.' He stopped, remembering who and where he was, and glared at the man across the table.

Robert Vernon was red in the face, his mouth a tight slit and his eyes narrowed in temper. The two men confronted one another, and Davidson, fascinated, sat frozen into his posture of dumb recorder.

'You and Francesca in one day is too bloody much.' Robert Vernon spoke explosively into the silence and Davidson jumped. 'All right, Sally wouldn't have done anything like that — she might have hit him, but she wouldn't have tried to kill him, and I should have known that. I shouldn't have interfered, and when I tell Sal I'll get my character read for the third time today. But, I'll swear she *didn't* know what I'd done. Fraser must have found it difficult, or else he hadn't had time, but he hadn't told her.'

McLeish nodded and in the pause remembered that it was Francesca who had somehow persuaded this tough old monster to produce his evidence.

'What made you tell Francesca?'

Robert Vernon hesitated. 'She read my mind,' he said, peering at McLeish to see if this rang any bells. 'Then she said I had to come and see you.' He brooded for a moment. 'I remember her when she was a very pretty baby,' he said sadly.

Davidson was seized by a fit of coughing and McLeish, taken by surprise, failed to keep his face straight. 'I know what you mean,' he managed to say. Robert Vernon grinned reluctantly at him and the atmosphere relaxed.

'I'm sorry, anyway. I'll get hell from Dorothy as well as Sally, if it's any comfort.'

Yes, well . . . Dorothy, McLeish thought heavily, conscious of her lack of alibi for the critical time last night. Despite his brisk scouting of the idea that the two crimes were necessarily linked, the odds were that they must be. Two separate murderers among the same small group seemed unlikely. And whoever had coshed Nigel Makin had meant to kill him and had not failed by very much, the doctors had made that clear. Indeed it was probably only McLeish's own arrival that had ensured Makin received treatment in time.

'Mrs Vernon was out last night, I see from her statement,' he said neutrally, and Robert Vernon looked at him in amazement.

'I've been married to Dolly for twenty-six years — I really don't have to wonder whether she's going to start murdering people. She's a Methodist.'

McLeish, who had known a multiple murderer who was a respected Congregationalist, forbore to comment.

'I mean you don't make that sort of mistake in your line of work, do you?'

'I hope not.' McLeish decided he had extracted all he could from this interview and that he would need, desperately, to talk again to Mickey Hamilton. He told Robert Vernon he would have to wait and sign a statement, and was mildly surprised when he accepted this docilely.

'It gives me a bit more time before I have to talk to Sal,' Vernon explained, openly considering McLeish. 'You're rather like Francesca's dad, now I come to look at you. He was a big chap too — thinner, of course, because he had what killed him in the end for years before.'

McLeish nodded, receiving confirmation of something he'd half suspected as being the origin of some of his troubles with Francesca. Fathers, by her definition, were much loved but intrinsically unreliable people who were ill at any moment when you really needed them and who died leaving you and the family bereft. He went back to his office, putting these thoughts resolutely from him, and picked up the phone to ring Francesca.

'I have just interviewed Mr Vernon,' he said, when he got through.

'Oh, good. He told you all? I mean, I'm sure you saw it straight away, but if Mickey knew Alan was getting him a place then he didn't have a motive to kill. Quite the reverse, indeed.'

'*If* he knew. Do you have a soft spot for Mickey?'

'No. Yes. He sings, you see.'

McLeish did see; the eldest sister to four brothers, all of whom sang, would naturally be predisposed in Hamilton's favour.

'I had a couple of men at the Savoy,' he said casually. 'Did you spot them?'

'Darling, how good of you. You needn't have, I was perfectly safe, but that was kind.'

McLeish put down the receiver a minute later, smiling to himself. It occurred to him sharply that she had not answered his question, and at that moment Michaels appeared in his doorway.

'Did she spot you?'

'I thought so, sir.'

McLeish sighed, and then brightened as he thought about it again. If the uncompromising Francesca was prepared to accept the police presence gracefully rather than insisting on unmasking it, that was definitely progress.

He realized that Michaels was big with news.

'Sir, you remember my brother-in-law at CabCall? Well, a driver who was off this morning came in at lunchtime and he was clearing his dockets. Sorry, that's the name for the procedure. Drivers call in all the jobs they've done and they give the destinations and the prices, so that the office can send the vouchers in with the monthly bills. He called in one on the Vernon Engineering account going from Harrods to the Western Underpass site. Mrs Vernon was the passenger: it was called in her name, and in any case he knows her slightly, he'd driven her before. He dropped her about seven-fifteen, the records say. He got to his next job in Notting Hill Gate at seven-thirty.'

McLeish sat and stared at him. 'She was there at the right time. She could have got on the site, too; the gate wasn't locked. Well done, Michaels, what a piece of jam! Where's her statement?'

He pulled it out of the top drawer where he kept the current case folder and found it quickly. 'Trun . . . trun, Harrods, trun . . . trun, left about eight p.m. just before it closed, reached her friend's house at eight-thirty. No word of a detour to the Western Underpass. Find out where she is, will you Michaels? I must talk to Hamilton, but I'd like to see that good lady, first.' He thought momentarily of her husband, waiting to sign his statement and dismissively confident that his wife of twenty-six years was not a murderess.

* * *

However, Hamilton was available and to hand, remanded to the Scrubs, and interviewing him was the most urgent duty. McLeish called for a car and sat, dictating memos, as he and Davidson worked their way out to West London.

Mickey Hamilton looked terrible — there was no other word for it. His skin was sallow and his bright brown hair dulled; he looked so bad, indeed, that McLeish searched anxiously for signs of physical ill-treatment. 'They're looking after you all right here?' he asked.

'What would it matter if they weren't?' Mickey asked with a momentary flash. 'How am I going to get to K6? I *had* that place — they won't wait for me. I never saw Makin, I had no reason to attack him. When is he going to come round?'

'No one knows that, and in any case he may well remember nothing at all. Happens with a bang on the head.'

'Oh God.' Mickey slumped again, his hands twisting anxiously, while McLeish decided how to begin.

'You told me that, if he had lived, Fraser was a more likely prospect for that place on K6 than you?'

'Yes, I did. It's true, but I didn't kill him. He was my mate and I miss him.'

'So you didn't know that he had an offer of a place?'

Mickey gaped at him. 'No, I didn't. When was he offered it?'

'The day before he died.'

'The Committee didn't tell me that. But they wouldn't, would they? Well, now you know — he *was* the better prospect. I got offered it because he was gone.' Mickey looked down at his hands, then suddenly scrubbed at his face. 'Damn, damn, damn! He was better known, of course.'

'You would have been very distressed if you had known he had the place?'

'As you see.' Mickey considered his hands bleakly. 'Actually, it doesn't seem to matter much, now — I mean, he's dead and I'm here and I've got the place.'

'If I told you that he had insisted that a place be found for you also, you would be surprised?'

He had his answer. Mickey stared at him, searching his face, then started very slowly to weep, his face contracting painfully. McLeish waited while he hunted through his pockets and failed to find a handkerchief, then offered a box of Kleenex.

'He did that, did he?' Mickey said, at last, through a faceful of paper handkerchief. 'But who made the offer?'

'A prospective sponsor. It was, of course, conditional on the Committee's being able to find room for you both.'

'There wouldn't have been a problem if there was enough cash. Who was the sponsor?'

McLeish did not reply and Mickey watched him for a minute.

'You're going to make me guess. Robert Vernon? To get him out of the way?' He considered McLeish's professionally unyielding expression. 'That figures, doesn't it? That old swine doesn't put himself at risk, he just pays people to go away. But Alan was going to make him pay for me as well, bless him. God, old Vernon would have hated that. Could he have hated it so much that he killed Alan sooner than pay?'

An interesting hypothesis, McLeish thought behind his dead-pan mask, and not one to which he had given consideration.

'No,' Mickey said, answering his own question, 'he'd still rather pay. He isn't the type to kill anyone, either.' He looked at McLeish. 'You're not saying much, Chief Inspector.'

'It doesn't seem to be necessary,' McLeish said drily, and a pale smile appeared momentarily.

'So I had a place, although I didn't know it?'

'You really didn't know it?'

Just for a minute Mickey hesitated, tempted. 'No, I didn't. I wish I could tell you I had, because I'd be in the clear, wouldn't I? But I didn't.' He looked over Davidson's head to the small high window. 'I must get out of here.' It was said softly, but he might as well have shrieked aloud.

'I don't know enough about Fraser's death or the attack on Makin to feel comfortable about letting you loose.' McLeish was equally direct. 'So what can you tell me? What about the lorry fiddle that Makin told me he had found, both here and at the Barbican?' Watching Mickey closely, he saw his hands move convulsively. 'We think that someone bludgeoned Makin to prevent him getting any closer to that fiddle. Maybe Alan was killed for the same reason — that he knew a bit too much?'

McLeish stopped and sweated out the silence as Mickey's eyes fixed themselves on the tiny grating. Finally he gave a long sigh.

'Alan was in it. And the Doolans. I wasn't.'

McLeish sat absolutely still but Mickey had exhausted himself.

'So how did it work?'

'I don't know how it worked on the actual sites. But two flatbeds that were supposed to unload at the Barbican never got there: they came to the Jennings site down the road and Alan and the Doolans unloaded them. They stayed on the Jennings site for a week — they clocked off at the Barbican and gave out they were going to Ireland for the week — and fixed all the steel. They did the same thing again last month, only this time it was RSJs and Alan said they had to work like blue-arsed flies unloading lorries at four different places. They weren't needed for the fixing at any of those, so they only missed a day at the Underpass. Too bloody tired to go in after that night. Told the GM they'd been on the beer.'

'It was just the three of them?'

'Yes. I don't know how it was worked on the sites — I mean, someone had to sign for the lorries that never got there, and I don't know who it was. Alan knew, of course: he had to, whoever it was, was part of the organization. But Alan wouldn't tell me, he said I didn't need to know and it was better to leave it that way.'

Typical of that cool, careful customer, McLeish thought, with a pang.

'What did they get out of it?'

'The Doolans got three thousand quid each for the Barbican job, and a thousand each for the night's work they did away from the Underpass.'

'Not a fortune, was it? Someone must have been making a bit more than that? It cost the firm £300,000 on the Barbican and about the same on the Western Underpass.'

'Alan got more.' It was the old, well remembered resentment. 'He didn't tell me how much, but he got more. If I knew who it was on site, I'd tell you, wouldn't I? Whoever it was had a bloody good reason to attack Makin if he thought he was getting close to the truth. Even allowing for the difference between buying and selling, there must have been £200,000 in there for someone.'

McLeish agreed silently that this was sound reasoning. It did not, however, improve Mickey Hamilton's position, because he simply didn't believe that Mickey had not been involved. It would have been the end of K6 for both him and Alan Fraser if they had found themselves with a prior engagement in a court of law, charged with theft.

'We can always find the Doolan brothers, you know, and ask them,' McLeish warned, and was taken aback to see Mickey look simply amused.

'That would do you no good. They'd never have met any of us before. It was maybe some cousins from Cork way that we were thinking of, and indeed none of them had been out of Ireland this year. We don't stamp Irish passports, do we? No, I thought not.' He looked accusingly at McLeish. 'You don't believe me, do you?'

It was as bad as having Francesca around, McLeish thought, momentarily unnerved. Perhaps being homosexual gave you the same kind of feminine ability to pick the thought in the mind of the other person out of the air.

'I don't operate on belief,' he said as formidably as he could. 'You *think*, Hamilton. Bring to mind everything you *know* about this theft. If I can prove there's someone with a better motive than yours then I'll move in on him, but for the moment you're it and you're staying here until I know different.' He looked at the light fading from the pale face in front of him, and felt a dreadful pang. 'Any time you think of something, get them to call me or Sergeant Davidson,' he ended lamely and swept himself and Davidson out of the room with what dignity he could manage.

He packed himself silently into the car, chewing his lower lip as he did when worried. 'He was in it, you know,' he said accusingly to Davidson. 'If we let Mickey out, he might just go and finish off the other link in the chain.'

'The laddie who organized it all, ye mean?'

The car phone bleeped at them and McLeish snatched it up to hear his secretary telling him that she had a message from the hospital that Makin had recovered consciousness.

'Message from Constable Woolner?'

'No, John, from a staff nurse. You had apparently told the Constable he was not to leave the patient under any circumstances, so he had bullied a nurse into ringing me up.'

'God, I meant to get him relieved,' McLeish said horrified, and told Davidson, who altered course to go to the hospital without being asked and looked amused.

'I'm concerned for that laddie. He'll be full to bursting if he's not left the patient.'

'I wonder how he has managed? Borrowed a bedpan, I suppose.'

Bruce Davidson suggested an alternative expedient and they were both laughing and proposing other outrageous ideas as they reached the hospital, and met DC Woolner, white-faced after a solid eighteen hours with his charge. McLeish apologized and congratulated him, disappointed but not at all surprised to hear that Makin had remembered nothing at all in the brief period before he drifted back to sleep.

'We'll get you relieved. Talking of which, Woolner, have you really not left him at all? No? How did you, er . . . ?'

Woolner blushingly indicated the wash-basin in the corner of the room and McLeish, dead-pan, fished in his pocket and handed Davidson a coin.

'That's why there should have been two of you here, but you've done excellently. You'll have a relief inside the hour. Write down anything he says, *anything* at all. We need all the help we can get.'

He was walking down the corridor when he saw Sally Vernon at the other end, looking pale and tired and plain.

He went up to her hesitantly, and said he was glad to hear that the news was better.

'Yes, Dad and Mum are very pleased,' she said dispassionately, and he considered the firm mouth and chin.

'How are you?' he asked, towering over her.

'About as well as can be expected, I daresay. Do sit down, John — Chief Inspector. There's too much of you.'

She sat down herself in a chair beside him and he remained silent, waiting for an opening.

'My father's just gone. He told me what he had done,' she said, turning to look at him, pushing back the blonde hair that was falling over one eye.

'Are you very angry?'

'Well, if Alan really didn't want to marry me, it was probably just as well. Dad meant it for the best.'

Her face crumpled and McLeish resisted the urge to put an arm round her as if she were Francesca. He patted her shoulder instead and used the other hand to find the handkerchief he knew she would not have.

'I'm sorry,' he said, inadequately, ignoring Davidson who had posted himself five yards away in a neat compromise between allowing McLeish to play the scene without interference and providing him with a witness if needed.

'I was angrier with Alan than with Dad. I mean, if he'd really loved me, Dad wouldn't have been able to bribe him, would he?'

'Perhaps he did love you but didn't want to get married?'

'Francesca's like that, of course.' Sally blew her nose on his handkerchief and looked at him with her father's bright brown eyes.

'Yes,' McLeish said, as evenly as he could.

'She'll marry you in the end though, if you hang on. She's not like Alan who only wanted his bloody mountains. I know it wouldn't have worked.' She blew her nose again. 'Who killed him, do you know yet?'

'No. But we'll find out, we mostly do in the end.' He patted her shoulder again, watching her to see that she was calm enough to be left. 'A young man of mine is in with Nigel, but there's no reason you shouldn't go and see him.'

'I've seen him — I've been here for some time. Jim is picking me up on his way back from the airport with Mum.'

'Your mother's been abroad?'

'Only to Paris for the day. We — Vernons — have a small operation there. It's really a sales office.'

Well, that explained why Dorothy Vernon had not been produced for him to interview, but since he was on the spot, he would wait. For hours if need be. 'What time are you expecting her?'

'Ten minutes ago. The plane may be late.'

McLeish felt rather than saw Davidson shift position and looked up to see Mrs Vernon trotting down the corridor.

'Hello, darling. Ah, Chief Inspector. I understand Nigel has been conscious. Can I see him?'

'Of course, you can, though he was asleep when I looked in. There's a man on duty in the room.'

He followed Mrs Vernon down the passage, determined not to lose her and stood behind the two women as Dorothy Vernon moved quietly to the edge of Nigel Makin's bed and looked down at him. Makin was sleeping uneasily, snoring slightly, looking older than his thirty-five years and very tired, the mousy brown hair, which he normally kept combed forward, receding from the forehead.

As they watched Makin's eyes opened wide in sudden alarm, and Dorothy Vernon said quietly that it was Dorothy and Sally Vernon, that he was in a hospital, and he was not to worry. He relaxed, intelligence returning slowly to his face, and focused on Sally. 'You all right?' he asked, faintly, and she moved forward to touch his hand.

'I'll be in the corridor, Sally,' Dorothy Vernon said quietly and turned to leave, starting slightly as she saw McLeish standing behind her. He followed her out and edged her down to a quiet part of the corridor, Davidson still hovering.

'I've been hoping to have another talk with you about last night,' he opened firmly. If he had not been watching he would have missed it, he thought, the tiny, instantly controlled tightening of the ringed fingers on her handbag and the swift sidelong glance at his face.

'Of course, Chief Inspector. I am a little tired now, but I would be happy to see you tomorrow.'

'There's a man in Wormwood Scrubs, Mrs Vernon, who isn't enjoying it very much. If your evidence helps us to decide to let him go, the sooner that happens the better.'

'I don't think anything *I* have to say is going to help to let Michael Hamilton go free, Chief Inspector.' She was holding herself as tense as a wire spring.

'You must let me be the judge of that.'

The look he got was not unmixed with respect and he followed up his advantage. 'Can we go and sit in your car? If that won't do, then I have facilities at Edgware Road police station.'

She followed him meekly to the big car, telling a surprised driver that he could go and get himself a coffee. McLeish sat sideways in the corner of the back seat, stretching his legs gratefully in the generous space.

'You told us last night that you went straight from Harrods to dinner in Clarendon Road. We have a report from a CabCall driver who took you to the Western Underpass site at seven-fifteen.'

'I didn't realize he knew me.' Dorothy Vernon was fidgeting with her gloves, visibly thinking. 'I decided I wanted to talk to Nigel Makin about his investigations. But when I got there I discovered I really did not have time for a proper talk — I was going to make myself late for dinner — so I just caught another cab back to Clarendon Road.'

'How long did you wait before changing your mind?'

'Oh, not long. A few minutes.' She would not meet his eye and McLeish regarded her with exasperation. The evidence of the CabCall driver placed her at seven-fifteen at the gates of the Western Underpass site. The friend with whom she had been dining some ten minutes from the site was equally confident that she had not arrived until eight-thirty.

That left an hour unaccounted for, and McLeish considered seriously whether Dorothy Vernon could have exerted sufficient weight to cosh Nigel Makin. He looked warily at her handbag before deciding reluctantly it was just not the right shape. A tyre lever, or something of that ilk, Forensic had opined. He tried again.

'Mrs Vernon, if you can't offer a more satisfactory explanation than you have, I may have to get a warrant.'

'Oh, don't be silly.'

McLeish blinked at her and she looked him in the face, flushed and irritable. 'You're an intelligent young man, you must see that whatever Nigel was finding out, he was doing it for us, for Vernon Engineering. Why would I want to stop him?'

'I really don't know. Unless, of course, he was finding out something you would rather not know.'

Dorothy Vernon fixed him with a singularly bleak look. 'I don't believe in ignoring unpleasant things, Chief Inspector. You're better off facing them, they'll do less damage that way. I came to talk to Nigel, then I realized I was short of time.' She paused. 'But that wasn't the only thing that changed my mind. I saw Michael Hamilton crossing the site — he went through the gate just as I arrived and why it wasn't locked as it should have been I do not know. I didn't want to talk to that young man, I don't like his sort, so I decided not to bother.'

'What time was this?'

'Seven-thirty. I looked at my watch.'

McLeish, sitting bolt upright, felt as if he was trying to pick up an eel with his fingers. 'Why did you not tell us all this, Mrs Vernon? What were you doing that you didn't want us to know about? It's your own site; you had every right to be there.'

She smiled at him tranquilly. 'I know that, but Robert would have been angry with me. And you'd arrested Michael Hamilton anyway, so I didn't need to tell you.'

McLeish sat back in the corner of the big Rolls, seething but clear on one point. This respectable church-going middle-aged lady was lying her head off, for reasons that were totally unclear.

'Oh yes,' he said calmly, not bothering to conceal his scepticism, 'just go over that again, will you, slowly, from the moment when you got out of the cab.'

She hesitated and looked at him sideways.

'Come to think of it, I'd rather have my sergeant take the notes, and I'd rather be at Edgware Road,' McLeish added, pleasantly. 'So if you don't mind, we'll just do that. You're entitled to have a lawyer present, of course.'

* * *

But three hours and a formal caution later, he had to give her best. She had stuck, undeviatingly, to her improbable recital in the presence of a worried senior solicitor, who had attempted one or two interventions before being told sharply to shut up and let her get on. Robert Vernon, unfortunately, was dining out at the Mansion House or McLeish would have welcomed him to the sight of his lady wife lying like a flatfish. Sally had been unceremoniously banished home to rest, and McLeish felt wearily two hours later that he had no alternative but to send her mother home too, after she had signed, in small careful handwriting, every page of what he was confident was an almost entirely mendacious statement.

CHAPTER 17

Dorothy Vernon woke up at six o'clock the next morning to daylight and got quietly out of bed, glancing across to the other side of the room where her husband still slept peacefully. There was no one like Robert, she thought, not wholly admiringly, for being able to sleep soundly through any crisis. He had that supreme gift for a successful man: once he had done everything he could, he stopped worrying and let matters resolve themselves as they would.

She hesitated a minute; for most of the forty years she had known him all their problems had been shared and discussed, but this one would have to be thought out alone. She sat down at the table in the pretty breakfast-room, telling a still-sleepy Luigi not to bother with an early breakfast for her, just to give her a cup of coffee and get on with his work. She stayed there for a full hour, slowly drinking two cups of coffee and going carefully over every point in her plan. By the time her husband got up to Luigi's breakfast, Dorothy had decided what to do and could read, with her customary attention, the *Telegraph*, the *Financial Times* and, since it was Friday, the *Construction News*.

She looked over the last paper, a neat, pretty woman with her pink housecoat and carefully arranged hair. 'I have to do some shopping myself this morning, Robert. I don't want the car, it's just a nuisance round Harrods, I'll take a cab. You're away to Bedford?'

'Yes. It doesn't matter when I get there. Would you rather I stayed with Sally?'

Dorothy Vernon hesitated, disconcerted by realizing she had actually forgotten about her daughter.

'She could do some shopping with you — might cheer her up.' Robert Vernon, without one shred of evidence to substantiate the theory, still believed that shopping was therapeutic for all women, and Dorothy Vernon considered him with love and exasperation.

'She doesn't like shopping any more than I do,' she pointed out. 'And she hates Harrods. I'll go up and see how she is.'

She was surprised to find her daughter, looking pale and tired, out of bed and buttoning up her housecoat, identical to Dorothy's but in blue. 'I thought I'd go and see Nigel, then go back to Spring Gardens today, Mum,' she said, watching her mother in the mirror to see if she was going to object. Dorothy sat on the end of the bed.

'I've got something I need to do this morning, but if you can wait till the afternoon I can come with you. I don't think you ought to go back there and unpack by yourself, not when you're still a bit shaky.'

'I thought it was this afternoon you and Dad were signing off Bill's settlement?'

'Yes, but I'm not needed. I thought we'd explained, Sal, that it's only your father's shares which are going to Bill. He gave me a lot when we married, and I would have been happy to put some of those to it, but he wouldn't let me. So it's your father's signature that's needed, and I think it's better if I'm not even there.'

'Dad wouldn't have done it if it hadn't been for you.'

'You'll not lose by it, Sal.'

'That's not what I meant, Mum. I think it's fair that Bill should have what he's getting and there's plenty for me. But *you* got Dad to do it.'

'That's why I'd rather not be there. Now, can you wait till afternoon?' She looked with pity at her daughter whose blonde hair was looking yellow and limp, sticking to her scalp. 'Have some breakfast and pop back into bed with the papers until I get back. Then we can go and see Nigel together, if everything's alright.'

'You mean if I'm alright?'

'Yes. Yes, of course.' Dorothy Vernon, disconcerted, looked for reassurance at her strong, stubby hands and the pale diamond rings which she put on automatically with her housecoat every morning of her life.

'I'm alright now, Mum. I'll go and see Nigel this morning, and you can come with me to the flat, later?'

Dorothy yielded, and kissed her daughter.

'I want to be there by nine o'clock, so I must get ready now.' She rustled away to get dressed, ringing for a cab as she went.

* * *

Mickey Hamilton had also been up early, woken at six for the routine of 'slopping out'. Although anxious about his cellmate, a silent and apparently deeply depressed West Indian in his early twenties, Mickey was not much physically affected by the communal living and general squalor of the routine. Anyone who had been stuck for two days at 20,000 feet with three companions in a tent in a blizzard, unable to move more than a foot in either direction for fear of falling off the narrow ledge, was inured both to squalor and the close proximity of other people. Emotionally, however, he was desperate, and greeted the unexpected appearance of a pale, irritable John McLeish with incredulous joy.

'I've not come bearing gifts,' McLeish said grimly, and Mickey's shoulders slumped. 'You were seen heading towards the Section I offices at seven-thirty the night before last, and I want to know what you were doing. Sergeant Davidson here will take notes, and you're on a caution already.'

Mickey sat down heavily and looked at him, appalled. 'Seven-thirty? But I never went back to the site, or the offices — I mean I picked up my pay around six and Bill Vernon and I had a drink, then I went to the caravan about seven-fifteen. I got packed up and left and then I realized I'd forgotten to check the Calor gas was turned off — I told you, that's what I was doing when you saw me. Who says they saw me at the site?'

'Mrs Vernon, who was around the site at seven-thirty. She says she saw you going towards the Section I offices.'

'Well, she's wrong and that's all there is to it. Unless she got completely muddled and saw me around six p.m. when I was there.' Mickey looked desperately at McLeish's unyielding expression. 'I mean, could her watch have been fast or something?'

His voice trailed away and McLeish said flatly that the time of Mrs Vernon's arrival had been confirmed independently. He persevered for another fifteen minutes but could not shake Mickey; despite the fact that the younger man was in a panic he was totally unyielding on the question of his whereabouts. McLeish, remembering his own reservations about Dorothy Vernon, sat back and gathered his concentration, mentally chasing an elusive reference, while Mickey Hamilton desperately denied being on the site at the critical time.

'Alright,' McLeish said, reluctantly, abandoning the attempt to get at the momentary flash of an idea and reverting to the other questions he had come to ask. 'This lorry fiddle and the bloke on site who signed for the loads that never arrived: who was he? You say you don't know, but you probably do if you think about it. I'm told he'd have to be staff. I mean, who did Alan know who was staff and around on both those dates?'

Mickey looked at him wearily. 'Alan had mates all over the place. Wherever you went, people said hello to him, and he turned out to have worked with them before. There must have been dozens.' He stopped, and his brain perceptibly began working. 'The site log will tell you who was there — I mean, it's a rule. Staff don't clock on but there's a list kept of who was there — not the hours they worked, of course.'

'Do you know where the logs are kept?'

'I assume in the agent's offices.'

John McLeish's heart sank. Of course in the agent's offices, where else? Leaving Davidson with Mickey he found a telephone, managed to get hold of Jimmy Stewart, and took ten minutes to establish that the site log had gone missing the day before yesterday. Nigel Makin had been the last person to have it. McLeish set a similar routine in motion to find out what had happened to the relevant Barbican log, but he knew already he wasn't going to find that either.

* * *

An hour later and four miles away in St Mary's, Nigel Makin woke up dizzy with headache and a sick taste in his mouth, and kept his head very still while he worked out where he was. His eyes focused on the end of the bed where a small committee was apparently waiting for his attention.

'John McLeish,' he said, still dazed, to the biggest of the three.

'Yes, and I'm only allowed a minute. Take it slowly and don't worry at all if you can't remember. Did you have the site logs for the Barbican and the Underpass?'

'The site logs?' He fought for clarity.

'We can't find them, you see,' the big man said gently.

'Yes, I did.' He gathered his breath. 'Nothing there. Six people there both times, but people you'd expect: Bill Vernon, John Williams and Pete Murray, all QSs. Two engineers, Jennings and Patel, and Sally, who is their apprentice. No one else in the log on both sites.' He felt his eyes close, and roused himself. 'Sally, is Sally here?'

'Yes, I am.' Makin felt her hand touch his and closed his eyes again gratefully.

'No more, Chief Inspector,' the consultant warned, quietly.

McLeish nodded, got himself out of the room fast and silently, and leaned against the corridor wall. Davidson came towards him, glancing at his watch — and McLeish straightened up, suddenly understanding how and why Nigel Makin had been attacked.

'Come on,' he said, urgently. 'Where's the car?'

'Where we left it, guv. Where are we going?'

McLeish told him as they half walked, half ran through the long corridors, people turning to watch them. Once liberated from the constraints of the hospital they raced for the car, and as Davidson switched the engine on, the phone rang. Michaels was on the line. 'Sir, CabCall rang in. I'd asked my brother-in-law just to let me know quietly when they were asked to take the Vernon family anywhere. They took Sally Vernon to St Mary's an hour ago — oh, you know that — and Mrs Dorothy Vernon to Hornton Street in Chelsea just after that.'

'Jesus Christ!'

'Sir? I'm sorry, my brother-in-law only just came on.'

'Not your fault. Get back to them, Michaels, and tell the driver not to let Mrs Vernon out of the cab if he hasn't already dropped her. Tell him to get lost in traffic, anything. Call me back.' He slammed the phone down, and glanced up. Davidson was doing well over the speed limit. 'Hornton Street, Bruce, off the King's Road. I'll check the number.'

'I have it.'

McLeish was dialling as he spoke and after an agonizing five minutes found his man at St Mary's.

'Where's Miss Vernon?' he said, peremptorily.

'She's just been here, but she isn't right now.' It was young Woolner again, restored to duty after a break. 'Shall I go and look?'

'No, don't leave Makin, stay right where you are. Go and look and tell me what he's doing?'

There was a slight clatter as Woolner put the phone down. Then, 'Asleep, sir, and all the indications are fine, heart, pulse, everything.'

Intelligent, competent bloke, McLeish thought, even through his worries, who had learned which of the appalling tangle of wires and screens in Makin's room did what. DC Woolner would certainly be asked to work for him again, if he himself remained at the Yard.

'Don't move, don't leave him, don't let any visitors in. Just say it's my orders and go on saying it, and keep them out by force if need be.'

The phone rang as he put it down.

'Sir? The driver dropped Mrs Vernon ten minutes ago.'

'Get me some help at Hornton Street, Michaels. Unmarked cars, six men. Now. No sirens. No one to force entry, they're to wait for me — we'll be there in ten or fifteen minutes ourselves.'

'Why not ring up Hornton Street, John?' Bruce Davidson, driving right on the end of the danger limit, shot the car through a gap to the accompaniment of outraged hooting.

'I'd been wondering about that. I don't want to cause panic.' He chewed his lower lip.

'What's the charge? We should at least start getting the warrant.'

'Well, that's the problem, isn't it?' McLeish rolled the window down to signal left across two streams of furious drivers. 'I can't actually prove anything at the moment.'

'It's no' as bad as that, John. You have motive and opportunity,' Davidson protested.

'Not enough as it stands. Right at this moment I can't see us being allowed to prosecute.'

'It'll have to be a confession, then?'

'Or another murder. Is traffic always like this here? Go on the pavement, Bruce, use the siren; we're still far enough away.'

The phone rang as he was hanging out of the passenger window, shouting at pedestrians to get off the pavement, and he ignored it until they had cleared the narrow street and had screamed round three sides of a square. 'Turn the siren off. McLeish here.'

'Woolner, sir. Miss Vernon isn't here: I think she may have left the hospital. Mr Makin is fine, still asleep.'

He chewed his lip. 'So she's on her way. Thanks.'

'It'll take her a long time to sort out where everyone is, John. We've got time.'

'I thought she'd missed it, actually. Clever of her. I thought we'd left her peacefully holding Makin's hand for the duration.'

Davidson sought for some comfort. 'At least Hamilton's under lock and key.'

'I bloody nearly let him out, you know. Thank God I didn't weaken.'

* * *

A mile away in the kitchen in Hornton Street, Bill Vernon was sitting, more frightened than he had ever been, his coffee steaming unregarded beside him, watching his stepmother drink hers. She was nervous, he thought dully, the diamonds in her rings flashing as her hands tensed round the coffee cup, but determined.

'Well, darling, you just got the time wrong. What can we do?' He heard his voice shake.

'I'd not feel able, Bill, to let your father go ahead with this afternoon without being clear in my own mind.' Dorothy put her cup down and looked him full in the face. 'I saw you, not twenty yards away from me, and I put my glasses on to make sure. I only saw your back, but I've known you nearly all your life. And it was seven-twenty, because I looked at my watch. So I decided I'd wait until you'd gone — as I've told you. Then you came out running and rubbing at your face. What happened, Bill? Did you find him hurt and dared not tell the police?'

Bill hesitated, considering his options very carefully. 'I was with Susy by eight-thirty, Dorothy,' he protested.

'Well, I don't know about that,' she said, sweeping aside his statement. 'I've not slept, Bill, for thinking that you might have left Nigel injured, dying perhaps. It wasn't you who raised the alarm, I know. It was Francesca's boyfriend who found him. I've lied to that young man, and signed the lie, because I wanted to talk to you first myself. He knows I was there, but he doesn't know it was you I saw.'

Bill's attention was caught by the phrasing. 'Who did you tell him you had seen?'

His stepmother blushed. 'Michael Hamilton: you're much of a height and I knew I could say later I might have been mistaken. Anyway, he'd been there earlier and he's the type to have been on the take. I thought the police had the right man.'

'Does my father know you're here?'

'No, Bill, I've always tried to bring you and your father together. I came to you first. But you haven't told me what happened.'

He looked back at her, frozen with panic, and watched with horror and a sort of relief as her expression changed.

'Was it you who did it, Bill?'

He nodded, unable to speak. 'I was frightened,' he managed, after a minute, feeling deathly tired and wanting only comfort.

'You were part of the lorry fiddle, and Nigel was getting close to you?' Dorothy Vernon looked out of the window, the coffee suddenly sour in her mouth. 'You were stealing from us. Why, Bill?'

'I needed money. I'd no idea you were going to persuade Dad to give me any, let alone such a lot. I didn't know you'd do that for me. I couldn't work in Vernon for the rest of my life, it felt like prison, and I'd spent what I had at twenty-one. I'm no good as a QS, but I'd be a good farmer. I'm sorry, Dorothy, I'm so sorry.' He reached out for her hand, then let his own fall back as she turned to face him.

'And what about Nigel?'

'I didn't mean to hit him so hard. I went in to talk to him about something else, and when I noticed the site log books, I just wanted to get them away. When you saw me I was, honest to God, on my way to a call-box to get help, but then I saw a police car come past and I thought the nightwatchman must have called it, so I ran.' He paused. 'I've rung the hospital; Makin's going to be all right.' He watched her steady face. 'Can't you forget it, Dorothy? I'll never, ever, do anything like that again.'

'Of course I can't, Bill.' She sounded, he registered dully, simply surprised. 'I have to talk to Robert and we'll decide what's to be done, though it would be better if you told him yourself.'

He watched, stunned, as she rose to go, collecting her coat and placing her coffee cup and saucer on the draining-board.

'I can't,' he said, agonized. 'I can't lose everything, I can't. I won't.'

She looked back at him, amazingly and appallingly unfrightened. 'I have to talk to your father. He'll want to know who else was in the theft with you, of course.'

'Alan Fraser and I organized it.'

He saw her slowly understand her danger. Her hands flew up as he approached her and he tasted blood as her rings cut his lip. He pushed violently back, banging her head against the wall, one large hand over her mouth to silence her, and had to suppress a shout of pain as she bit him. Using all his strength, he smashed her head against the wall once more and, as her knees sagged, lowered her to the floor. Not dead, he thought, frantically, I must get her out of my flat and I must kill her and leave her somewhere where no one can ever find her. Once this afternoon is over it doesn't matter what anyone thinks, I'll be free.

He picked up the unconscious, astonishingly heavy bundle, slippery and difficult to grasp in the thick fur coat, and kicked open the door from the kitchen. He staggered through the passage and into his garage, walking round to the back of the big Volvo. He was trying to free one hand from his burden to get the boot open when a dreadful volley of thuds and kicks started up outside and he froze. Then, unbelieving, he heard the splintering crash of his own front door being broken off its hinges, and the passage filled with running men. Bill stood, transfixed, his burden still in his arms, and the big man in the lead stopped so sharply that the following squad was taken off balance and piled up behind him.

'Hello, John,' Bill said, relieved to see someone he knew.

'Is she dead?' John McLeish asked calmly, and Bill wondered, distracted, why he was breathing so hard.

'I don't think so,' he answered, and gave the bundle a shake.

'Let me take her.' John McLeish was beside him and another man, and they were laying Dorothy down in the passage and John was kneeling beside her while the other man was speaking urgently into his radio, asking for an ambulance. Then McLeish straightened up, breathing more easily now and looking enormous in the narrow corridor.

'William Vernon, I hereby arrest you on the charge that you did on Tuesday, September 20th, feloniously assault Nigel Makin, with intent to kill. You have the right to remain silent, but anything you say will be taken down and may be used in evidence against you.'

Bill stared at him and felt the corridor start to move: blackness came up and swallowed him as his head went back and his feet slipped from under him.

'Sorry, too quick for me.' McLeish was kneeling beside Bill Vernon, who had gone down like a tree. 'Clipped his head on the bumper. We'll need another ambulance.'

* * *

In the event, they sent Bill Vernon, a huge pad tied incongruously to the side of his head, off with Davidson and a constable in the first ambulance, to get him out of the way. McLeish was kneeling in the corridor beside the young male nurse who was getting an oxygen supply into Dorothy Vernon's mouth when he saw, over the concentrated bent head, Sally Vernon bang the door of a cab and come rushing over to them.

'Mum,' she called, agonized, as she ran towards them. 'Mum!'

McLeish caught her before she bumped into the stretcher.

'She'll be all right, Sally, she's just had a knock on the head.' He let her through, keeping a restraining hand on her arm, and she dropped on her knees beside her mother. 'Mum?' she said, in agony, stroking her mother's cheek. 'She looks awful. Oh, Mum.'

The young male nurse observed that people always looked worse without their dental plates, but it was still a bad injury. She would be much more comfortable in hospital if he could now have space to move her.

Sally stood up looking horrified and clutched at McLeish, who held her back to let the stretcher pass. 'Never mind that young man, he's maybe missed the bit of the course where they tell you about reassuring the patient's relatives. Just you go with her.'

She watched while they packed the stretcher. 'It was *Bill*, then?' she asked, painfully.

'Yes. Your mother must have seen him on site although she lied to me about it. He had put his watch back, and his girl never noticed that he picked her up much later than eight-thirty. His watch was still wrong the next day, but I didn't connect that with the facts till mine stopped this morning.' He considered Sally severely. 'I may not have been at my best, but your mother deliberately lied to me. She's bloody lucky to be alive. And a good deal of credit goes to Makin for remembering what was in the logs.'

'I was on both the sites too.' Sally turned back to face him as she climbed into the ambulance.

'You didn't need the money.'

She looked back at him, and McLeish saw her suddenly as she would look in twenty years' time. Then the doors were closed and they were gone.

McLeish surveyed his remaining troops; one sergeant and three DCs which, added to the two who had gone in the ambulances, pretty much exhausted the CID force available at Chelsea that morning. He asked the sergeant to stay, and released the rest, to their obvious disappointment.

Upstairs in the flat with the sergeant, he was unwilling to disturb anything until the Forensic team could arrive, so confined himself to looking but not touching. He stopped in front of a small landscape, recognizing the town: it was Jedburgh, viewed from a distance across rolling hills. The picture was pleasing, although he could hear in his head one or other of the Wilson family observing that there was a lot of this sort of painting about, particularly in Scotland. But whether good or indifferent, it represented a long-held ambition which its owner was not now going to realize, and for which he had been prepared to kill. McLeish stood looking at the picture, wondering if there was anything or anyone for which or for whom he would kill. Would he kill to protect? Well — yes: anyone who tried to harm Francesca would not be safe. But would he kill to acquire? He was roused from this contemplation by Michaels on the telephone telling him that Forensic would be with him in fifteen minutes, and that Robert Vernon had been found and was speeding back from Bedford. What, he asked, should be done about Mickey Hamilton, if anything?

'We can't prove that Vernon killed Alan Fraser. Hamilton may be our best witness. Don't do anything; leave him there.'

He waited for Forensic, and watched as the search started. The site logs and the torn-up remains of the computer programme were in the desk, thrust into a bottom drawer; a smudge of blood on the opening page of one log would presumably match that of Nigel Makin. There were also two bank-account folders, one for an account in Geneva and one in Jersey. But there was nothing to connect Bill Vernon with the murder of Alan Fraser; even the bathroom cupboard was innocent of anything more lethal than soluble aspirin.

McLeish wandered through to the kitchen and looked longingly at the kettle. No, Forensic had not yet got in there. He would maybe just go and see if he could get the thermos which Francesca had given him filled while Forensic made some more progress. He peered out of the window to see if he could spot a likely café, and stopped, frozen. Everything was suddenly unnaturally quiet and all the colours around him were very bright, as he stood unmoving, waiting for the thing that had snagged his attention to declare itself again. His eyes focused on the windowsill. A depressed-looking plant, two milk bottles and a blue-and-white thermos. McLeish gaped at it as if it were a bomb and shouted for the nearest member of the Forensic team.

'Print it and measure it,' he said, urgently. 'Can I use the phone?' He picked the receiver up, sticky from the fingerprint powder, and nearly dropped it. 'The Fraser case, Fred,' he said as it was answered, no longer feeling tired or conscious of a desire for coffee. The thermos — the one the dope was in, of course. I don't mean dope, I mean antihistamine. What does it look like?' he waited, barely able to breathe while the patient man at the other end went off to look.

'One clear print, one partial, John. Not the flat owner's.' It was the leader of the Forensic team.

'Put it in a bag. Yes, Fred?' He repeated the description and the measurements of the thermos that reposed in the custody of his people at the Yard to the Forensics man, who was nodding. 'Thanks, Fred. Don't lose it, will you?'

'A duplicate, John?' the Forensics man at his side asked, interested.

'Yes, please God. I must get it back to the Yard and match those prints.'

'Whose will they be?'

'Alan Fraser's, I hope.'

CHAPTER 18

'But they weren't Alan's? They didn't match?'

'No. They were Bill Vernon's girlfriend's prints, and two of his.'

John McLeish had arrived unannounced at Francesca's house and found Peregrine and Charlie there. Both had immediately declared their intention of leaving and were poised in attitudes of imminent departure on kitchen chairs, but neither of them, blast them, was actually making a move. He roused himself to explain, realizing that it was probably the only way to get them to go.

'I hoped, you see, that we'd be able to nail Bill Vernon. A duplicate thermos is the only explanation that makes sense: it just isn't possible that the antihistamine was in the milk, the sugar or the tea. Too indirect, too risky — we all saw that once we settled down to think. You couldn't be sure that Alan would take enough sugar or milk, and you also couldn't be sure someone else in the gang wouldn't knock himself out or turn giddy and ruin the whole plan. It had to be some method of delivering the antihistamine infallibly to Alan, and to Alan alone.'

'But you can't pin it on Bill Vernon?'

'Not yet. But I had a team going round the local chemists with photographs, looking for anyone who had bought several packets of any brand of antihistamine at one time — and I've now sent them back to ask about blue-and-white thermoses.'

Charlie and Perry gazed at him. 'Who is on that sort of team? The ordinary copper?'

'No, no, a detective sergeant with a few detective constables. I did it when I was starting. Most police work is routine,' he added, noticing the disbelieving, sidelong looks both younger men were giving him.

'I see,' Perry said, recovering himself and putting down his glass in a way that inspired McLeish to hope that he was actually now going to leave. Charlie destroyed this possibility by asking, diffidently, what was actually happening at this moment. 'I mean, you have a team out at all the chemists, but where is everyone else? What is happening to all the Vernons?'

It would be Charlie, the most contemplative and thoughtful of the gang, who had asked after Bill Vernon's family, McLeish thought. He deserved an answer.

'Well, Bill is still in the Scrubs hospital, pretty much in a state of shock. He'll have to come up tomorrow before magistrates, and we'll ask for him to be remanded on bail. We've charged him with attempted murder of his stepmother.'

'What about the attack on Nigel Makin? Did he not do that?' Perry asked.

'Oh yes, but we haven't got the case absolutely clear. We need to go over a witness's statement again.'

'How is Dorothy Vernon?' Francesca asked.

'She's in the Wellington, conscious, but not able to talk. Sally is rushing between her mother and Nigel, who is still in St. Mary's. He's doing all right — he'll be out in a couple of days.'

'I saw Robert Vernon today, but I didn't like to ask about the others,' Francesca said, soberly. 'He came in just to talk to Bill Westland and me for five minutes and said that we would understand, of course, that he could do nothing for the moment other than try to look after his family. We made noises of inarticulate sympathy — even my good godfather couldn't manage to say anything sensible to someone whose wife had been half killed by his son.'

'Bit like being faced with Oedipus Rex at a cocktail party,' Perry observed, thoughtfully. 'Absolutely no subject you could raise without falling into a trap.'

'And how is your dear mother?' Francesca offered, side-tracked. 'So sorry to hear. And your father?' She and Perry started to giggle.

'Very poor taste,' Charlie said furiously.

Francesca scowled at him and McLeish realized that he must have interrupted an earlier quarrel, a rare event in that close-knit gang.

'What about Mickey? You've let him go presumably?' Perry was hastily moving off dangerous ground.

'No. There are reasons why I can't do that.' McLeish hesitated; he had, indiscreetly, told Francesca about Dorothy's statement that placed Mickey Hamilton on the spot when Nigel Makin was attacked but was not prepared to add to his indiscretions by telling her brothers. He was perfectly confident, as he had been all along, that Dorothy was lying, but it would simply be unprofessional to release Mickey before it was clear beyond all possibility of doubt that he was not implicated in the attack on Makin.

Perry and Charlie gazed at him expectantly, but, seeing that nothing more was forthcoming, politely forbore to press him. Charlie swung his chair forward with a crash; like all Wilsons he had been sitting with the chair tipped perilously on its back legs. 'I really am going. I must go round to Tristram's.'

Francesca opened her mouth to comment and closed it again, while Perry looked exasperated.

'Give him my love,' Francesca said, finally. 'I'll find your jacket.' She went into the corridor leaving her brothers watching each other.

'He wasn't singing well, Charlie,' Perry said, defensively, ignoring McLeish as completely as if he were not in the room.

'You could have said no thanks, you wouldn't audition! They'd be bound to want you rather than Tristram because you're better known.'

'He fucking sang badly.' Perry's mouth was set hard and he was colouring steadily.

'He was nervous because you were around.' Francesca, returning and seeing battle rage, threw herself into it. 'He is jealous of you and he sings less well when you are there, although he is the better singer in many ways.'

'He bloody isn't!' Perry was now blazing with temper and McLeish watched, wonderingly, deciding with interest that Perry was that angry because he was feeling guilty.

'Look,' Perry said furiously, 'it's a big world out there. Tris has more than just me to compete with: if I hadn't been singing, Richard March or Alun Edwards would have got it, believe you me.'

'So let him lose to someone else and hate *them* for it. You're his brother.' Francesca, now as angry as he, glared at him, the two scarlet faces like mirror images of each other.

McLeish moved to intervene, but subsided on Charlie's warning scowl.

'Perry,' Francesca now had herself in hand and had drawn breath, 'you may be right and Tris would not have got it. But you know he is jealous of you, and you have a secure career — why get in his way?'

'I very much wanted to sing that Requiem with Andrew Goldberg conducting, that's why. It's only done about once every three years, and who knows where I'll be next time?' Perry, in instant reaction to his sister, had returned to rationality as well. 'I'm sorry about Tris; I know I make him nervous. I've asked Goldberg if he'll take him for the second tenor part, but he sang so badly at the audition that it's an uphill fight. I *have* got Goldberg to agree to hear him again, as I'd have told Charlie if he'd only bloody listened.'

Charlie might not have bloody listened, but McLeish had, hearing even through exhaustion the echo of Alan Fraser bargaining for a place on the expedition for Mickey Hamilton as well.

Charlie picked his moment to suggest that, since John was plainly exhausted and needed food and the company of their sister, it might be a good idea if he and Perry went away. He bustled his brother into a beautifully cut denim jacket, while Francesca and Perry kissed each other, ceremonially, rather in the manner of chieftains concluding a truce over the bodies of murdered kinsmen.

'God bless you, Charlie,' McLeish murmured to him as they stood in the corridor watching Perry trot back up the steps with some offering for Francesca, hastily garnered from the back of the car.

'Oh, *they* won't quarrel for long,' Charlie said, with just an edge to his voice. But Perry and Tristram might, McLeish added silently for him as he waved the brothers into the Rolls.

'Must telephone,' he said urgently to Francesca, who was belatedly offering the hospitality of her house in terms of a bath and food. He made three phone calls from the living-room and realized he was falling asleep at the end of the last one. Francesca found him five minutes later slumped uncomfortably on the end of a sofa, and bullied him upstairs and out of his clothes into her substantial double bed. McLeish's last thought was that he must stop doing this or she would never marry him; what use was a man who arrived only to fall asleep? Vowing to wake up again when he had got a couple of hours in, he went out like a light.

* * *

When he woke he could just see daylight at the edge of the thick curtains and it took him a minute to remember where he was. He felt round the bed for Francesca, but she was not there and her side of the bed was cold and neatly tucked in. He sat up on the side of the bed, chilled by this, and reached out for the bathrobe she kept for him on the back of the door. At least that was still there, he was somewhat reassured to find. On the landing, sunlight streamed in and he realized it must be at least eight o'clock. He opened the door of the spare bedroom next door and sighed: Francesca had slept there, her nightie was on the floor. A very poor omen. She had never done that before, but had always crawled into her own bed beside him, no matter how good an impersonation of a dead man he was giving.

He pulled the belt tight on his bathrobe and went downstairs, grimly wondering if this was what happened to so many police marriages — after a bit your wife moved into the spare room and didn't even bother to wake you in the morning? Well, it wouldn't do. He paused to brush his teeth and put a comb through his hair, and marched into the kitchen, surprising Francesca loading the dishwasher.

'Did you have a good sleep, darling?' As always when angry, she was gathered, coherent and formally polite.

'Why didn't you wake me?' The only way to deal with her in this mood, as he had learned from her brothers, was to go straight into the attack.

She straightened up, holding a plate like a shield, but he rested secure in the knowledge that her upbringing would prevent her from throwing it at his head. He walked over, took it away, and put his arms round her, feeling her stiffly resistant. 'You weren't even in bed when I looked for you,' he said reproachfully, and she exploded.

'John! Bloody liar. You were dead to the world. I came and looked at you at midnight, I switched on all the lights and marched round the room, collecting clothes and dropping shoes. Absolutely no response.'

He held her firmly, blessing the advantage that eight inches and a good three stone offered in these circumstances. 'Sorry. Can we go back to bed now?'

'No, you cuckoo. Neither together nor separately. I have staved off two people wanting you but both will ring back in a few minutes. And I have a nine-thirty meeting, and I haven't read the papers. Not that it matters all that much, given that it is an inter-departmental one and there are at least twenty of us, but still. John, stop it, we do not have time. And you're all bristly.'

'What were my phone calls?'

'Someone called Pryce at seven-thirty and Bruce Davidson at seven-forty-five.'

McLeish looked down at her. 'Commander Pryce?'

'S'right.'

'My guv'nor.'

'Only ranks to Under-Secretary, doesn't he? I wasn't going to wake you at seven-thirty for one of those.'

McLeish wondered aloud for whom Francesca would wake him.

'Well, I nearly did for Bruce because I know he doesn't call you here unless he must. He said it would wait an hour, but you must call him back before you start the day.'

'You should have woken me — the phone calls could have waited, but we could at least have had breakfast together, if nothing else. You were cross with me.'

'Absolutely.'

He was kissing her when the wall phone rang behind her head. He picked it up, holding on to her with his free arm. 'Sir.' He listened patiently to Commander Pryce's qualified congratulations.

'No, we haven't charged him with Fraser's murder yet. No proof, sir . . . Yes, as soon as he's making sense we'll be talking to him . . . With a solicitor present, sir, yes, I don't doubt. There should be no problem about charging him for the attack on Nigel Makin — there's just an inconsistency in Mrs Vernon's statement that I'd like to clear up. He's safe enough where he is.' McLeish promised to keep in touch, keeping to himself the thought that in as much as the Commander expected to spend the next two days in Devon, this might have its difficulties, and put the phone down.

Francesca had escaped and was sorting papers methodically into a briefcase. 'I was right, wasn't I?' she observed from the other side of the kitchen table. 'Not worth waking you for, he was just being an Administrator and keeping up Morale. Of course, that's all chaps at that level really do.'

McLeish opened his mouth to argue that whatever the principles obtaining in the unarmed branch of HM Civil Service, a Commander in the Metropolitan Police Force carried real responsibility for real actions, but the phone rang again. He ignored it long enough to cut Francesca off at the door and kiss her goodbye, then dived back to it. He listened, his eyes widening.

'Jesus Christ! A fingerprint! No way *that* could have got there by accident. On the inside of a piece of paper in the pocket of the jacket?'

'A *partial* fingerprint,' Bruce Davidson warned. 'The chap in Forensic is in no doubt, but he thinks it's shaky as evidence. Not enough points of comparison for a court, he says.'

'What took them so long, anyway?'

'They only got the jacket yesterday from Scotland. It's yellow oilskin and it had been lying out and there was nothing there — just smudges from gloved hands. But then this wee piece of paper was in the right-hand pocket. It had got wet, of course, but the inner fold was dry. They were actually very quick, once they got the jacket.'

But it won't quite do to convict a murderer, McLeish thought, shivering slightly as the cold of the tiled kitchen floor struck through his bare feet. 'Look, Bruce, I must get dressed and eat — I missed supper. Make sure the lads do *all* the local chemists again for that thermos. He can't have bought *that* in three different shops, like the pills, so we may have a chance there.'

'Can I tell the sergeant in charge about the wee print? That'll cheer him on his way.'

'Yes, of course. It's not to go beyond him in detail, but he can tell the lads there's some new evidence. These shop enquiries are hard graft.'

They rang off and McLeish raced upstairs to dress, noting gratefully that however cross Francesca had been it had not impaired her domestic efficiency. Clean underclothes, socks and shirt awaited him, tucked in a corner of a drawer, and he threw the ones he had worn for thirty-six hours into a linen basket, knowing that they would be dealt with.

He realized he was noting these domestic details in order to control mounting tension; it was always like this when all the pieces started to come together. He knew he had this one right now, and the problem that was winding him up was how to prove it. A confession might well be more than he could achieve — particularly if a good lawyer was present — and the conventions governing fingerprint evidence were rigorous. No matter how confident he and Forensic might be that they had their man, a partial fingerprint would cut no ice in court.

McLeish was downstairs, hunting through the fridge for bacon and eggs, before he understood suddenly that he would not be able to bear it if Alan Fraser's murderer went free. He would never climb with Alan again, he could probably never bring himself to climb with anyone at Culdaig, but he could avenge Fraser's death and he would, if he had to choke a confession out of the murderer.

He ate his bacon and eggs without tasting them, put the plates mechanically in the dishwasher, then walked into the big cloakroom in the extension at the back of the house, washed his hands and stood contemplating his own face in the mirror above the basin. Very dark hair above brown eyes and a broken nose and strong, wide jaw — despite the straight mouth it was basically a good-tempered face, he thought detachedly, and indeed he considered himself a rational, mild-mannered bloke, not obsessive like so many good coppers. But he understood, looking himself in the eye, that there were two things he had to have in order to go on living with himself, and he didn't much care what it took to get them. First, he had to get Alan Fraser's murderer sewn up so tight that he would never escape the web of evidence. Second, he had to get away from his position as privileged visitor in Francesca's house and honorary brother to all the Wilsons, by persuading her to marry him. That, he observed coolly to his reflection, would take a little time: nailing Fraser's murderer was today's job. He picked up his raincoat and was out of the house and into his car seconds later, not looking back as he went.

* * *

News of various sorts awaited McLeish at the office: Dorothy Vernon had a good night and had expressed an urgent need to talk to him. He sighed; this was a necessary piece in the jigsaw, but he wanted to stay at his desk, at the centre of the investigation, and he already knew what she was going to tell him. Nonetheless, courtesy and ordinary humanity demanded that he go and see her as soon as possible, and he asked his secretary to ring the hospital and tell them he would be there in an hour. Robert Vernon had also rung him twice, and, while anything he had to say was probably stale news by now, he was owed a return phone call at least.

'Chief Inspector. Thank you very much for ringing back.' The words sounded rusty, and McLeish realized it must have been a long time since Robert Vernon had to thank anyone for ringing him back.

'I just wanted to tell you that Sir Richard Brown of Brown Taube will be acting for us in connection with this affair. Our usual people, Freshfields, say that he is the best.'

McLeish, with effort, murmured something non-committal. The head of that firm had an absolutely unparalleled track record in persuading judges that his distinguished clients had not really meant to defraud insurance companies, cause inconvenient ex-lovers to be physically intimidated, or embezzle millions via funny offshore islands, or else that they had been driven to it by pressures that would have caused anyone to do the same. Hardworking policemen, who tolerated conditions that would, on the evidence, have driven these particular defendants to justifiable homicide, were not keen supporters of Sir Richard.

'I hear you're seeing Dorothy — Sir Richard will be there. I thought I should let you know.'

'Thank you. But I'm pressed for time, so I'd be grateful if Sir Richard would be punctual or make another arrangement.'

'He'll be there. I made sure he cleared his diary.'

McLeish waited out the pause, realizing that Robert Vernon had more to say.

'What about Hamilton?'

'He is still in custody.'

'You haven't let him go, then?'

'No.'

'Of course, you've to talk to Dorothy. I mustn't keep you back, Chief Inspector, I'll see you at the hospital at eleven.'

McLeish signified what pleasure he could at this prospect and returned to his list. He rang the Scrubs hospital to discover that Bill Vernon, although still heavily sedated, was making sense and could, if necessary, be questioned, although it was the registrar's view, offered unhopefully, that they would get more sense out of him after another twenty-four hours.

'Is he well enough to be put in an identity parade?'

'Today? Just about. If you must.'

'I don't know yet if it will be necessary. You'd better make a note that Sir Richard Brown is acting — yes, him — so I want all this done kosher.'

McLeish got himself transferred to the remand wing and learned that Mickey Hamilton was being visited later that morning by another distinguished member of the English legal fraternity. Mickey's uncle's position in Edinburgh must be all that he'd said it was, to get Roy Butterworth himself. Seeing that Sir Richard was presumably due there later in the day also, the Scrubs would be unusually honoured. He felt the familiar tension pressure at the back of his neck, and picked up a paper-clip and chewed it anxiously, hearing in his head Francesca telling him to stop it or he would take all the enamel off his teeth. On this thought the phone rang.

'I'm sorry I was cross, but I might as well not have a lover.'

A typical Francesca opening, he thought, amused, combining a due apology with a direct attack. 'That's all right. And it may all be over by tonight.'

'Well, that'll be nice. And for poor Mickey — he must be tired of being in jail.' She was, he could hear, in a rush as usual. 'Darling, ring me later? I'm not doing anything else tonight.'

The phone remained stubbornly silent thereafter, until the time came for him to leave for the Wellington. He borrowed Pryce's driver, called Bruce Davidson, and went off, taking the in-tray with him. He had been prepared to take a stern line with Dorothy Vernon, but she greeted him, looking very white and old, with a bandage going right around her head, two burgeoning black eyes, and diamond earrings sparkling incongruously against the bandage.

'I don't suppose anyone has thanked you for saving my life, John,' she said, seeing him smile, 'but I do thank you.' She bent a stern eye on her husband who, embarrassed, murmured some approximation.

Sir Richard Brown, McLeish noted with respect, had effectively effaced himself from this scene. He was a slight man in his fifties, narrow-faced, with mousy brown hair, sitting placidly in an uncomfortable hospital chair. For all his stillness, though, it was like having a nest of machine-guns trained on you.

'I did not tell you the truth in one particular, Chief Inspector.' Tears came to Dorothy Vernon's eyes but she pressed on. 'It was Bill, not Michael Hamilton, whom I saw coming away from the site offices that evening.' She looked at his unmoved face. 'You knew that?'

'I knew you weren't telling the truth. What was Bill doing?'

'He was walking very fast, pulling at his face. I recognized him then — he walks with his toes turned in, it's very easy to pick out. Then I saw his face clear under the site lights.'

'You didn't speak to him?'

'No. He was looking frightened and angry. So I left it and walked to Clarendon Road and had a drink in the pub there before dinner.' She pressed her hands together and the diamonds in the rings glittered in the light from the window. 'He told me, when we were talking yesterday, that he had attacked Nigel but that he hadn't meant to kill him, he'd just been terrified. He didn't mean to kill me either, you know.'

McLeish quickly took her through her conversation with Bill, conscious all the time of Sir Richard, who, however, intervened only once, laying the groundwork of his prospective defence by ensuring that McLeish had logged Bill's reported statement that he had been on his way to telephone for an ambulance for Makin.

She reached the end, obviously exhausted, and McLeish rose to go, saying over her head to Sir Richard that a typed statement would follow, for signature.

'You'll convey my apologies to Michael Hamilton,' Dorothy said, with a recovered gleam of authority. He smiled at her and removed himself and Davidson to the corridor, finding that Sir Richard had followed them out.

'Will you be charging my client, William Vernon, in connection with the assault on Mr Makin?' he asked.

'Yes, I imagine so, when we have Mrs Vernon's statement signed. You'll want to be present when I interview him, I take it?'

'Yes. I wonder, might I have copies of any statements he has made so far?'

'Certainly.' McLeish had been ready for this one, and Sir Richard nodded. 'I understand from Roy Butterworth that you also have a Michael Hamilton in custody, charged with the assault on Mr Makin?'

McLeish was momentarily gravelled, but then it came to him: Sir Richard would undoubtedly have been the first choice for Mickey Hamilton's well-connected father, but he had been booked for Bill Vernon by the time the phone call came.

'Yes,' he confirmed stolidly, and waited, fixing his eye on a cupboard to the right of Sir Richard's head.

'Are you considering charges against my client in connection with any other offence?'

'Considering charges, yes.' McLeish found himself feeling very young and inexperienced against the formidable presence, and fell back on his training. 'I'm sorry, I can tell you nothing more at the moment.'

To his enormous relief he became aware of activity in the passage and Bruce Davidson was fidgeting at his side.

'Excuse me, Sir Richard,' he said thankfully, and turned to find the uniformed constable indicating that he was urgently required on the phone.

'Yes?' he said into the phone which was placed on the Sister's desk. 'You haven't? Oh, well done. Is she sure? What's she like — all right, is she? How old? Well, she would be older, wouldn't she, because the kids in shops don't look at you. Fantastic. Get hold of her — we'll fix an ID parade at the Scrubs. *I'll* speak to the manager. She *is* the manager? Better yet . . . Don't lose her.'

He stuck his head into the corridor and shouted for Bruce Davidson, noticing thankfully that Sir Richard had either rejoined his clients or vanished into thin air. They made for Scotland Yard.

* * *

Across in St Mary's Hospital, Nigel Makin was out of bed, gingerly testing his ability to walk, when Sally arrived. He kissed her, and felt his head starting to ache again.

'Sally, how is your mum? I've to wait here till I see the consultant.'

'Recovering.'

She looked pale and drawn, all the colour gone from her face.

'I know I look awful.'

'No, you don't, just a bit tired. What about Bill?'

'He's been charged with the attack on Mum. This upmarket lawyer Dad has brought in says he'll be charged with the attack on you, too. Apparently they haven't charged him with killing Alan.' She was watching him carefully. 'They haven't charged anyone else either.'

Nigel bit his lip. 'Sal, it must have been Bill. I know Fraser was in that scam, and if Bill was, too — there's your motive. I'm sorry, it's bad for you all.'

'Dad says the lawyer reckons John McLeish isn't sure about it.'

'Well, he would say that, wouldn't he? Two assaults are bad enough, but it must be better if he can keep Bill off a murder charge.' He sat down on the bed, looking for the bell, as his headache became suddenly worse, then said abruptly: 'Jesus, they don't suspect you, do they, Sal?'

'I don't know what John thinks. He is clever, just as Francesca said. *She's* not rung me up, you know.'

'Well, she can't really, can she? She can't interfere with the boyfriend's work.' He watched her anxiously as she sat picking at her nails. 'Or is it me they suspect?'

Her head came up and she blushed. 'I really don't know, Nigel, but Dad's arranged with our new lawyer that you should use someone else in another firm.'

'*I* didn't do it.' Nigel was outraged. 'I could willingly have killed Alan, but I didn't.' He hesitated. 'I'd still like to marry you,' he said to his counterpane, and looked up to find her weeping. 'Oh, Sal. Don't. It'll be all right.'

'Wait until you're better, Nigel.' Sally wouldn't look at him and he withdrew his hand.

'Sorry, I'd better go and see Mum. I'll be back later.' She hesitated but did not kiss him, and he watched her go through a headache that seemed to have taken over his whole body.

* * *

Half an hour away, at the Scrubs, the elaborate preparations for an identity parade were being made.

'No, I must have both of them,' John McLeish was trying hard to control acute anxiety. 'If he isn't well enough today, we'll have to postpone it. What's the lawyer say?'

'Well, he isn't keen, but I think he'll play. John, could you come and have a look at the other people we've got lined up? It's not the easiest specification, but we've got two of the uniformed branch, one at the CID here, and we're borrowing two from up the road.'

McLeish plunged into the perennial problem of all identity parades, which is how to secure enough people of at least superficial resemblance to the accused to constitute a parade.

'I hate these things,' Davidson confided moodily. 'Particularly with two high-priced lawyers here, shouting the odds.'

'They're both here?'

'Yes. Engaging in polite legal chit-chat, weighing each other up. Asking for you.'

'OK. Get the uniformed lads into civvies. The cars are on their way. I'll go and have a word with the briefs.' He took a deep breath and plunged into the waiting room to greet Sir Richard and the smaller, plumper Roy Butterworth, who was younger and noisier but no less formidable. He took them both to another room where they could observe the parade and sat there beside them, leaving Davidson to do the organizing. Hardly breathing, he watched as the parade formed up, his eyes on the man he was certain in his own mind had succeeded, at his second attempt, in getting rid of the threat to his future represented by Alan Fraser.

Davidson shepherded in Mrs Sylvia Williams, who was a tall woman, big-boned, black-haired and nicely dressed, and stood back to let her go down the line. McLeish, who had met her earlier and thought she would make a good witness, sat absolutely still and prayed. She went down the line of eight men, all six foot or more, all dark, all in their late twenties or early thirties, and he observed with one part of his mind that Davidson had done well, even if one of the policemen did appear to be standing to attention. Sylvia Williams was stopping in front of each man, taking a careful look as she had been instructed. McLeish stopped breathing as she took an extra few seconds or so in front of Bill Vernon, but she passed on steadily and finished the row.

McLeish shot out of the room, nodding to the lawyers, and arrived in the little room to which Sylvia Williams had been taken.

'Did you recognize anyone?' he asked.

'I was just telling the sergeant here . . . I knew him straight away, but I looked carefully at everyone, just as you asked.'

'Thank you very much.' McLeish smiled down at her and she smiled back at him hopefully, pink with excitement. 'You've been a tremendous help. We'll ask you to sign a statement now, and then it's over until the case comes to court.'

He sent her off with Davidson and stood for a moment, feeling literally sick with rage. He waited until he had himself in hand, then walked back to the little room where both lawyers were waiting, both silent now.

'Mr Butterworth, could I have a word?' He held the door for the smaller man and took him to a next-door office. 'Mrs Williams has identified your client as the person who bought a blue-and-white thermos flask on the morning of Alan Fraser's death.'

'Thank you, Chief Inspector.' Butterworth had understood immediately but was far too experienced to give away any points. 'I had understood from Sir Richard that the existing charges against my client in connection with the attack on Nigel Makin would be dropped.'

'That is correct. It is in connection with the death of Alan Fraser that I expect to be making a charge. You can see your client, but we will oppose any application for his release. He has not been told yet, of course, that he was identified by Mrs Williams.'

But Mickey Hamilton had known, McLeish thought murderously; he had flinched when he saw her, he'd remembered who she was.

He arranged for both lawyers to see their customers, feeling less than satisfied. 'Difficult in court, these ID parades. You could see the briefs working out how to rubbish it.' Bruce Davidson sounded just like the voice inside McLeish's own head.

They both looked up, startled, as an apparition in black oilskins appeared in the doorway. The figure peeled off a motor-cycling helmet to reveal himself as DC Woolner, who wordlessly held out a plastic bag containing a blue-and-white thermos.

'Bottom of the skip at the back of the site offices, sir. We did the prints straightaway — Alan Fraser's and *Michael Hamilton's*!'

'Oh, good man, well done!' He took the package from him, sniffed the air thoughtfully, and Woolner stepped back.

'All sorts of rubbish in that skip, sir.'

'Honest dirt. Go and have a shower, and well done.' He waited till Woolner had left before he and Davidson grinned at each other briefly. 'I want that one, Bruce. We'll have him at the Yard, even though they'll hate my guts at Edgware Road.' He paused. 'It's there, isn't it? Even with a good brief?'

Davidson chewed the inside of his cheeks. 'There or thereabouts, John. I'd like something a bit more.'

'If it takes me the rest of my life,' McLeish said calmly.

* * *

'So Bill has been charged with both attacks?'

Francesca and John McLeish were eating lunch in the tiny café opposite the entrance to New Scotland Yard, just over twenty-four hours later. Bill Vernon had appeared that morning in front of magistrates on a second charge: attempted murder of Nigel Makin. He had been remanded in custody because of the seriousness of the charge.

'Yes. Makin is coming out of hospital tomorrow, and will be back with the firm after a rest, to be chief executive. Sally's going with him on his convalescence.'

Francesca stopped eating, and gaped at him. 'But she was in love with Alan Fraser.'

'Who didn't want to marry her.'

Francesca opened her mouth to speak, and closed it again, her sequence of thought written all over her face.

'Makin hadn't got round to suspecting Bill Vernon of the fiddle at all, interestingly, because he was looking so hard for traces of Alan Fraser.'

'Of whom he was, reasonably, very jealous.'

'Yes, and for whom he had considerable respect. He said to me that Alan was a good tradesman as well as a good climber, though an arrogant bastard. He didn't reckon much to Bill Vernon at all.'

'Neither did I,' Francesca said soberly. 'But I suppose he only wanted one thing — his farm in Scotland.' She looked at him, anxiously, wondering how to go on, and decided to be brave. 'And are you getting any closer to pinning Mr Hamilton down?'

'We know what happened. He decided in Scotland to have a go at Alan, probably on impulse, and took the first jacket at hand to disguise himself a bit. He ditched the jacket because he had seen us below and guessed, quite correctly, that you had seen him. He'd left about half a fingerprint on a piece of paper inside it. He loved Alan, who didn't love him in the same way. And he was bitterly jealous.'

'Because Alan was the better climber?'

'And, as we now know, because he was the more effective organizer. Alan was the one who got the book written, he set up the fiddle on the sites and he got the lion's share of the cash.'

'He knew what he wanted, did Alan,' Francesca said, reflectively, 'and was prepared to hustle to get it. He really didn't believe the world owed him a living, whereas Mickey did — does.'

'Then Mickey made another, successful attempt in London. He thought, quite correctly, that I was coming to warn Alan. There must have been a leak from Scotland.'

'You can hear it, can't you?' Francesca agreed. 'Everyone within twenty-five miles knows everything up there and Mickey only needed to have rung up for a gossip to get it all. *Not* your fault, darling; I don't see how you could have avoided that. Even if you hadn't been known to be coming to the site, Mickey would still have had another go. Alan was still in his way.'

'I think that's right.' McLeish sounded calm, and she held his hand, relieved. 'No, I made myself miserable for a few days there, but he was quite obsessed and he was going to try again, anyway.'

'Will you get a conviction without a confession?'

'Maybe. We've got a lot of good circumstantial evidence. But I'd prefer a confession. The prison doc says he's in an anxiety state, so he can stay in a small room with a West Indian nutter till he tells us.'

Francesca blinked, but decided not to comment. 'Meanwhile you have to go to Scotland and explain?'

'Yes. Can you come too? I'll have to spend a day in Glasgow, and half a day in Carrbrae, but we could go on to Culdaig afterwards, if you don't mind the driving?'

'Of course I'll come — you won't like it on your own.'

EPILOGUE

John McLeish stood at the entrance to the VIP lounge at Heathrow Airport, Bruce Davidson at his shoulder, contemplating the tableau presented to him. Francesca, Perry and Tristram were standing, their attention fixed on the television which hung from the ceiling in the centre of the vast room, Perry's arm round his sister's shoulders and Francesca's left hand tucked into the crook of Tristram's elbow. Most of the lounge was watching them, but the trio was unconscious of any scrutiny, totally absorbed in the screen. They looked ridiculously like each other and utterly self-contained, Perry's bodyguard-cum-driver waiting behind them. McLeish, knowing it could only be music that was holding their attention, moved quietly to see what it was.

'Handel or near offer,' Perry observed to his siblings, without taking his eyes off the screen on which someone in knee-breeches and a frockcoat was, confusingly, declaring his love in a high, clear voice to a young woman conventionally clad in a ballgown.

'It is Handel, peasant. An opera called *Xerxes*,' Tristram said. 'The counter-tenor is the king's brother.'

'*Not* very easy,' Perry observed. 'And most unfair to tenors.'

'Not much fun for counter-tenors — I mean, darling, they were castrati,' his sister pointed out.

'Ah, there's his brother, the king.' McLeish felt Bruce Davidson stir uneasily beside him as another character clad in the same sort of knee-breeches and frockcoat, but blatantly female this time, emerged on to the screen.

'Now, why isn't he a counter-tenor?' Francesca wondered aloud, as the newcomer launched into a declaration of undying love for the same begowned young woman.

'Oh Frannie, can't have a king played by someone not quite all there, as it were — or not in those days. *Lèse majesté*,' Tristram said, reproachfully.

McLeish, deciding this could go on all day, leaned forward and tapped Francesca on the shoulder. 'We need to get over to the Glasgow shuttle service.'

'Sorry, darling, is that the time? Quick, everyone.'

'Are the boys coming too?' McLeish sounded openly dismayed and Bruce Davidson managed to turn a giggle into a cough.

'No, darling, they're both doing a concert in Berlin tomorrow. I was just keeping them company while they wait for their flight.'

'Nice to see you, John, however briefly,' Perry said, punctiliously. He hesitated. 'I'm glad you got him — the murderer, I mean, but I don't suppose it's much consolation. Was it because of the lorry fiddle that Alan was killed? Or can't you say?'

McLeish looked round carefully, but the Wilsons and their attendants were the only people within earshot. A bold spirit, seeing the Wilsons diverted, had substituted *East Enders* for Handel, effectively distracting attention from them.

'No, it was because of K6. Hamilton has now made a statement.'

'Pure anxiety,' Tristram volunteered. 'Mickey saw a chance and thought he would never get it again — or at least not at a time when he so needed it. What *I* don't understand is why Alan stole money from Vernons.'

Francesca, looking worried, said that perhaps it was just that everything Alan knew how to do, everything he was, depended on his being in top physical health. If he was injured or sick he had nothing to fall back on; perhaps that was why he had stolen — to build up a nest-egg?

'It's the Highers he didn't have all over again,' Perry said affectionately.

'They might have changed his life,' his sister pointed out. 'Might have made it unnecessary for him to go in for casual theft.'

'You didn't like him,' Tristram said, with interest.

'It's not that.'

She looked to McLeish for help, but it was Perry who spoke. 'You're frightened by people who only want one thing and want it that much,' he said, as if they were alone in the echoing lounge, and Francesca looked away to think.

'I'm frightened *for* people who are like that,' she said, turning back to him abruptly.

'It's all right, Frannie, *I'm* not like that.'

'You've always had everything you wanted,' Tristram observed.

'Now that is perfectly true,' Francesca said, with some spirit, as Perry protested and McLeish told her in exasperation that if they missed the last shuttle up tonight it would mean the seven o'clock one the following morning and towed her towards the boarding-gate. She followed him on to the plane, clutching his hand and turning back to wave to the boys.

They settled into their seats with Davidson, tactfully, two rows behind them.

'You're not looking forward to Scotland, are you, darling? Not your fault — Alan was killed before you could even warn him. Mr Hamilton was jolly quick.'

'Yes, he was. He was a great deal more competent and decisive than I would have believed. He bought a thermos exactly like Fraser's at lunch-time that day, and lots of anti-histamine at the same time in the same chemist, near the site. It's a very busy branch of Boots, and we were bloody lucky to find a manageress who remembered him. He switched the thermoses at tea, as we finally realized, and threw Alan's own one away. Young Woolner found it — that was a good piece of work.'

He looked away out over the wing of the aeroplane and Francesca put her hand over his.

'We could try and do the Coire Dubh walk this weekend? I love you.'

He looked sideways at her and leant over to kiss her. 'We ought to decide what we're doing on a longer-term basis.'

'I know. If you can't get what you want you'll go away. I do know. I'm getting there.'

She kissed him back and they sat, holding hands and watching the sun set over the wing, as the plane flew steadily north.

THE END

THE JOFFE BOOKS STORY

We began in 2014 when Jasper agreed to publish his mum's much-rejected romance novel and it became a bestseller.

Since then we've grown into the largest independent publisher in the UK. We're extremely proud to publish some of the very best writers in the world, including Joy Ellis, Faith Martin, Caro Ramsay, Helen Forrester, Simon Brett and Robert Goddard. Everyone at Joffe Books loves reading and we never forget that it all begins with the magic of an author telling a story.

We are proud to publish talented first-time authors, as well as established writers whose books we love introducing to a new generation of readers.

We won Trade Publisher of the Year at the Independent Publishing Awards in 2023. We have been shortlisted for Independent Publisher of the Year at the British Book Awards for the last four years, and were shortlisted for the Diversity and Inclusivity Award at the 2022 Independent Publishing Awards. In 2023 we were shortlisted for Publisher of the Year at the RNA Industry Awards.

We built this company with your help, and we love to hear from you, so please email us about absolutely anything bookish at feedback@joffebooks.com

If you want to receive free books every Friday and hear about all our new releases, join our mailing list: www.joffebooks.com/contact

And when you tell your friends about us, just remember: it's pronounced Joffe as in coffee or toffee!

ALSO BY JANET NEEL

WILSON & McLEISH MYSTERIES
Book 1: A FATAL BLOW
Book 2: A FATAL FALL

Printed in Great Britain
by Amazon

37368795R00151